EIGHT

VERY

BAD

NIGHTS

EIGHT VERY BAD NIGHTS

BAD NIGHTS

A Collection of Hanukkah Noir

Edited by Tod Goldberg

WITH CONTRIBUTIONS FROM:

Ivy Pochoda • David L. Ulin
James D. F. Hannah • Lee Goldberg
Nikki Dolson • J. R. Angelella • Liska Jacobs
Gabino Iglesias • Stefanie Leder
Jim Ruland • Tod Goldberg

SOHO
CRIME

Published by
Soho Press, Inc.
227 W 17th Street
New York, NY 10011

Library of Congress Cataloging-in-Publication Data
Names: Goldberg, Tod, editor, author. | Ulin, David L., author. |
Pochoda, Ivy, author. | Hannah, James D. F., author. | Goldberg, Lee, author. |
Dolson, Nikki, author. | Angelella, J. R., author. | Jacobs, Liska, author. |
Iglesias, Gabino, author. | Leder, Stefanie, author. | Ruland, Jim, author.
Title: Eight very bad nights : a collection of Hanukkah noir / edited by Tod Goldberg.
Description: New York. NY : Soho Crime, 2024. | Identifiers: LCCN 2024025281

ISBN 978-1-64129-613-7
eISBN 978-1-64129-614-4

Subjects: LCSH: Noir fiction, American. | Hanukkah stories, American. |
American fiction—21st century. | LCGFT: Noir fiction. |
Hanukkah fiction. | Short stories.
Classification: LCC PS648.N64 E54 2024 | DDC 813'.08720806—dc23/eng/20240610
LC record available at https://lccn.loc.gov/2024025281

Interior design by Janine Agro

Printed in the United States of America

10 9 8 7 6 5 4 3 2 1

EIGHT
VERY
BAD
NIGHTS

TABLE OF CONTENTS

FOREWORD

Tod Goldberg

There's an old bromide in crime fiction that says there's only four ways a person can die: Homicide, suicide, natural causes, or an accident. Maybe that's true. But for anyone who has managed to spend Hanukkah with their extended family, they would argue that there's also a fifth way: Habitual annoyance. Is it possible to expire from listening to Cousin Roberta's open-mouth chewing of brisket? If Uncle Arnie tells the story about meeting Sinatra in an airport one . . . more . . . time, will you simply collapse? Can you slip this mortal coil if Mom tells you what a disappointment it is that you're not a doctor? This is the challenge of Hanukkah. Sure, it's a festive time, but after eight nights with family, almost any exit sounds appealing, even those from this life. Because unlike Hanukkah's seasonal partner, Christmas, which celebrates a birth, Hanukkah is a memorial holiday. Eight days meant to remind you that some seriously bad shit went down in the second century and, because of a miracle, you're alive to eat kugel.

The miracle itself—that in the midst of the Maccabean revolt, one day's worth of oil used to light the holy menorah lasted eight—is recreated in homes around the world beginning on the twenty-fifth day of Kislev in the Jewish calendar, which translates to a date in late November through December, which is to say: the date changes every year on the standard calendar, which as a child was very frustrating. You never knew when, exactly, you were getting presents ... or when, exactly, the influx of family would arrive on your doorstep, smelling of Chanel #5 and cigar smoke, ready to tell you the horror of their travel. Oy vey, Auntie Esther, you made it! That fifteen-minute drive across all of Walla Walla sure *does* sound oddly reminiscent of your family's escape from Russia in 1919 ...

The first Hanukkah I can remember happened in 1975, when I was four. The photos from this time reveal a series of menorahs all over the house—an electric one on the window sill in the living room, a standard fire-operated model on the mantel in the family room, and then one from the Old Country on the dining room table—all surrounded by Santa figurines, stuffed elves, twinkling lights, a billion ornaments, and, in the family room, a six-foot Christmas tree, covered in blue tinsel. "Christmas," my mother told me then, "is just more convenient." And so it was. We'd light the menorah every night—well, most nights, sometimes Mom went out on a date—and open a small gift—usually some candy-corn, or the kind of gift you might put in a stocking, like jacks or a PEZ dispenser—but the real action happened on Christmas. One generation removed from her parents' escaping pogroms, our mother was already a non-religious Jew living in the San Francisco Bay Area, raising four kids on her own, and teaching them that sometimes, celebrating miracles is hard to fit into the schedule around work, school, soccer practice, Girl Scouts, and this nice man she met at Toastmasters who was taking her out to dinner in the City. Yes, this man had just been released from San Quentin, where he'd done seven years for robbing a bank in Marin, but it's not like he had a *gun*! (This may well give you some insight into how my brother Lee and I ended up how we are . . .)

Eight nights is simply too long to celebrate anything. As these eleven stories show, eventually, someone is going to drink too much. Eventually, someone is going to say the wrong damn thing to the wrong damn person. Eventually, even the people you love the most are going to make you want to kill somebody. And if you happen to be celebrating Hanukkah at work? Oh, there will be blood.

IVY POCHODA

Ivy Pochoda is the author of the critically acclaimed novels *Wonder Valley, Visitation Street, These Women,* which was a *New York Times* best thriller of 2020, and most recently *Sing Her Down,* which won the *Los Angeles Times* Book Prize and was named a CrimeReads Best Crime Novel of the Year. *These Women* was a finalist for the *Los Angeles Times* Book Prize, the Edgar Award, the California Book Award, the Macavity Award, and the International Thriller Writers Award. *Wonder Valley* won the 2018 *Strand* Critics Award for Best Novel and was a finalist for the *Los Angeles Times* Book Prize and France's Le Grand Prix de Litterature Americaine. *Visitation Street* won the Prix Page America in France. Her books have been widely translated. Her first novel, *The Art of Disappearing,* was published by St. Martin's Press in 2009. Her writing has appeared in the *New York Times,* the *Wall Street Journal,* the *Los Angeles Times* and the *Los Angeles Review of Books.* She teaches creative writing in the Low-Residency MFA at UC Riverside and the Studio 526 Skid Row.

JOHNNY CHRISTMAS
Ivy Pochoda

Over in the Gulf I got some bad ink. Prison style shit. Given all the bad things that happened over there after the towers fell and the bad things I did, this was the least of my worries. But still. I brought home enough scars that I didn't need this one.

It was supposed to be my girl's name—same girl who would visit when I was locked up in the Brooklyn House of D on Atlantic awaiting trial for one of the things I narrowly escaped having pinned on me. Like many of the girls whose boys were locked up, she stood outside the jail and hollered at me. Voice like the A train screeching into Jay Street.

When I shipped out, I wanted her name on my arm to remind me someone cared enough to shout herself hoarse in the dark.

Problem was, the name came out all lopsided like it had been slurred by a 2 A.M. drunk. Didn't heal right either, what with the sand and sweat and all out stress of war. And that heat. Ten thousand pounds of heat.

BACK IN BROOKLYN THE world kept spinning in my absence. While I was in basic and then three tours in the desert, my neighborhood got a fresh coat of paint, some fancy lipstick, croissants instead of rolls. You'd have seen it coming if you were paying attention instead of causing trouble. I don't have to tell you what came and what went. That story is everywhere and there's a bunch of quasi old-timers like me haunting the last dive bar in Cobble Hill who will fill your ears with that shit.

Let's just say, we fought, the world got more expensive, it was harder to find my place when I got back. And I still had that tattoo on my forearm even though the girl was long gone and the Brooklyn House of D shuttered. Rumor had it, and still does, that someone's gonna turn it into luxury housing, but ask me, the juju in that place is gonna rain nothing but bad luck. So I figure it's best to let it sit and let ghosts be ghosts. Sometimes it's okay to be reminded of the way things were instead of transforming them into something better.

Regardless. The neighborhood started filling with families and cool kids. And bistros. Boutiques selling Brooklyn back to locals and newcomers. A cat café—whatever the fuck that is.

And between it all on Smith, next to the last of the last old school diners, a tattoo shop—Black & Blue. Not that there's anything special about that. So much ink on the kids these days if you came from space you'd think they were born with it. But what caught my eye about this place was the art in the windows. Fisheye, wild style paintings of the hood like I remember it. The Wykoff PJ's. The BQE over Atlantic Ave. And a big old painting of the Brooklyn House of D. Down in the corner of that piece the artist's name—Johnny Christmas.

Who the fuck wants to paint a jail, I don't know. But there was something in that painting that got me.

Started to happen that every time I walked past the place, my forearm began to itch. Like Lorraine's name was dying to jump off my skin. Sometimes I'd peer in at the dudes at work. A bit older than you'd imagine. More my age than not. Worn out, like myself.

Time came when I met a lady serious enough that Lorraine's presence on my flesh started to pose a problem. And next thing, a week before Thanksgiving, when I'm fixing to be trotted out in front of her whole family, I found myself inside Black & Blue scanning the books for something to erase my past mistakes.

A clock I thought. Because time is supposed to heal all wounds even though I know this is a lie.

THE GIRL BEHIND THE desk was a sagging pincushion of piercings—speaking of past mistakes—and asked me if I had a particular artist in mind for my cover up.

"That guy work here?" I said, pointing to the House of D art in the window.

"Johnny Christmas? Come back this evening."

I'M NOT GOOD WITH faces—paying attention to them I mean. When you're trained to kill and to expect to be killed, you learn pretty quick not to spend time making eye contact. You never know how quickly someone's going to exit your life and how. Better not to make attachments.

All of which is to say, I didn't take much notice of this Mr. Christmas, even when he was about to ink my arm. Over the years I've become a taciturn guy which solicits a taciturn response.

I could feel the needle before it hit my skin and before

it hit my skin I heard him say, "Lorraine, huh. Let's get her gone."

And then I knew.

I would have known it anywhere.

This wasn't any Johnny Christmas. No Christmas about it. What we had here was a straight up Jew. And not just any Jew. This was Mikey Goldfarb. One of the baddest boys I encountered in the Brooklyn House of D.

"LORRAINE. LOR-FUCKING-RAINE."

Never mind that it was snowing that fucking inconsequential snow that hasn't made up its mind whether to stick around on not—the sort where the wet flakes hit with a sound like a bug on a windshield. Never mind that it was wet, cold, and fucking miserable. We were all in the outdoor exercise pen up top the Brooklyn House of D because from there we could see down to the street. And down on the street was where our girls were hollering up at us.

It was coming up on Christmas which meant the activity down on Atlantic was popping. I don't mean the cabs and jittery Christmas lights—but that too. I mean the crowd outside the jail clamoring for our attention. The closer to the holiday, the more tricked out the women got—antlers and Santa hats, jingle bells and light up sweaters. The colder it was, the skimpier some of them dressed.

Just thank fuck Lorraine wasn't the type to give the goods away for free.

"Yo, Davo." I heard her nasal Italian voice. "I fucking love you, Davo."

That was my clue to shout, "I fucking love you, princess."

Normal times, men like me wouldn't have been shouting

about love in front of each other. Normal times, men like me wouldn't have been freezing our nuts off in a shitty outdoor gym.

But there's nothing normal about cooling your heels in a cinderblock pen while waiting for trial.

My crime—tangled with the wrong Mexican outside a bar where I was too young to be drinking. The evidence— the mess of his nose and shard of his tooth implanted in my knuckle.

Fact is, I did what I did so I counted myself lucky Lorraine was down there shading her eyes from the falling mess, trying to tease me out from the rest of the dudes clinging to the ex-pen's fence.

"I fucking love you, Lorraine."

Not much more to say than that. Not with the other twenty or so dudes yelling at their girls and their girls yelling back. Sex talk. Baby talk. Fucking promises. And let me tell you, some of those ladies had pipes that could blow your house down. Blow your house and then some.

Lorraine and I had this thing—she'd be the last to go, as would I—toughing it out after the crowd thinned. Usually one or two ladies gave her a run for her money but with weather like we were having, I knew Lorraine would have them beat.

Except not that night. One by one the other women peeled off until it was Lorraine and someone I swore I'd never seen before, though it was pretty hard to tell from a couple of hundred feet up.

It was coming up on dark but I could still see this woman wasn't like the rest—older, huddled, covered. Couldn't make out much of her besides the fact that she was carrying some kind of candlestick, now and then sheltering the flame from the slop dropping from the sky.

If you made the effort to come visit your boy or son at the jail, I woulda bet he'd get himself up to the ex-pen. Except for it was just me looking down on Lorraine and this lady. And let me tell you, it was the loneliest thing in the world—her holding vigil for exactly no one.

THE NEXT EVENING, SHE was back. This time there looked to be an extra light on her candelabra.

Before I got called inside, I heard Lorraine once more. "Yo, Davo! You got a Mikey up there?"

Mikey Goldfarb—well, he wasn't like the rest of us.

Smart kid it seemed. But dark. Dark as fuck.

It takes all kinds in the House of D. Lots of dealers and thieves. A few stick-up guys. Some repeat offenders and car jackers. Mostly misdemeanor charges.

And then there was Mikey Goldfarb—the nerdy kid with the dead-eyed stare who ran over his grandmother's landlord on Pacific. Not ran over. Pulverized.

Story went—Goldfarb targeted the guy from half a block away. Saw him in the crosswalk, bending down to pick something up from the street. He must not have been a fast moving motherfucker. But anyway.

Story went—Goldfarb sighted him, crosshairs style. Then, pedal to the metal, accelerated down Pacific, miraculously taking his grandmother's Caprice from basically zero to sixty in a few seconds.

Story went—the landlord had no chance. Car sent him flying across Hoyt. That would have been enough. But Goldfarb kept driving. Ran over the guy again, the Chevy's left tires crushing him from pelvis to skull, deep into the asphalt of Pacific Street. Or so they said.

"You got a Mikey up there?" Lorraine called again.

"Sure fucking do."

"Tell him to come see his grandma."

Now, this was before I learned to keep my head down and my eyes to myself. This was before I learned that not everyone's business was my business and the best way to stay out of trouble was to keep quiet.

Which didn't mean I relished the idea of searching out Goldfarb. Kid gave me the heebie jeebies. Didn't talk much. Didn't come up to the ex-pen. Mostly sat in his cell staring at the wall—cold as stone. Still as a fucking statue.

One of the boys timed him. Motherfucker went nine hours without moving.

Like I already said, coldest boy in the House of D.

But you can't leave your grandmother to cool her heels in the snow. Some shit just isn't right.

So I found Goldfarb—you guessed it—sitting on his cot, staring down his cinderblock wall.

He didn't look around when I said his name.

"You had a visitor down on the street today."

So still I could hear him blink if he so chose to do so.

"Older woman looking for you."

Let me tell you, I'd seen rocks with more life than this guy.

"That's some cold shit, Goldfarb," I said, "leaving an old lady out there in the snow."

Before I left, he turned his head—a scary slow-mo movement that froze me to the spot.

"You ever hear someone's sternum crack under a three-thousand-pound car," he said.

Didn't blink. Barely opened his mouth to speak.

"You ever *hear* it."

Back then, these words were some straight up psycho-killer, horror movie shit. After my first tour, they acquired real meaning.

"Jesus Christ," I said.

"Don't tell me about cold," he said. Then, like he was moving through molasses, rotated his head back to the wall.

THAT NIGHT THE TEMPERATURE took a tumble. Our cells trapped the cold, the cinderblocks ice to the touch. Our breath hung like storm clouds.

In a few years, people would remember this week as one of the coldest in ages—the whole city iced over. The sidewalks frozen solid. From up top in the ex-pen, we could see people inching down Atlantic, gripping storefronts, signposts, and mailboxes for balance.

Buses jackknifed across the avenue.

The city stopped dead.

But that didn't deter the women. They lined up below the jail like a bunch of deranged carolers all singing a different song to a different man.

And in the middle of it all, not singing, was Mikey's grandma, still holding those candles.

"Yo," I said to no one in particular. "Someone wrestle Goldfarb out of his cell. Asshole's grandma is down there freezing her titties off."

And maybe to escape the cold or maybe because we were all looking for an excuse to mess that quiet motherfucker up, two dudes did just that.

So here was Goldfarb, no jacket or nothing. They walked him over to the fence.

"Yo, Lorraine. We got Mikey here. Tell his grandma!"

The women below parted for Goldfarb's grandmother and her candles.

It must have been below zero that night. But Goldfarb didn't shiver. Didn't even rub his hands together or jam them in his pockets. Just stared down at this grandmother like he stared down his wall. Kept on staring until those damn candles burned down to nothing.

Now I've seen some pretty messed up shit since.

I've seen bombs fall on schools.

I've been in ground battles in marketplaces and taken sniper fire.

But nothing has ever scared me as much as that look Goldfarb was giving his grandma. Stared down at her so hard and unblinking, it's a miracle his eyelids didn't freeze open.

Then he turned his back and headed for the stairs.

"The fuck is going on here," I said. "Goldfarb, she holding a vigil over your cold, dead soul?"

"It's a menorah, motherfucker," he said.

AFTER THAT, THE RUMORS about Goldfarb began to swirl. When you're locked up, everything becomes epic. As far as I know, he'd barely said a word to anyone since he came in, but suddenly everyone knew everything about him.

Lurker.

Creeper.

Virgin.

Orphan.

That summer of all the dead cats—Goldfarb.

That empty warehouse that burned down with the homeless dudes inside—Goldfarb.

And so it went.

THE HOLIDAYS WERE A strange time inside. Lots of forced and trapped joy. An extra carrot cake at dinner courtesy of the bakers at Rikers. Tinsel drooping in the cafeteria. A plastic tree in the day room frosted with fake snow. The crappy TV playing *It's a Wonderful Life* even though we all goddamn know it isn't.

This was around the time that there was a push to get Kwanzaa on the holiday calendar and some of the tougher customers had been grumbling to the COs that they were being disrespected by the presence of the sole Christmas tree. Like that tree was responsible for all of their systemic ills or what have you.

Never mind that these were the same dudes whose women stood outside decked out as Rudolph the Horny Reindeer.

But anyway. We were inside and the real joy was outside and there was no amount of tinsel or holiday music that could distract from this fact. So I'm not sure whether the lack of Kwanzaa décor was the culprit or the communal knowledge that we'd all be sharing a slop of a Christmas dinner because our trials had been pushed into the New Year.

A few days into the epic cold spell—everyone feeling extra amped up and cooped up—and one of these Kwanzaa guys flat out coldcocked the Christmas tree, took it out with a right hook that sent the red plastic ornaments rolling all over the linoleum. And then it was on—a full on crusade in the cafeteria. Kwanzaa versus Christmas. Fists and trays flying.

In the middle, there was Goldfarb, just sitting at his table like the whole place wasn't exploding around him—so stone cold still that it's like he's emitting his own vibration. So fucking placid that there came a moment when everyone stopped the battle and just stared at him.

Then one of the Kwanzaa guys held up his hand, backing his boys off.

"Yo, Goldfarb. You just gonna sit there?"

Goldfarb didn't meet the guy's eye, which spelled trouble.

"You gonna sit there while they straight up disrespect us non-Christmas motherfuckers? That's what kinda guy you are?"

Now everyone could see that this dude is getting straight up agitated by Goldfarb stonewalling him.

"Your motherfucking grandmother has the balls to stage her own Hanukkah protest outside and you got nothing to say about it in here."

Then, a slow turn of Goldfarb's head—as if he had all the time in the world for this exchange and the all-out battle was on hold until he said his piece.

"That's right—your grandmother. She's standing up for your people's faith while you let this institution jam their fucking Santa shit down our throat."

You know those nature videos of a cobra strike? I swear Goldfarb was faster than that. In a hot second he had the dude on the ground, bitch-slapping him with his dinner tray until he sprayed teeth.

That was the last time I saw Goldfarb.

There's no solitary at the House of D. Maybe they took him to Rikers. I don't know.

What I do know is that his grandmother still turned up outside for two more days. He didn't even let her know he was gone.

AS IT HAPPENED, A few days later, I got lucky.

Mexican guy whose teeth I rearranged, got deported. No victim, no crime. So the evening before Christmas, I walked out of the jail to find Lorraine waiting for me on the steps.

And my girl was pissed.

"Yo, Davo," she said. "How come you can't get that Mikey asshole to take notice of his own goddamned grandmother."

Next to her was the woman in question, bundled up in a fur coat that looked to have traveled all the way from the Old Country, wherever that might have been.

"You got nothing but time in there, Davo. You can't do that at least?"

"Goldfarb's a scary motherfucker," I said. "Can't make him do a thing he doesn't want to do."

Then the grandmother clutched my arm with the hand not holding the menorah. "Not my Michael," she said. "My Michael's a very good boy." She gave me a hard look—same eyes as her grandson. I didn't like them on her any more than I did on him.

But still, I didn't want to tell her the depth of her good boy's disrespect. Why ruin an old woman's holiday?

"He loves you, Mrs. Goldfarb," I said. "He talks about you all the time."

I could feel her stare icing over.

"He's just having a hard time is all. A boy like that never forgets his grandmother." I knew I was laying it on thick, halfway high with the freedom of release.

"What does he say?" There was a hard note in her voice that signaled her disbelief.

"That he loves you."

"I doubt that," Mrs. Goldfarb said.

I've heard a lot about the tough love of Jewish parents—but this straight up stole the show.

GOLDFARB'S TRIAL TOOK PLACE right after New Year's around the time that I first considered enlisting.

Although I'm not much for the news, I followed it in the paper and on the local stations. After all the holiday cheer, the press seemed eager for something to sink their teeth into and that something was Goldfarb. Through the week-long trial he didn't say a word. Didn't defend himself. Didn't explain or show remorse. Reporters lapped it up—splashed him on the front page for two days.

First-degree manslaughter. Twenty-five years.

A FEW MONTHS LATER I found myself in a recruiting office. Hard to stare at the hole in the skyline without taking it personal.

The night before I headed to basic, Lorraine and I went to dinner at this new French place down at the end of Smith Street. First time I spent two hundred dollars on a meal in my life. But that's a different story.

On our way out, we passed a woman struggling with a shopping cart in the next doorway. I was at her side before I realized it was Mrs. Goldfarb.

How the hell she bumped that cart up the stairs to her three-floor walkup on the regular, I still can't figure. When we got to her door, she asked us in. Now, I could think of a million ways I rather spend my last night in Brooklyn, but just thinking of this old lady standing on the freezing sidewalk eight nights in a row touched something in me I was ashamed to admit I had—something I knew I'd have to keep in check when I shipped out.

The apartment was small. Railroad style with the front window onto Smith and the back mostly obscured by a rusted fire escape. The hall lined with moving boxes.

"Mikey would have unpacked those for me," Mrs. Goldfarb said. "He is a very good grandson."

We all have our own moral compass and our own definition of good and evil. But even back then, before I'd seen people do all sorts of fucked-up things on account of their twisted moral obligations, I was having trouble placing the stony eyed kid who left his grandmother out on the cold on the spectrum of goodness.

Anyway, good people don't crush their landlord's sternums and cheekbones under Goodyear tires. Fact.

"Why don't you sit down," Mrs. Goldfarb said. "You're the first company I've had since I was forced to move. I was a model tenant for nearly forty years. Paid the father. Paid the son until he raised the rent. And now I'm here in this box. Who knew I'd spend my last years alone, priced out of my own home while people from Manhattan are paying twelve dollars for a hamburger downstairs? That's not a fate anyone would wish on their grandmother."

She fetched a bottle of wine the color of motor oil and wiped dust from the bottle.

"I raised Mikey's dad in that apartment. Then I raised Mikey after his parents died. You think my landlord had any respect for all I'd done for my family? You can't get a two-story place in Brooklyn for that price anymore. You can't get one with a parking spot either."

Lorraine and I nodded because what can you say? She was right. An apartment in Boerum Hill with a parking spot was outta sight.

"Anyway, what use do I have for a car anymore. Everyone's abandoned me. And I was the only one who drove in the first place."

I don't remember much about the rest of our visit, only that I was itching to go and had trouble swallowing Mrs. Goldfarb's musty wine.

At the door she grabbed my wrist. "You might not think that Mikey loves his grandmother. But he does." And there it was, that same cold look that I'd seen on her grandson.

I couldn't wait to get away.

OVER IN THE GULF, I replayed this visit many times and each time Mrs. Goldfarb's words sounded more sinister in my head. But then again, I was kinda losing it in the desert.

PAIN IS UNRELIABLE. A papercut or a blister can be more intolerable than an open wound or a dog bite. I'd have thought that after taking shrapnel and being hammered by cinderblock after a grenade attack, a needle tapping into my arm would be no big thing.

But that clock Mikey Goldfarb inked on my arm set my heart racing. Felt like I was going into A-fib. Sweat poured down my forehead. After twenty minutes I had to take a break before I passed out.

If this bothered Goldfarb, he didn't let on. Stoic, that one, always. He came back with a bottle of whiskey that raised my temperature but lowered my blood pressure.

After a few decent swigs, it lowered my inhibitions as well. "Goldfarb, right?"

Probably not wise to try and startle your tattoo artist while he's on the job. But I shouldn't have worried.

"I was in the House of D with you. Saw your painting out front."

"It's Johnny Christmas now."

"Last time I saw you was on Hanukkah," I said. "Saw your grandmother after, though. Tough lady. She still around?"

"Died. At the start of my sentence. Fucking waste."

"Let me ask you something," I began.

"Worst fucking driver in the entire world," Goldfarb said. "Until she wasn't."

"She told me you were a good grandson," I said.

"Worst fucking grandmother too. But what can you do? Guilt runs deep even when it isn't yours."

He finished the clock in silence.

I paid the pincushion girl at the front desk and left Goldfarb a tip in a small envelope. I also bought the painting of the Brooklyn House of D.

It's hanging in the living room of the place my girl and I got right after Thanksgiving.

WHEN YOU ENLIST, THEY tell you a whole lot of shit about loyalty, patriotism, laying down your life for your country and your fellow soldiers.

But that painting of the House of D—well, that's a masterclass in loyalty no Army brochure or puffed-up Colonel could give.

I've taken bullets, like I told you.

But doing twenty-five for an old lady. Well, that's a whole other thing.

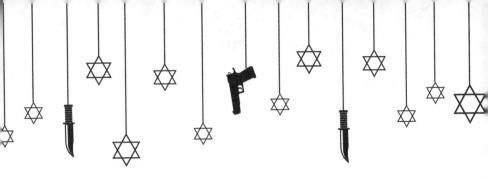

© NOAH ULIN

DAVID L. ULIN

David L. Ulin is the author or editor of nearly twenty books, including the novel *Thirteen Question Method* and *Sidewalking: Coming to Terms with Los Angeles*, shortlisted for the PEN/Diamonstein-Spielvogel Award for the Art of the Essay.

SHAMASH
David L. Ulin

His grandmother's menorah
sat on the mantel like a weapon. Which was and wasn't
what it was. Ornate, with filigreed branches of inlaid silver, it had been less gift than confrontation: a reminder to
her daughter and son-in-law of their roots. The December after he turned four, his father brought home for the
first time neither dreidel nor gelt but a pine bush no more
than three feet vertical, the family's first Christmas tree. To
decorate, his parents bought ornaments and tinsel from the
Lamston's on Columbus Avenue.

The next year, his grandmother dropped the menorah
like a bomb.

They were living, then, in an Upper West Side walk-
through: two bedrooms, living room, eat-in kitchen, and a
foyer large enough to count as a room of its own. This was
where the tree was set, clamped into a bowl of water, towel
around the base. Six weeks earlier, in November, there had
been the blackout. He remembered that too, the disruption
and the thrill. The grown-up world, its noise and mayhem,
falling dark and silent. Everything shutting down. His parents did their best to make it an adventure. The sensation
was of a project they had improvised. They raised a pup tent

in the living room and made cocoa on the gas stove. All the while, he could see the trouble in his mother's eyes. Even then, he understood the unreliability of her psyche, that she might at any moment turn on—or (worse) *from*—him.

His father, at least, was consistent, although that was not to say: engaged.

Now, nearly six decades later, his mother no longer remained among the living. His father was ninety if he was a day.

He had arranged the menorah in the living room, above the faux fireplace, not long after his mother's death. This was when he moved back. *Moved back*, he laughed. *Don't get me started.* The anger could take on a life of its own. Sixty-two and living in his father's house like some fucking travesty. The one who never got away. It was a narrative he never wanted to be a part of, but that was all in vain. In the aftermath of his mother's . . . evaporation, it had become apparent the money was gone. The final asset was the apartment—not on the Upper West Side (that had been a rental) but a small co-op in Murray Hill for which his parents had scraped together a down payment during the fiscal crisis of the 1970s. The irony was not lost on him. When else had they ever been in the right place at the right time?

Now it was what kept the household afloat.

Or would have been, if the property hadn't been so leveraged. One day soon, perhaps tomorrow, the lenders or the co-op board would swoop in and take it all.

Recovering the menorah had been easy. It was how his parents were. Carry your baggage with you, never let anything go. He was like this also, although he preferred not to think about it much. What was the point if you had no other choice? One evening, after he'd gotten his father to bed and set up breakfast, made sure there was water and the mattress railing was secure, he'd dug through the hall closet until he found it, at the back of the top shelf among the family photos and the super eights, the tax documents and financial forms—all of it equally obsolete and irresistible: hieroglyphs, petroglyphs, lost languages, lost lives.

And yet, how to know how long his father might linger? How to know how long he might hang on? This wasn't the way he would have supposed it. Physically, at any rate, his mother had been the sturdy one. Cognition was a different issue, but her body maintained a certain flinty stamina. Then she caught a respiratory virus and vanished from the world. They mourned her—he and his father. He propped the old man up at graveside, whispering the details of what they were undertaking, what they were experiencing, easing him through the day. It did not come naturally, this . . . generosity. It had not been how he had moved during the time before. There comes a moment, however, he had learned, when everything you ever thought or wanted falls into irrelevance before the overwhelming weight of necessity. He was not a good son, he had spent so much of his life in retreat from those who raised him. In the end, though, what was he to do? No friends, no other family to speak of; his parents had existed for so long as a universe of two that when it all began to crumble there was no one else. The image in his mind was of a lean-to, slowly settling, shedding shape, definition, as it collapsed into decrepitude.

Well, such a collapse had happened, hadn't it? The forces of chaos were at hand. He thought about his father as he prepared to light the shamash. Without death or intercession, he would end up in a public facility, where all his mishigas, his rules, would no longer matter. No one would care how he presented, who or what he claimed to be. You might say he had it coming. You might say it was his fate. But fate was hard to read even if you clung to it. Fate asserted itself in unexpected ways. Fate meant doing whatever was necessary. This was another thing he understood.

Once, he'd imagined himself as a prodigal. Such a status would render his homecoming a return. But that, he knew, was inaccurate—both to himself and to the parable. The prodigal had been the younger of two brothers and had forced his father's hand not once but twice: first, by coercing him to divide the estate while he was living, and again after, in his profligacy, he ran through his share and came crawling home. It was a cautionary tale, although since he didn't have a sibling, maybe not so much in this house. What mattered to him more was responsibility. The menorah represented a case in point. Resurrected in a living room his father didn't enter and his mother never would again, its presence felt restorative, as if something had been given back. His grandmother, yes, but even more, a new unraveling. Even more, a long-discarded territory of light. Every night, he recited the blessing as he lit the candles. His father slept through it, as he did now, dreaming who knew what or where or how, waiting to be consecrated to the dust.

This evening was Zot Hanukkah, the eighth night, for which he'd fitted the menorah with eight tapered candles. They stood pristine and perfect in their row. As he struck a match and held it to the shamash, he thought about the Maccabeans, who regained control of Jerusalem and the Second Temple—the real Hanukkah miracle—and in so doing redeemed, for neither the first nor the last time, their heritage.

Wasn't that what he was seeking: a miracle, to help his father die at home?

Might miracles still exist, in the tumult of this fallen world?

Baruch atah Adonai Eloheinu Melech ha-olam, asher kid'shanu b-mitzvotav, v-tzivanu l'hadlik ner shel Hanukkah, he whispered, touching the shamash to each of the candles, one after the last, until his grandmother's menorah was aglow.

Old man

was what his father liked to call him. Beginning when he was a boy. *Hello, old man,* he'd say, suddenly expansive, as if they were members of a club. This was not pretension but something more elusive. His mother was the one who put on airs. Once she had described the shame she felt at her father's immigrant legacy, the privations he'd had to overcome. Awakening at four, in the dawn of the previous century, to deliver ice before school. She had never recognized, even as she gasped her last, that life was a contagion, that it burned itself out like fever, that the only legacy that mattered lay in death. His father was a little bit more open; he would wax philosophical on occasion, although to recall such conversations was to be reminded of their abstraction, their air of intellectual as opposed to existential concern.

Now it was impossible to say what his father thought or did not think, how much he registered; he had stopped speaking, for the most part, leaving his bed only rarely, to sit in the same brown armchair he had occupied for decades, sinking into its well-worn cushions, slipping between the seams. Between the seams, yes ... of breath and not-breath, disappearance and decay. Once in a while, he would ask where she was, or pull himself up—each limb ratcheting as if independent of the others, a danse macabre, all joints and angles, like an enormous bird trying to escape its nest. It wasn't despair, or even desperation; he was too far gone for that. Rather, it was the routine of recognition, as if he could sense that something was incomplete. His eyes were rheumy, faded. They sat in his face like a pair of runny eggs. In each, incomprehension formed a glaze through which he could see no longer, not a wall so much as a dirty window, irrevocably smeared and blurred.

Old man, he thought as he stepped into his father's bedroom. *Well, who is the old man now?* The air inside was gray and soft with snoring. He could not imagine it ever having been different. He did not remember very much from before. In the house of forgetting, the amnesia was contagious; there were moments he felt worry for himself. The weight of everything, the density of it, would sweep over him, not like a wave but like a landslide, as if he'd been buried alive.

"Good night," he said to his father or might have said. Or maybe he said not a word at all. Then he crossed to the nightstand, where he had placed a small plastic battery-operated menorah. The lights flickered as he switched it on.

His father's pen

lay on the kitchen table. He had left it after breakfast, with the unfinished crossword. Each day, he rose at dawn, anxiety driving him from bed. *Rose?* More like: *capitulated*, gave up any hope of sleeping, just as he had given up on everything. He'd taken early retirement when he moved in, Department of Education more than happy to accommodate an older teacher, four decades in the system, vested, earning low six figures, twice what a new teacher would get. There was a youth movement at the Department, there was a youth movement everywhere, no place for age or experience, no place for a living wage. The money was banked at a separate institution than his father's. He felt the need to stay apart. He was his father's power of attorney but not financially liable for his losses. His teacher's pension belonged to him alone. An escape pod or a lifeline, he thought if he thought of it. But mostly, it felt as though he were living in an endless present, the weeks and days, the seconds even, no longer a progression but, rather, a stasis. Entropy. He'd been a high school physics teacher so he had taught the concept, but what he loved was that entropy was multidisciplinary. It applied in physics, yes, and biology and economics, cosmology and philosophy. At its simplest—and he had made a career explaining complex ideas in straightforward language—it represented a measure of disorder in a system. A writing implement, for instance, running out of ink after it was too much used.

Which was what, this morning, had happened to his father's pen.

It was a black Diplomat, anodized aluminum with inset orange piping. The barrel balanced like a stiletto in his hand. Unlike his father, he had never cared for pens, buying Papermate gels by the boxful, throwing them away once they went dry. The old man, on the other hand, had spent decades collecting: Parkers and Watermans, Mont Blancs and Ancoras, seventy-five of them protected in a pair of zippered calfskin cases. This had been the first delicate subject he broached after his mother died, after he and his father had reconfigured as a family of two.

"We're going to need to sell the pens," he said one night at dinner. He had prepared hamburgers and his father was picking at the bun. Five-thirty, and through the kitchen window the winter sky was waning, that thin and dissolute solstice light.

His father stared back at him limply, out of a face that might as well have been made of mashed bone meal. His hair was sticking up and he was in pajamas. He barked out a noise that sounded, if one listened hard enough, like: "What?"

"The pens," he repeated. "We need to sell them. I'll take care of it."

The look of confusion on his father's face made him want to quit. Was it really worth it? Then, he recalled his research, if a bit of after-hours googling could be classified in such a way. Those seventy-five pens might bring in fifteen thousand dollars. It could keep them afloat for a couple of months.

"How about," he said, unsure if he were being comprehended, "we look at the pens and have you pick one. That will be the one you keep for yourself."

He'd only been home a few weeks but he had learned it was best, in dealing with his father, to narrow the options, to liberate him from the freedom of choice.

"Are you ready?" he went on, as if it had already been decided.

He chose to believe he saw a nod.

"Great," he said, withdrawing the cases from where he had them on his lap under the table. Before he could work open the first zipper, his father's eyes went flat. "How about this one?" he asked, withdrawing a vintage Cross, thin, sterling, elegant. It brought to mind the communicators from *Mission: Impossible*, which he had watched on television as a kid. Was this the pen he had played with, pretending he was Hunt Stockwell or Ilya Kuryakin, speaking into it as he tried to outsmart T.H.R.U.S.H.? The image brought him up short, and he felt pressure in his throat, behind his eyeballs. He turned so his father would not see him wipe the tears.

In the end, he couldn't continue. It felt gratuitous, even cruel. More coercion, more degradation. *Loss of control* was how his father had once phrased it, but they were well beyond that now. Gently, he reminded the old man to choose the pen he wanted. With quavering fingers, the old man withdrew the Diplomat and handed it his way.

"This one?" he asked.

His father nodded, he was sure of it this time.

Then, the old man started speaking, not much louder than a whisper. He could see the effort it took to force the words out, throat cording and tensing, the difficulty of pushing enough air through the larynx for the language to take shape.

"Excuse me?" he said, unsure of what he'd heard.

His father began again. "I want you to have it," he said or something like that, he wasn't certain, the two of them seated in the kitchen, the universe like a clock ticking within them and without them, winding down to entropy.

It was a shanda
that they had come to this. Or maybe just bad luck. Either
way, it was another story to tell. Experience was neutral,
he had learned this also. It was the response that counted,
that dictated everything. Briefly, he recalled his mother,
eyes rimmed with resentment when she didn't get her way.
How many times had he seen it? How many times had he
felt he was the cause? She was gone and still the thought
of her could make his breath go shallow and his pulse race.
Growing up, he had tried to keep his distance, although
that was impossible in an apartment this concise. Even
her rare moments of concern came steeped in distance,
in unknowing, as when she'd told him (for his own good,
she made sure to mention, as if he were unable to come to
a responsible decision) not to study physics because he'd
never find a job.

This, in its way, was another shanda, the shanda of their
insufficient love.

The pen had run out in the middle of the crossword. He
had been waiting for it to happen but also thinking, perhaps, that it never would. Like the oil in the lamps of the
Maccabees, the ink had outperformed expectation. Like
the oil, and his father too. His mother had never liked the
pens; she considered them a waste of money, and a threat
because of the attention his father directed their way. *You
love those pens more than you love me*, she had said on more
than one occasion. True or false, it explained how much the
gift of the Diplomat had meant.

It had been some months before he started to use it.
He'd had to adjust to the idea. All those years teaching
public school, living in apartments across Manhattan and

Brooklyn, he had dutifully come to see his parents once or twice a month, sometimes here and sometimes in a restaurant, always on their turf. It was a given, that they would not visit. It would have never occurred to him that it could be another way. He was the child, wasn't that the case? Even at thirty, forty, fifty? But in truth, he didn't want them in his house. Another thing to lose sleep over, not guilt exactly but regret. Regret that it couldn't be otherwise, that there was so much ceremony to stand on, that this was as true of him as it was of them. He regarded their relationship as a matter of accountability. He had done what it was necessary to do. Nothing less, nothing more. And he bore no grudges. Moving back in had been, at first, no different, a form of retreat, a way of playing out the string.

The pen, however: It was magnetic, a lodestone. Since he was no longer teaching, he didn't need to write much: no grades, no reports, no evaluations. No syllabi or lesson plans. Just the occasional check or list and the daily crossword. An ink cartridge could last a good long time. Even so, after seven or eight months, he began to wonder if the pen would ever run out. He began to imagine it as an omen or a sign. Each morning, when he filled the first clue of the puzzle in black ballpoint, it was as if something had been affirmed. As the year lurched into December, he found himself in a delicious anticipation. Maybe the pen, the endless flow of it, might come to represent a Hanukkah miracle all its own.

Then, this morning, as he worked the right bottom quadrant, it had run dry.

He didn't know what to think and didn't want to. He didn't want to divine what it might mean. Instead, he went about taking care of his father, only retrieving the pen in the stillness of evening and carrying it into the living room. On the mantel, the candles had burned down a little more than halfway. Dripping wax had begun to pool along the silver branches in rivulets of white and blue.

The shanda involved not his mother but his father. It had to do with the two menorahs, this and the small one by his bed. The old man would have been livid if he'd known about it. But that was the point—he didn't know. He had brought the Christmas tree home and turned his back on Judaism, and in the process cut off access to their heritage. It was like trading up; this was how his parents thought of it, that they'd had graduated to a higher class. His mother, he knew, had laid the groundwork. But his father had been the catalyst. She needed him to make it real.

Now she was gone, and he was going. The menorahs shone as a rebuke. He thought of his grandmother, whom he had loved; she would have been approving. He placed the pen on the mantel next to the menorah and watched the candles flame.

At night he walked

after he had his father settled. It was necessary to remove himself. All day in the claustrophobia of that apartment, waking his father, feeding him, making sure he was comfortable and clean, that he'd had his medications, putting him to bed. It was like caring for a baby, another chore he'd never sought. And yet, a baby? A baby grew and learned things. A baby became a toddler and went to school. A baby grew into a teenager who despised you. This was just a winnowing into the grave.

His father was no longer capable of getting out of bed

without assistance, which—in this regard, at least—was a
blessing. He'd wait until nine, when the old man's snores
were steady. Then he'd call and put the old man's phone
on speaker, leave it on the nightstand when he left. On
the way downstairs, he'd put in ear buds, listen to his
father breathing as he walked. It made for a peculiar balance between presence and absence, between being there
and not. He'd once had a coworker who every morning
would call his mother, in assisted living in another state,
and keep the line open throughout the day. He lacked the
stamina for that, or maybe he was too drained and angry
to care. Still, he was here, wasn't he? He'd given up his life
for this. He understood none of it was workable, that the
present was a way station between a past no longer extant
and a future spelled out in collapse. He knew nothing was
getting better, that he had consigned himself to purga-
tory, a form of living death. The secret was he was ready.
If not for the dying then for the silence.

He was ready to withdraw.

This is what happened when he was walking. He withdrew, or lost himself. A couple of hours spent slipping
through the night-dark streets of the borough, starting
with Park Avenue South. The Empire State Building was
just a few blocks west, hovering like a three-dimensional
facsimile of itself. So much of the city seemed to him like
that now, in some way smaller than it was. Maybe it was the
proximity, the closeness; it was hard for a single structure,
even this one, to stand out. Maybe it was the smallness of
his life. The Empire State had been built over the course of
thirteen months, in 1930 and 1931. Neither of his parents
had yet been born.

When he thought about the building, he thought about Evelyn Frances McHale. In 1947, at twenty-three, she'd stepped off the observation deck on the eighty-sixth floor and entered oblivion. The photo of the aftermath had become legend: her body, left ankle crossed demurely over the right, supine on the crushed roof of a parked sedan. Her face made up, gloved hands raised. *The most beautiful suicide*, she would come to be called, but he understood this was sophistry; just turn her body over to discover the real effects of her jump. In her purse, a note. Seven sentences. *Tell my father, I have too many of my mother's tendencies*, read the last.

Some nights, he would head downtown, past Union Square, through the Village, Soho, all the way to the Battery. Others, he would turn the opposite direction, walk Fifth Avenue to the northeastern edge of Central Park. He sought out sectors that were quiet, empty—residential and commercial. He moved across them like a shadow, a specter in the cityscape. As he moved, time seemed to flatten, not to stop exactly but to slow. Through it all, every step, his father's aspiration echoed in his ear buds, counterpoint to the beat of his disembodied rambles, reminding him that they were receding together, yoking them in their shared and primal destiny.

Many nights he wished his father would stop breathing. Many nights he hoped he'd come home to find him dead. His father wasn't cruel but he could be cutting, although most often he was merely cold. Now that he couldn't speak, their lives together had settled into silence, which had felt like a reprieve at first but had settled into its own form of gloom. Before that, his father had been demanding about all he could no longer handle, more than once leveling accusations of improprieties.

"What improprieties?" he'd roar back. "You used up all the money."

It would be funny if it didn't make him want to die.

The thing was, when you hit a certain point none of it made a difference any longer. There was only this, the here and now. Here, they had no money. Now, his father's existence had gone empty except for eating and shitting, except for being bathed. This—the daily washing of his withered body—was a rite of passage, a duty to be taken on. How much more until his father was no longer?

As he roamed the city the only answers he could conjure turned up blank.

The casualty department

was how he referred to the apartment. It was a joke for him alone. The phrase was British, what they called an emergency room, and like so many Britishisms, this one had a charming practicality. Why not, after all, just say it? Why not just call it what it was? *Emergency* was a euphemism. *Casualty* reeked of rage and blood.

His mother's love

had never been sustaining. This was the reason he was an only child. She'd only had room in her heart for a single person, his father, and she had been shattered by terror that she would one day be left alone. It wasn't that she wanted to die first, although, as it turned out, this was how it happened. More that she refused to reckon with death on any level, to admit that she lived at the mercy of the world.

And yet, the world had been merciful for a long time. She and his father had possessed all they needed, until they did not. Like the ink in that pen, the money had lasted longer than anyone could have anticipated—longer, even, than his mother had. As she lay dying, rain had fallen. In a strange room she emptied herself. The room was the room of death, which she had never acknowledged she would enter.

She and his father both.

He remembered a conversation not long before her death. He was visiting, and they were in the living room. In the bedroom, his father slumbered dreamlessly. If he watched closely, he could almost see the sequestering wall breathing in and out.

"How does he seem to you?" she asked. It was not the first time. To talk with her was like listening to a closed loop. Her short-term memory was almost entirely gone. Mostly, she peppered him with questions about his father's health.

Her mind like an eddy of water spiraling around a drain.

"What do you mean?" he said, part of the routine. It felt like acting in a play.

"I think he's improving. Don't you agree?"

"I can't give you the answer you want."

"What answer do you think I want?" she sparked, and there they were, those eyes again, like lasers, looking for the point of egress, looking for the fight.

He tried, when he was with her, to be gentle. Bygones being bygones and all that. She was old and dying also. Her dread was like a rat in the cage of her mind.

Some days, though, he couldn't take it. Some days, though, he took the bait.

"You have to accept," he told her, "the situation."

Her eyes kept probing him, as if for cracks.

"He's going to die," he went on. "You have to accept that."

"No," she answered. "I do not."

Zot Hanukkah

was almost finished. The candles had nearly burned through to the nubs. Tomorrow, he would clean the guttered wax and for another year, the menorah would stand like a sentinel on the mantel, his grandmother's angry ghost.

Tomorrow? The idea of it made him want to laugh. He was becoming his mother, so enmeshed he couldn't imagine the world without his father, although their love for one another had not been love, exactly. Or, at least, it had not been smooth. He recalled the early days of her forgetting, the old man shouting at her about her lapses, as if that would counteract what was happening to her mind. When he was there, he would put a stop to it, but mostly he kept his distance, still working, still in his apartment, stopping by when he could avoid it no longer, for an hour or a meal.

Outside, a soft rain had begun to fall, like the night his mother died; it brushed against the windows in a faint caress. Like a hand, a set of fingers smoothing the world and its troubles, washing clean the boundary between desire and despair. He shut off the lights and sat in grainy grayness, the only light from the menorah. He could almost feel himself disappearing. What would happen if he refused?

On the mantel, the candles began to flicker; he watched as, one by one, they went out. Right to left, the reverse of how they'd been ignited. Almost like there was an order or a plan. And yet, a plan, what did that get you? His mother had a plan but it didn't include a way to behave in the face of death. Evelyn Frances McHale had a different plan, which did not include a way to behave in the face of life. *Tell my father, I have too many of my mother's tendencies.* Sing it, sister, he wanted to say. These two women, dying seventy-five years apart, and still his father lingered on.

The candles made him think of stars imploding. The last one to stay lit was the Shamash. The Shamash, the helper candle, its purpose to light the others, and to replace any candle that might happen to fail. And wasn't that what he was, too, a helper candle? A Shamash in human form? But even a helper candle must eventually burn out. He held his breath as he watched the final wick go dark.

Today had been a day of endings. Zot Hanukkah. The pen going dry. Now, the candles had finished also. All of it seemed to him related. It felt like the last night of the world. He'd known since this had started that they'd run out of options; now, there was only one way for things to go. Tomorrow, they might find themselves evicted. Tomorrow, the bank might foreclose. He still had his money, but even if he used it, what would it matter? It would only forestall the inevitable.

There would never be enough.

No, it was up to him. It had always been up to him. From the moment he had moved back, he'd been on a one-way ticket, and now he had arrived. In the dark, he listened to the sound of his own breathing. It was too indistinct, almost, for him to hear. On the other side of the window, the rain continued falling faintly through the universe and faintly falling upon all the living and the dead.

The shamash

entered the bedroom to the low wheeze of his father's snoring. The semidarkness here felt liminal. He thought for a moment about switching off the menorah, but his father's feelings, whatever they may or may not have been, no longer were a matter for consideration. They had moved beyond the point of caring or dispute.

He reached across the mattress railing to lay a palm upon the old man's forehead. It was warm to the touch. The casualty department. If the casualty refused to die, however, it would become an open wound. An open wound might easily become infected. An infection could spread. He imagined himself at the edge of it, where the raw red blister of the casualty went white with maceration. He imagined himself falling in. What's that he'd been thinking about mercy? He could use a little mercy now. But mercy, it was a complicated business. Death could be a mercy as much as living. *For everything there is a season*, the Kohelet proclaimed. And yet, this same book of the Mikra also declared, *Everything is meaningless.* How to reconcile these apparently opposing points of view? The Mikra was the Hebrew Bible. His reading of it was, like all his forays into Judaism, impressionistic, vestigial, one more abstraction: a physics problem undertaken by a student who had been kept out of class. On the internet, he'd learned about the Mercy Seat, the golden lid that sat atop the Ark of the Covenant, where a pair of cherubim, one at each end, stretched their wings to create a sacred space in which Yahweh might come to dwell.

Of course, for Yahweh to appear, it would have to be the Day of Judgment. Otherwise, Yahweh had gotten good at getting gone. How else to explain the circumstance in which he found himself, taking mercy into his own hands?

He was so tired it felt as if he were being suffocated. All he wanted was to close his eyes. He leaned over the mattress railing to take one last look at his father. "I love you," he said. He bent to kiss the old man's derelict skull before retrieving one of the pillows from the bed and placing it over his face.

Outside, the rain ticked up, scratching at the window like the fingers on a pair of hands. Maybe it was Yahweh and this *was* the Day of Judgment, although when he went to look, nothing was there. Just the wet sidewalk below and the buildings across the street, trees with their bare branches gesticulating at the sky. *What now?* he thought, or might have thought. Or maybe, he didn't think anything at all.

On the bed, the pillow kept moving; it kept rising up and rising down. Briefly, he allowed himself to hope that this would stop, that the pillow's soft weight would be all that was required. His father, though, had never made anything so easy. His father had never made anything so clean. He could leave the pillow on his face all night and come back in the morning, only to be greeted by the sluffing of his snores.

If this was going to happen, he was going to have to do it. He was going to have to decide. He could walk right out of this room and take his chances. He could remove the pillow and go on with the way it had been.

But that time had passed. He understood this. It was not now or never because that implied a choice. And the notion that mercy was a relief or a consolation ... well, that would be mistaken, wouldn't it? Mercy was never easy, some sort of gauzy benediction. Mercy was a form of rigor. Ruthlessness might be a better word.

He had not known it would end like this or he would never have moved back. He would have cashed out his pension and run. To California or beyond, some place where he knew no one. But that, he'd come to recognize, was not who he was.

No, he was the Shamash, he was the helper. He would do what needed to be done. A good son? Maybe, yet that had never been the point of it. More a necessary narrowing, beyond memory and emotion, to this act of responsibility and love.

He wasn't certain how to start but once he did, it seemed as if he'd known all along. He leaned over his father's body. He placed both hands on the pillow and brought his weight to bear. At first, there was no reaction. Until the old man began to fight. His snoring yielded to an anguished rasping, and after that, a kind of wordless bellowing. He almost stopped then, thinking of his mother. This was how his father had bellowed at her. The old man raised his arms and swatted at him; he had to let up on the pressure as he pulled away and out of range.

He nearly quit again when he felt his father grasp his forearm. He roughly pushed the shriveled hand away. His eyes began to fill and he could see no longer. Everything was blurring, bleeding, the grayness of the room receding, black wings like death at the edges of his vision as if this were a Mercy Seat of mourning.

He continued to press the pillow into his father's face.

And as he did, he could feel his burdens lifting. He could feel them begin to fly away. Was that his father's soul he could sense departing? He didn't know what he believed. His tears were dripping on the pillow. He closed his eyes to press the tears away. And there, he found he could see himself, not in the closed space of this room but walking Manhattan with his father on his back. They were not in a state of struggle but communion. He was carrying the old man through the stations of his past. First, the Upper West Side, where they had lived all those many years ago. Then, the Empire State Building, lit up in blue and white, trinkets festooning many of its windows. As he drew closer, he could see that they were fancy pens.

On the bed, his father was thrashing no longer. He opened his eyes, and they were dry. The old man was not quite still but quieting. He understood that he would have to remain present for this part. Just a little more, he thought, pressing harder on the pillow. He held it down until his father ceased to move. After counting to sixty in his head to be certain, he removed the pillow, revealing a face that was not placid: mucus hanging weblike from the compressed nostrils, mouth open in an angry maw. He checked the old man's pulse and closed his eyes before wiping his face.

In the bathroom, he stared into the mirror, steadying. His father hadn't been what you'd call living, really, but he was still awake. Now, all that was done, like the pen and the menorah, that makeshift monument in the living room, a monument to what? *Baruch atah Adonai Eloheinu Melech ha-olam, asher kid'shanu b-mitzvotav, v-tzivanu l'hadlik ner shel Hanukkah*, he recited. It was the only prayer he could recite. Himself not quite a Jew, less Maccabee than wannabee.

Still, like the Maccabees, he'd had the strength to see it through.

Time felt suspended, although the rain kept falling against the window. He remembered this from his mother's death, as well. Another in-between space, in which it was as if nothing happened until it was reported, as if, were he simply to stay silent, no one would know. He would let the dust collect, sift quietly from room to room, and bury him. He felt like he could sleep for one hundred years.

Later, he would tell himself it had been a mitzvah. Later, he would recall the promise of the Mercy Seat. Later, there would be some sort of reckoning.

But in the first moments of his orphanhood, the Shamash wept.

JAMES D.F. HANNAH

James D.F. Hannah is the Shamus Award-winning author of the Henry Malone series, including the novels *Because the Night* and *Behind the Wall of Sleep*. His short fiction has appeared in *Best American Mystery and Suspense 2022*, edited by Steph Cha and Jess Walter; *Ellery Queen Mystery Magazine*; *Playing Games*, edited by Lawrence Block; *Under the Thumb: Stories of Police Oppression*, edited by S.A. Cosby; *Vautrin*; *Rock and a Hard Place*; *Shotgun Honey*; and *The Anthology of Appalachian Writers*. He lives in Louisville, Kentucky, where the bourbon is.

TWENTY CENTURIES
James D.F. Hannah

Crash's cell is set to vibrate, and it's still enough to wake her. It's Virgil McCoy, her chief deputy, on the phone.

"Hey, Virgil," she says.

"Hey, Sheriff. Sorry to be calling so early, but we got a situation."

The bedside clock glows 3:32 A.M. in green luminescence. The line between night and morning, Crash thinks. Is it early or late? Depends on which side of things you're on.

She sits up in bed and repositions a pillow behind her back. "What's going on?"

Virgil clears his throat. "Nine-one-one got a call on a dead body here in Diggtown."

She takes her watch—a Timex she bought at Target last year—from the nightstand and straps it onto her wrist. "Homicide? OD?"

"That's part of the situation. He's laying here in a front yard, no clothes on. He's all cut up and bandaged, Sheriff. Looks like someone was trying to skin him alive."

Taylor stirs. Crash thinks she's waking up, but she only makes a small, indistinguishable sound, like a response to a dream, and rolls onto her other side.

Crash slips from bed and heads toward the kitchen. A chill hangs in the old house. The furnace clicked on and off throughout the night, fighting a losing battle against a weather forecast that called for an overnight low barely in double digits.

"You at the scene?" Crash says to Virgil as she takes a can of Maxwell House from a cabinet.

"Yes, ma'am."

"Lay off the 'ma'am' bullshit, Virgil. Text me your location. State police shown up?"

"No, Sheriff. Just me."

"All right. Secure the scene and I'll be there quick as I can." Crash ends the call and rests the phone on the kitchen counter. A quick shower and the coffee'll be done. Time for a cup, fill a thermos with the rest, take it with her.

"Charlotte? What're you doing?"

Taylor, in the doorway. She's the only person besides Crash's own parents to call her by her given name. She's wearing joggers and a tank top and an expression of sleepy-eyed curiosity.

Crash kisses her on the forehead.

"It's nothing. It's—"

"If it was nothing you wouldn't be making coffee in the middle of the night," Taylor says.

She has a point.

They are a study in contrasts. Taylor Davies is taller, Black, her hair in braids. Crash is white, boyish looking, with muscular forearms and a string of tattoos along her left arm. Taylor is also an FBI agent, assigned to the Criminal Justice Information Services Division in Clarksburg. Acting like she could be shocked by a dead body is probably insulting. But this relationship is only a few months old, and Crash treats it with kid gloves still.

She explains the phone call while the coffee pours through the machine. She makes herself that first cup and Taylor gets herself orange juice. Taylor listens, sips her juice, and when Crash is done, kisses her.

"It's cold, and it's late," she says. "I'm going back to bed. Please be safe."

Crash rinses Taylor's glass in the sink. The wind howls and rattles the windows. Snow sparkles under the cool white moonlight. A person wouldn't make it long in this weather.

Did Virgil say the body was naked?

DIGGTOWN USED TO BE a coal camp built by one of the coal companies as a home for its miners. But then the mines closed, the jobs left, and the people left with them. Now the neighborhood's a shadow of a shadow, houses in various states of care or disrepair. Christmas lights shine from some windows. An inflatable Santa Claus snaps in the wind like a parade float almost out of control, tethered to the earth by a rope.

Then there are houses like the pale yellow one at the address Virgil sent, sitting beneath a streetlamp's sodium vapor light. The wooden siding is cracked and hangs loose, whipping and smacking like gunshots. The interior of the house is dark. No fence, but Virgil's marked off the boundary with crime scene tape already.

The LED readout on the cruiser dashboard claims it is twelve degrees. A cold that'll suck the air from your lungs. Crash pours coffee from her thermos into a Yeti mug. Adjusts the heavy cap around her head, pulls up her gloves, zips her jacket to the neck, and gets out of the SUV.

A dog barks from inside a neighboring house as Crash approaches Virgil, who's also dressed in the warmest gear the department has to offer. Snow crunches beneath her feet, and it's an effort to pull them free and move forward with each step. Virgil's face brightens as Crash hands him the Yeti.

"Much appreciated, Sheriff," he says as he sips the coffee.

Wind and snow stings her face as Crash sweeps the shine of a six-battery flashlight across the yard until it lands on a shape lying in snow tinted pink by blood.

The dead man had been young, younger than Crash, and gym-ripped, thick muscles threaded with ropey veins beneath his skin. He's wearing blue boxer shorts, so not as naked as Virgil had implied, but still, damn near naked, and definitely not clothed enough for twelve degrees.

Blood-stained bandages cover the man's torso and legs. The right hip. The smallest at the top of his left arm. The bandages all affixed with duct tape. Around the bandages swim a variety of tattoos. Snakes, skulls, flames, images Crash can't quite make out in the darkness.

"Call came from next door, a Eugene Miller," Virgil says. "Says his dog was out here barking and going crazy. He came to see what it was, found the deceased here."

Crash takes her cell phone out and snaps pictures of the dead man.

A man's voice calls out, "Y'all gonna be all night? Some of us gotta work in the morning."

"That's Mr. Miller," Virgil says.

Crash stands. Looks toward the voice. "So I gathered," she says.

Crash approaches the porch. Eugene Miller's standing in the doorway, white hair a swirl atop his head, skinny legs sticking out from the bottom of a ratty blue robe pulled around himself. He seems oblivious to the cold. Warmed by the anger of inconvenience and lost sleep, perhaps.

"Mr. Miller, I'm Sheriff Landing," Crash says.

"I know who you are." Miller purses his lips. "I didn't vote for you."

"But you voted nonetheless. Deputy McCoy says you found the body."

Miller stares past Crash, toward the dead man. "Didn't used to be this way, you know. People worked. Now it's nothing but druggies and bums, and I don't see the sheriff's department doin' much about it."

Crash gestures toward the yellow house. "You know who lived here?" she says.

"Used to belong to Terry and Maggie Mason, but Terry had a stroke and his kids put him in a home somewhere. Maggie got cancer and died last year. The family moved the furniture out in the fall. I've heard they've tried selling the place, but no one's rushing to get here."

"Is there a chance you knew the deceased?"

"Young lady, I—"

"It's 'Sheriff,' Mr. Miller," Crash says.

"Fine then, Sheriff. I work, not like these bums. I mind my business."

Crash steps closer to the house. Pulls up a photo of the dead man on her phone and holds it in Miller's direction. "Then you don't recognize him?"

Miller twists his head away when he realizes what he's looking at. "Jesus," he says. "Do you mind?"

Crash doesn't move. "So he doesn't look familiar at all?"

Miller turns his head back, a reluctant gaze settling on the phone.

"It might be that Parsons kid, lives a few miles up the road," he says. "His old man's in a wheelchair. I think the kid takes care of him."

"Either of 'em have first names?"

"I'd imagine they would, but it ain't my business to know 'em."

Crash tucks the phone into her coat pocket. "It was your dog that found the body, correct?"

"Yeah. I was done drinking around eleven, and I didn't feel like listening to the news lie to me, so I put Grace out for the night and went to bed. She started up about two or two-thirty, and when I came to yell at her to hush, I saw what got her so riled." Shakes his head. "If I'd known you'd be here all night, I'd have gone on back to bed. Not like he was going nowhere. Cold enough, he'd have kept till morning."

A soft whine comes from behind Miller, and Crash sees a midsized mutt standing there. A shaggy Heinz 57 of a dog, watching her with nervous, chocolate-colored eyes.

Miller stomps his foot. "Hush it, Grace."

"Glad she's inside," Crash says. "Awfully cold tonight."

"She's got a place." Miller jerks his chin toward a ramshackle doghouse half-buried in snow. "She's fine. Now you mind if I get back to bed?"

"Don't let me stop you. Sleep well, Mr. Miller."

He slams the door shut behind him. Crash waits until the lights go off and the house is dark.

"Asshole," she says. She walks back to Virgil, who hasn't moved, still standing watch over the body.

"Seems Mr. Miller thinks our deceased lives a few miles up the road. Last name of Parsons."

Virgil finishes the last of the coffee with a loud slurp. "That's not much in the way of help, Sheriff. You've got Parsonses all up and down this creek. Probably can't swing a dead cat without hitting one."

"Okay, but this one has a father in a wheelchair. Think that'll narrow it down any?"

"Only by a bit." He scratches his chin with gloved fingers. "Reckon it gets to morning, we can drive up and look for houses with ramps, might have their names on the mailboxes out front, too."

Crash checks her watch. Four forty-five A.M.

"It's morning already." She cuts the beam from her flashlight to the body, traces a single set of footprints, from the dead man back to the edge of the yard. There's blood in each step, the drops like cherry blossoms. "Don't know we can wait. If his father's an invalid, the old man might need medical attention that's not gonna hold on till sunrise. You wait for the coroner. I'm going to go and see what I see."

"In this dark, this weather, what'll you suppose you'll be able to see?"

Crash holds the flashlight under her chin, letting the six-battery lamination set her face aglow. "It's why they give us the big flashlights, Virgil."

CRASH DRIVES FIVE MILES an hour, feeling the tires occasionally spin or the SUV slip on the ice-slick road. The road's barely wider than the vehicle, and it wouldn't take much to send her in one of two directions: headfirst into the creek on the left, or into the ditch line to the right. She keeps one hand on the steering wheel and the other on the flashlight, raising it whenever she sees a house with a wheelchair ramp. So far, they've all had unblemished snow surrounding them, no signs of footprints.

Two miles up she finds a bundle of clothes piled next to the road. A man's jacket, a hoodie, blue jeans, boots, a cell phone with a spiderwebbed screen. The inside of the hoodie has blood on it. She bags everything and puts it in the trunk for the state lab to examine.

It's another three miles later when she sees the trailer, a double-wide on an elevated foundation. A wheelchair ramp to the porch, a prefab metal storage building in the yard. A TV antenna shudders in the wind.

She sees footprints across the front yard, and "Parsons" written out with vinyl letters on the mailbox. She parks in the driveway, approaches the front door. It's cracked an inch or so already, and she pushes it open the rest of the way.

The doorway spills out onto a living room decorated from thrift shops and discount stores. She calls out, "Parker County Sheriff's Department!"

The stink hits her along with a blast of heat. She smells smoke and death. She pulls her service weapon.

"Parker County Sheriff's Department!" she says again. The extra intake of air to yell makes her nearly gag. She holds back bile.

The living room flows into the kitchen. She sees the empty wheelchair there. Steps around the counter dividing the spaces.

The toes of her right boot skim the edge of a pool of

blood, thick as spilled jam, haloed around the head of a man face down on the yellowed linoleum. This new dead man lies at the foot of the wheelchair, the back of his skull caved in, his body twisted in a way you'd think his bones had been removed.

Mired in the blood is a bowling trophy. Clumped onto one corner of the wooden base are strands of hair and clots of blood and bits of flesh.

She checks the man for a pulse. Knows the answer, but the question has to be asked.

No surprises there.

She surveys the area. Finds more blood in the living room, a path of it, trailing down a hallway. She follows the blood and the smell of smoke, the droplets getting larger, the smell of smoke stronger, leading her into a bathroom.

Here the blood's still red and livid and angry, pooled onto the tile floor. Thick and viscid in the sink. Bottles of isopropyl alcohol and lighter fluid scattered across the floor. Half-empty rolls of duct tape and packages of gauze bandages. A blood-stained razor blade balanced on the sink's edge.

The porcelain's charred black and filled with spent matches and ashes. She takes a pen from her coat pocket and pokes through the mess. It's the remains of photos, edges blackened and curled and eaten away by fire. Blackened images of the past, of the dead man, younger and growing and changing, still unmistakably him.

There are blobs of something bubbly and crispy stuck to the inside of the sink, cooked onto the porcelain. It reminds Crash of how fat on a steak burns.

She looks at the razor blade, so coated in dried blood it's adhered to the sink.

For the first time she looks up and notices the mirror. The words scrawled in blood. Thick, finger-drawn letters.

I'M NOT WHO I AM.

She stares at the reflection in the glass, the words seemingly etched across her face like a mask, like a sign, like a proclamation.

THE DEAD MAN IN the wheelchair is William Parsons, though Crash would bet people had called him "Bill." Perhaps "Billy." She's staring at a framed photo on the mantel of the double-wide's fake fireplace. The picture is of William Parsons and a woman and someone who was most definitely the naked dead man, though in the picture he's no more than ten or eleven, his features soft and rounded and unformed. The picture likely taken at a Sears or Olan Mills studio at the mall in Clarksburg. Everyone's smiling. Everyone's happy. The photo's set in the middle of several other cheap-looking bowling trophies.

Virgil comes up behind Crash, pulling off his big hat, his hair sweaty and matted to his head. Behind him the coroner attendants wheel out the covered shape of the person who had been William Parsons. Maybe "Bill," probably "Billy."

"Neighbors said it was just the victim and his son living here," he says. "Well, the victim in the kitchen."

"Have a name on the son?" Crash says.

Virgil removes his gloves, brings a notebook from his coat pocket, thumbs through the pages. "Dennis. The father was Billy."

"One mystery solved," Crash says.

Virgil pauses, lets the notebook drop to the side. "What was that, Sheriff?"

"Nothing, Virgil. What about a wife or girlfriend? For either of them."

"There was a mother. Catherine Parsons. Neighbors don't know her maiden name. She and the deceased—the one here, I mean—met in college and married and moved back. They divorced, she left town, died a few years back."

Crash looks at the family photo above the mantle. That frozen-in-time moment of familial bliss.

"They know what Billy or Dennis did for work?" she says.

"No. They moved here after the elder Parsons and his wife divorced. Dad started hitting the bottle, put his car into a tree coming home from town one night, landed himself in the wheelchair. The son's been taking care of him ever since. Neighbors said the son was quiet, awkward, but he'd gotten into working out. Really transformed himself. Last few years, they've always been getting boxes dropped off and packages picked up. They didn't know what it was about, but there was a lot of activity around that metal shed outside."

"Seems these neighbors paid a little more attention than Mr. Miller."

Crash feels her ass vibrate, realizes it's her cell phone going off. She doesn't recognize the number as she answers.

"Parker County Sheriff's Department," she says. "Sheriff Charlotte Landing speaking."

"Sheriff, this is Joseph Mason. I know it's early, but I heard you found a body outside my grandparents' house." The voice on the other end sounds young, sounds nervous.

"Morning, Mr. Mason. Appreciate you calling," Crash

says. She motions for Virgil to walk away. He puts his hat and gloves back on and heads outside. "Any chance you know a Dennis Parsons?" she says.

"Dennis? Jesus, yeah, I know Dennis. Why you asking?"

"How'd you know him?"

"We went to school together. We were friends, but then his mom left and his dad had a car accident and Dennis didn't do much more than take care of the old man after that. Was it Dennis in the yard?"

"It was."

"Goddamn. Poor guy never had a chance, did he?" Crash hears the consideration going on in Joseph Mason's head. "Don't know if anyone's told you, but Dennis and his dad had gotten into some weird shit these last couple of years."

"Can you narrow down 'weird shit'?"

"I came to clear out my grandparents' house and Dennis volunteered to help. I hadn't seen him since we graduated high school, and I almost didn't know it was him. He'd got jacked, covered in tattoos. He's telling me about the conspiracy theories he and his dad were finding. Fall-down-a-rabbit-hole stuff. White supremacy and Nazis, storm-the-Capitol nonsense. And the tattoos matched the crazy, Sheriff. Swastikas and numbers that were supposed to have secret meanings. I couldn't keep up with everything. He said he was discovering how it all was connected."

"What was connected?"

"Everything. Politics and religion and science and the media. He said there'd be a 'great awakening,' and we'd elevate our consciousness, and we'd take everything back from the power brokers. You ever had it, Sheriff, you're talking to someone and you think they're normal and then you realize they're crazier than a shithouse rat? This was that."

"What did you say?"

"Nothing. I thanked him for helping and couldn't wait for him to leave. I started law school this fall; I don't need that nonsense. Can't say I'm surprised. Him and his dad up that holler, having to schedule to see sunlight, what else was gonna happen?" A pause. "His dad. Oh hell. What'll happen to him now?"

Crash doesn't answer this question. She instead tells Joseph Mason goodbye and hangs up. Stands in the doorway and narrows her sight onto the aluminum building. Virgil gets out of the cruiser parked behind Crash's and stomps through the snow back into the house.

"Something up, Sheriff?" he says.

"You got bolt cutters, Virgil?"

"I surely do. Why?"

"Fetch 'em, then."

THE LOCK COMES OFF with the cold solid snap of steel, the cutters slicing through the shackle, the body dropping into the snow. Virgil lets the cutters fall and goes to open the door on the metal building when Crash says, "I got this."

The door whines on rusted hinges as it swings open. Crash brings her pistol up in one hand, the six-battery flashlight in the other, the beam cleaving the building's darkness, landing on a Nazi flag hung up on the far wall.

"Well shit," Virgil says.

The building's four-deep full of cardboard boxes, stacked so there's a narrow path through the middle. Crash moves the light throughout the building interior. She's looking for extra security. Not just a video camera, but trip wires or motion detectors. She's read the reports, white supremacists setting boobytraps for law enforcement or anyone unlucky enough to stumble onto their operations.

Virgil stands directly behind Crash. His breath crackles in the cold air. She checks the floor for pressure plates.

"In for the penny," she says. "May as well be in for the pound."

She steps into the building.

Nothing explodes.

Another step.

Still nothing.

She checks at the edges of the boxes, the spaces between each one stacked atop one another. All neat and organized. No dust. This wasn't a place where things were piled away and forgotten.

One of the boxes is open already. She holsters her service weapon.

"What are you doin'?" Virgil says from the building doorway.

Crash pulls back on the box flap. "What's it look like I'm doing?"

"You don't know what could be in that box, Sheriff."

"That's why I'm opening it, Virgil. Didn't you learn anything from Christmas mornings? Though if something jumps out, you have my permission to shoot it. Just don't shoot me while you're at it."

Crash shines her flashlight into the box. It's half full of folded T-shirts in clear plastic bags. Black with WHITE LIVES MATTER in block lettering, underneath that a hooded figure and a noose and a fist raised in a white power salute.

She opens the box beside it. More of the same. She tells Virgil to check the other boxes. Hoodies and more T-shirts, different sizes and colors, all with similar messages.

A few years ago there'd been a white supremacist compound located close by. Shut down now, and the government had impounded the property. But it doesn't matter if you tear the house down, Crash figures, because the roaches and the rats are always going to find somewhere else to live.

Virgil's holding a sweatshirt with a German eagle over a black sun.

"You suppose we should call the Feds on this?" he says.

"Probably," Crash says. "I know someone."

TAYLOR AND CRASH HAVE salad while the lasagna warms in the oven. Taylor eats her salad plain, ranch dressing on the side to dip in. Crash floods her bowl with Italian. The radio's playing Christmas songs—has since the first of November—and this is an oasis of normalcy after the whole of the fucking day.

Finally, Taylor says, "Well?"

Crash pauses with her fork poised above a plate half-empty of lasagna.

"Are you going to tell me about it or do I have to decipher it from the local news?" Taylor says.

Crash tells her the whole story. When she's done, Taylor shakes her head, gathers the dishes, rinses them in the sink.

"I'm amazed sometimes how it's not enough to hate people, that they've got to merchandise it as well," she says.

"It's the world," Crash says. "It gets smaller and it bleeds everywhere. Bleeds back to places like here."

"That's not true, Charlotte. Disney and Andy Griffith and the idea the world used to be one way and that's the way it's supposed to be, and maybe it was that way for these dead men you found. But it wasn't that way for everyone, and it never was."

"I know, Taylor."

Taylor drops the rag in the sink, drops her shoulders, practically lets her entire body collapse. She presses the heels of her hands into the edge of the sink to hold herself in place.

"I don't think you do. Because you are a small white woman living in a place designed to protect people like you."

"Have you gotten a good look at me? I look like a fourteen-year-old boy, and that's not the most popular look around here for a grown-ass woman. It was always obvious I was never going to marry a dumb boy and push out two-point-five kids and sell cookies at the church bake sale."

"You have choices about what you show the world. That dead man, the one with tattoos, it sounds like he was making it clear who it was he wanted the world to see. And when you're making those choices, it's telling other people they're expected to hide who they are, and I can't do that, Crash. And I won't."

"No one's asking you to, either. The only thing I've wanted is for you to be you. Nothing more or less."

Taylor turns off the faucet, but doesn't turn around.

"I know. Which is one of the reasons I love you."

There it is.

The thing they've never said to each other. Not yet. Not until now.

Crash comes up behind Taylor, dries her hands with a paper towel and holds on to them.

"I love you, too," she says.

"Though you shouldn't be expecting me to stay home and make dinner for you, either," Taylor says. "I am not really housewife material. I know maybe four good recipes."

Crash looks into her dark brown eyes.

"We should go to bed," she says.

CRASH GOES THROUGH TUDOR'S Biscuit World on the way to the courthouse, gets herself a sausage biscuit and coffee before she drives through town. Serenity, decorated for the holidays. Wreaths and red bells hang from twinkling lights strung from streetlamps. Christmas trees flicker with fake candlelight. Menorahs glow in store windows.

She slides the cruiser into her parking space, drinks the coffee, eats the biscuit.

Taylor was restless all night. Crash lay awake and listened as she seemed to hold each breath in anticipation of something. Before getting dressed and going to church, Taylor mentioned she was heading back to Clarksburg right after. Crash had already called the Feds, and she expected them to arrive at any time. Taylor didn't want to be around when they showed up, someone see her there, complicating things.

The compartmentalization of Taylor's life. Everything in small, neat little boxes. Say "I love you" and then leave.

Life in discrete units.

Crash told her okay. Said she needed to go to the office anyway. Once she's there, she sorts through the bag of Dennis Parsons's belongings and plugs his phone into a charging cable.

Her desk phone rings. The coroner's office. The coroner's a fussy little man named Ted Quarrier.

Quarrier. Coroner. She's never thought of how those words sound together and it makes her laugh as she's answering the phone.

"Good morning, Coroner Quarrier," she says.

"Morning, Sheriff. Finished up on both of your dead men. Care to hear the good word?"

"Hit me with your best shot."

"For the son, cause of death by hypothermia exacerbated by blood loss. The way he made those incisions, there stands a good chance he'd have bled out anyway, but the weather, the temperature, only made it worse."

"Any idea what would have made him stomp out into the snow in underwear? Drugs?"

"Tox screen was clean. I'd say it was paradoxical undressing. Fairly common in hypothermia cases. The muscles in the body trying to reduce heat loss become exhausted and release warm blood from the core to the extremities. It's essentially a hot flash, and since the individual is typically already disoriented and confused, they believe they're burning up."

"And they strip down to their skivvies."

"How old are you, Sheriff, you're using the term 'skivvies'?"

"What about the father? William Parsons?"

"He's dead also. Best guess of time of death is Friday evening. Traumatic blow to the back of the skull. Severe hematoma. Severe skull fracture. Whoever clocked him with that bowling trophy wanted him really most sincerely dead. Are you liking the son for this one?"

"It's what's showing up when I shake the Magic 8 Ball."

"What's the world coming to, Sheriff?"

"I doubt the world's going anywhere it's not been already."

They wish each other a happy holidays and Crash replaces the receiver in its cradle. She moves her computer mouse to stir the monitor to life and navigates her way to the photos she took yesterday at the Mason house. Dennis Parsons stares at her with expressionless eyes.

The fractured screen of his cell phone now glows with life. She bets dollars to donuts there's things on this phone that would tell her more about Dennis Parsons. Help her understand him. She might not understand totally why he bashed in his father's skull, though.

She taps the screen. The device predates biometrics, where a fingerprint or facial recognition would open it. What it needs is a four-digit passcode.

She's found the website William Parsons was running. Thing is a goddamn white power eBay, a smorgasbord of hate iconography in every style and size you can imagine. T-shirts, flags, banners, books, digital downloads, sweatpants with "WLM" instead of "JUICY" written across the ass.

A red banner on the site identifies its biggest seller is a plain white polo shirt. Looks like the ones you buy at Old Navy on sale for five bucks. This one's priced $14.88. Some other items priced the same. She knows about the fourteen words, and the mental gymnastics to make eighty-eight into "Heil Hitler."

Could it be that simple?

She taps the numbers onto the screen. The phone unlocks.

It is that simple.

Crash goes to photos first. Mostly memes with the stupid cartoon frog these idiots are into. Others use a comic book skull or variations on a German iron cross. They are nothing if not repetitive.

Into the calendar. Not much there. Not that Crash expects Dennis Parsons would have a full social life.

Contacts. Not many names, but a load of what feels like code names or aliases, which makes sense. In case of a situation like this, a cop gets hold of the phone, why make it easy to identify people?

Text messages. Dennis has been blowing shit up. He's in a half-dozen group chats, and every conversation's the same: racist jokes, racist memes, frustration no one's getting laid, and, more than anything, a seething anger at change. Rage that they weren't consulted. Indignation their parents' and grandparents' country wasn't entirely theirs anymore. A questioning of why should they have to listen or care about what people who don't look like them think or feel or want? What had happened to might making right?

Apps. Anything here? Well, Dennis Parsons's Instagram seems dedicated to following women with OnlyFans accounts. Dude was a thirsty motherfucker. Some online betting he sucked at—he's lost twelve of his last fourteen bets—and a Reddit account best described as a garbage fire.

Crash notices an app with an alert message. It's one of those places that tests your DNA. Send them a vial of spit and ninety-nine bucks and they'll tell you what far-off lands your ancestors escaped.

Guys like Dennis Parsons must love stuff like this. Confirmation of their very white heritage. German or Nordic or all the Scot-Irish blood pulsing through Appalachian veins.

Crash opens the app and moves through the findings.

Got those strong Celtic roots, Broadly European, roughly 50 percent, it states.

About that other half, however.

Those are Ashkenazi Jewish. Also right at 50 percent.

This is not the plot twist Crash expects on her Sunday morning.

Included in the app are ancestry reports and DNA relatives. There's no report for a father, but there is one from a mother, listed as Catherine Beckman.

The former Catherine Parsons, Crash thinks.

Which means Dennis's mother also spit into a tube and sent in ninety-nine dollars.

And that, despite Billy Parsons's protestations, Catherine Parsons isn't dead.

According to the app, Dennis got this information two days ago. Times to around Coroner Quarrier's determination of when someone chunked the corner of a bowling trophy into Billy's occipital lobe.

Crash imagines young Dennis Parsons, attached to his mother by an invisible umbilical cord, and then she's gone, and he's left with a father who teaches him to hate—perhaps to hate this very person—only to discover she's not dead. She is, it seems, very much alive.

Wouldn't take much for Dennis Parsons to be flooded with memories and resentment, followed by harsh words and accusations and questions and anger, as thick and cloudy as the bottom of a lake dredged for a body.

Where had the trophy been? On the fireplace mantle, with the others. Dennis Parsons, walking across the living room, bringing the trophy back into the kitchen.

Billy Parsons, trapped in his wheelchair, watching what would happen next like it was happening to someone else, until it happened to him. Then Dennis Parsons had stood in the bathroom, cranked by adrenaline and anger, and methodically cut away at the parts of his flesh that reflected back onto the father he had murdered. Watched it all in the mirror. Burned photos and those pieces of flesh in the sink.

I'M NOT WHO I AM.

Trying to destroy the lie of who he is before wandering out into the freezing cold.

Crash isn't one to stare into the darkness and ask the void what sort of world is the world becoming. She'd been the chief deputy for the previous sheriff, Matt Simms, and he'd definitely been that person, however. He'd served in the Army after 9/11. Told Crash how the whole thing— "Operation Enduring Freedom"—had begun with purpose but frayed quickly. The clarity of the mission muddied so fast.

"Things fall apart," he had told her. "The center cannot hold. Mere anarchy is loosed upon the world."

"I studied that poem in college," Crash said to Matt.

"Then you got to the part where he says 'the best lack all conviction, while the worst are full of passionate intensity.' Sometimes I think that's what the world needs, is the passionate intensity. It feeds on that. The world demands you burn bright and burn out and move on for the next in line."

"To what end?" Crash said.

"The world doesn't care about ends, Crash. No more than a clock cares about what we do with our time. The clock's job is to mark the minutes."

Crash wants something to have meaning. This could be the Methodist in her. The idea that it's not all random molecules bumping against one another. There's a reason for things.

She checks the phone log. Dennis Parsons didn't call people he didn't know.

Except the last phone call he ever made. The only time he ever called that number, at least from this phone.

The time. Friday evening, about six. Bill Parsons probably already dead.

Who do you call at a time like this?

Crash takes the receiver from the desk phone and punches in the number.

A woman's voice answers.

Crash says, "I'm trying to reach Catherine Parsons."

The break on the other end of the line seems to hang there for forever. Then, finally—

"It's not Parsons anymore," she says. "Hasn't been for a while."

THE COUNTY SPRANG FOR a system a few years ago, a video camera in the coroner's office transmitting to a monitor in the sheriff's office, the idea that it was less traumatic for families when they had to identify a body. That it wouldn't be like in the movies where they watch as the white sheet's pulled back and there's your brother or son or wife on a stainless-steel slab. No, this would offer a disconnect for the nexts-of-kin, they were told. It wouldn't be like in the movies, but rather it'd be like watching a movie.

Now compound that with more than a decade of time, and the next time you see your son, it's on this monitor? Can you even imagine that? Is it still like watching a movie?

Crash thinking this as Catherine Beckman stares at the monitor, at the face of her son, at the face of someone who may now just be a stranger to her.

She has hair the color of a sky full of rain, carefully tanned skin, simple earrings, tasteful rings on her fingers. Her clothing is dark and fashionable, from the type of boutique that doesn't need its name on a sign in front. Her eyes are wide and wet and she bites at her bottom lip, scraping away lipstick.

"The last time I saw him, he was so small," she says, and looks away.

Crash turns off the monitor and sits back in her chair. She puts her hand around her coffee cup, feels it cooling already. Catherine Beckman has her own cup on the other side of the desk, untouched.

"As your son's next of kin—"

"I can't describe how weird that sounds. It's been a long time since someone even suggested I have a son, Sheriff." She glances at her coffee cup. "You think Dennis killed Billy."

"The investigation is ongoing, and we don't have anything conclusive, but we also don't have any other suspects."

She nods.

"When I met Billy, he was a different person. He wanted to teach history. That's how we met, was in a history class in college. The plan was to move back here, get a job at the high school, except he couldn't find an in with the county. He taught some community college classes, and we'd go bowling a lot, but he was frustrated he couldn't do what he wanted. He started working watchman jobs at night to help make ends meet. He was bored and spent his time online. That's where it started, him in these online forums, talking to strangers all night. At first, he told me it was a whole new way of looking at history, and then it became about the purity of blood and protesting when towns took down a Confederate statue."

"He did this knowing you're Jewish?" Crash says.

"Of course. I never hid who I was until I came here. But by then, my parents were both gone, and the rest of my family was scattered everywhere. I had no more community, Sheriff. I was married. Billy and Dennis were my family. I even started going to the Baptist church with them."

"Then you made the decision to leave?"

"Because I'd had enough. I'd made dinner and Billy hadn't raised his head from his phone the entire night and it was Dennis and me alone at the table eating. I told Dennis to go to his room, to pack some clothes. It wasn't until Dennis and I had suitcases at the door that Billy even got up off the couch, asked us where we thought we were going."

Catherine Beckman's voice falls until Crash has to lean forward to hear her.

"He hit me," Catherine Beckman says. "It wasn't the first

time, but never with Dennis watching. It put me on the floor. He said I wasn't going anywhere with his son. Said if I walked out the door, I walked out alone, and I was never coming back for any reason."

"What did you do?"

"I did what I needed to do to survive, Sheriff. I kissed my son and told him I loved him and I left. I told myself I'd get stronger and I'd come back and I'd save him, but I knew what Billy was doing to Dennis already. I didn't know how to make him not hate me. Now I'm certain I wouldn't have liked the person Dennis became." Her eyes glance toward the blank monitor. "Dennis was Jewish. Judaism is matrilineal descent. The ultimate Jewish mother joke, someone told me. All Billy did was teach Dennis to hate himself. I only did the DNA app because of a project at temple. Tracing family lines. I don't put much stock into such things, but my husband, he loves it." She shakes her head. "What do I do here, Sheriff?"

"We have some paperwork you'll need to fill out, so we can release the body to the funeral home of your choice, then—"

"That's not what I mean, Sheriff."

"I know."

Catherine Beckman sighs. "Do you suppose Billy suffered? When Dennis killed him?"

"I don't know. That's well outside my field of knowledge."

"I hope he did. I hope he suffered unimaginably to the very end." She stands. "I need to get home. It's the fourth night of Hanukkah. My husband likes for me to be there to light the candle together."

Crash walks Catherine Beckman out of the courthouse, back to a Range Rover. From the courthouse steps Crash watches as the SUV doesn't move. Catherine Beckman sits behind the wheel and cries. What Crash imagines must be giant, gushing wails of immeasurable, impossible grief, burying her face into her hands and her shoulders shaking before finally taking a long, deep breath, wiping her face with a tissue, starting the engine, and driving away.

© ROLAND SCARPA

LEE GOLDBERG

Lee Goldberg is the #1 *New York Times* bestselling author of dozens of books, including *Malibu Burning, Calico, Dream Town, True Fiction, The Walk* and *Lost Hills,* as well as the bestselling and acclaimed Fox & O'Hare series he co-authored with Janet Evanovich. A two-time Edgar Award nominee, Lee also co-created the popular Hallmark mystery series *Mystery 101* and has written and produced hundreds of hours of network TV, including *Monk, Diagnosis Murder, seaQuest, Hunter, Spenser: For Hire* and many others.

IF I WERE A RICH MAN

Lee Goldberg

On the fourth day of Hanukkah, Ray Boyd decided to go on a treasure hunt. The idea hit him while he was passing the outlet mall off Interstate 5, an hour north of Los Angeles, in his old black-and-white Ford Crown Victoria Police Interceptor.

So he stopped at the mall and bought a carry-on roller bag, some polo shirts and slacks, and went to the mall bathroom to change out of his T-shirt and jeans into the new clothes. He stuffed his old clothes in the trash, put the rest of his purchases in the roller bag, and returned to his Crown Vic.

Ray dumped his bag into the massive trunk, which could comfortably fit three corpses, not that he'd ever tried, but it was important information to have in the back of his mind. The only other object in the trunk was the cardboard box that held his other earthly possessions: a Jack Reacher novel, a Ka-Bar knife, and a burner phone. There was also about $100,000 in cash, all the money he'd earned over the last few months from acting on sudden ideas and unexpected opportunities, hidden behind the door panels and inside the seats, along with some fake IDs and credit cards that he'd picked up in Las Vegas.

He slammed the trunk shut, got into the car, headed north on I-5 for a few miles, then took the turnoff onto Highway 99 toward Fresno.

The Crown Vic was stripped of its badging, sirens, and light bars before it was sold to him on his first day out of prison. But it still had its monster engine, two side-mounted spotlights, the smash bar on the front grill, and its fearsome disposition, so when he roared up behind cars, they quickly moved out of the way.

Ray got off the 99 in Fresno, found a pawn shop, and bought himself a gold wedding band, a money clip to replace the rubber band around his cash roll, and one of those necklaces that he'd seen all the old Jewish men wearing in Palm Springs, their garishly colorful, open-necked golf shirts revealing a golden Hebrew symbol lying in their curls of gray chest hair.

He was all set to see an old friend.

THE HAMPTON INN OFF Highway 99 was clean, crisp, and contemporary. Accented with fake wood paneling and stacked-stone facades, the lobby doubled as a breakfast room in the mornings and as a lounge the rest of the day, though nobody was using it. There were vases full of fake flowers everywhere and a bowl of red delicious apples, waxed to shiny perfection, on the counter at the check-in desk, where a fresh-faced young woman stood waiting to greet him.

She was athletically slim and in her early twenties, her long blond hair tied in a ponytail. She wore a smoothly pressed blue button-down dress shirt, open just far enough to show a slight hint of cleavage, and a pair of crisp black slacks with vertical creases that could cut loaves of bread.

"Welcome to the Hampton Inn," she said. "Do you have a reservation?"

"No, I don't," he said, wheeling his suitcase up to the counter. Normally, he stayed in the kind of places where they didn't ask for ID and no one made reservations. "Is that going to be a problem?"

She shook her head. "Of course not. This is Merced. We always have vacancies."

"Mazel Tov. I'd like a ground floor room, please." He handed her one of his fake California driver's licenses. This one was under the name "Mitchel Stein" and had a Santa Monica address.

As she typed the information into her computer, she asked: "Do you have a physical disability, Mr. Stein?"

"None at all. I'm full of youthful vigor."

"I could see that when you walked in, but I had to ask in case you wanted one of our ADA rooms."

He knew what they were. Americans with Disability Act suites wide enough for wheelchairs to navigate, with handrails in the shower and by the toilet, and with low sinks they could reach without getting up. They even had a few in prison.

"I understand." Ray leaned closer to her, close enough to see the band of freckles sprinkled across her slender nose, and to smell the coconut-scented shampoo she'd used that morning. "The truth is, I'm afraid of heights."

That was a lie, of course. The truth was he wanted to be able to escape out of the window if necessary and to have his car parked right there for a fast getaway.

She nodded knowingly. "We all have our crosses to bear."

"What's yours?"

She smiled again, but this one had a mischievous quality to it. "Impulse control. Would you like a king-size bed or two doubles?"

"One king. I'm on my own."

She typed something in the computer. "Are you in town for business or pleasure, Mr. Stein?"

"Hanukkah. My daughter Mindy is a student at UC Merced and she couldn't make it home for the holiday. So, I came to her. It's four days into the celebration, but it was the best I could do with work."

"I'm sure she'll appreciate it. What is she studying?"

"Cognitive science. What about you . . ." He let his voice trail off as he glanced at her name tag, intentionally letting his gaze linger on her breast for a second too long. " . . . Britney?"

"Psychology," Britney said. "With an emphasis on human sexuality. How did you know that I'm a student?"

"An educated guess. The population here is fifty-eight percent Hispanic. The economy is terrible, driven mostly by agriculture, so it's not a place people come to look for work, unless it's in the fields and, frankly, most of those people are Hispanic as well, a big chunk of them illegals. You're white, young, attractive, and not knocked up, so odds are you're not from here, because if you were, you'd have fled by now. So, the only reason you'd be here is the same as my daughter—you think state colleges are for losers and Merced is the only University of California campus you could get into with your mediocre grades."

"You're very observant," Britney said.

It was all bullshit he'd made up on the spot, but he was sure it was accurate. Merced was an easy place to size up.

"I'm an insurance adjuster, I have to pay attention to potential risks and meaningful figures." He flicked his gaze to her chest again, making sure she caught him at it. She seemed pleased rather than offended. She was proud of her rack. "Is it okay if I pay in cash? I don't like credit cards."

"Cash is fine, but we require a two hundred dollar-per-night deposit in advance against your final charges."

"I'll be here four nights at most." Ray took out his money clip and he noticed her eyes went wide, if only for a second, when she saw the wad of cash. He peeled off ten C-notes and slowly laid the bills on the counter. "This should cover it."

"That will be fine." Britney picked up the money, typed something on her keyboard, and the cash drawer popped open. She put the cash inside. "What's your problem with credit cards, if I may ask?"

Ray looked her in the eye and tried to match the smile she'd given him earlier. "Impulse control."

Britney smiled back at him, as if to say she understood the danger of quickly accumulating credit card debt, or perhaps to convey an entirely different understanding.

She ran two key cards through a machine of some kind, slipped them into a tiny folder, and wrote a number on the outside. "You're in room one twenty-three. Here are your keys."

Britney placed the card folder on the counter like a wrapped present.

Ray opened the folder, removed one of the key cards, and held it to her. "I only need one."

"Don't you want one for your daughter?"

"She won't be coming by."

"I see." Britney took the card, set it on the desk, then carefully picked an apple out of the bowl and offered it to him. "Enjoy your stay, Mr. Stein."

Ray accepted the apple and held it up for emphasis. "This is what got Adam and Eve in trouble."

Her mischievous smile was back. "It's also when the fun started."

He took a bite out of the apple, which was hard and juicy, and wheeled his suitcase down the hall to his room. He wondered if Britney flirted with all the men who came in and if she did it with actual intent, or just to make her day less boring.

Ray opened the door to his room. There was a bathroom to his left, and just past it, an enormous bed covered with four fluffy pillows behind four purely decorative pillows, and a ridiculously puffy comforter. The bed's padded headboard was bolted to the wall, which didn't make sense to him. Was there a big market for stolen headboards? Or was it secured to the wall so it wouldn't bang when people were fucking?

The bed faced a huge flat-screen TV, a low dresser/work desk combo, a two-seat dining table, an easy chair, and a small refrigerator. He dropped his bag on the easy chair, parted the blackout drapes behind it, and looked out the window, which gave him a view of the parking lot and the highway.

He closed the drapes, sat on the edge of the bed, and ate his apple while he used his burner phone to get directions to Phil Zarkin's retirement home.

He tossed the apple core in the trash, took a piss, and headed out again.

But instead of going through the lobby and flirting some more with Britney, he walked the opposite direction down the long hall to familiarize himself with the layout, security, and exits. He walked past the stairwell, the windowless business center, the small gym, the vending machine cubby, the doorway to the fenced-in pool, and then went out the door at the end of the corridor. There were cameras everywhere. He wondered if Britney was watching him.

RAY VISITED A RALPH'S grocery store, found his way to the Kosher section, and bought a box of Yehuda Matzos, because it looked very Jewish, and a jar of gefilte fish for the same reason, then drove another few blocks to the Peachtree Meadows Active Senior Living Home.

The two-story, boxy building had a garishly large portico and was surrounded by a parking lot filled with old sedans with Peachtree logo stickers on their bumpers and blue handicap placards, shaped like hotel "Do Not Disturb" doorknob signs, dangling from their rearview mirrors.

Once inside the assisted living facility, the air reeked of flatulence and incontinence with a slight *frisson* of decomposing flesh. It reminded Ray of most of the prisons he'd lived in.

A heavy-set, red-haired woman in her forties wearing a cardigan sweater over nursing scrubs sat at the front desk. She typed away at an old computer, where he imagined she was doing a Google search on "how to restore your chin if it has been completely absorbed by your neck."

"Good afternoon," Ray said. "I'm here to see Phil Zarkin."

She jerked, as if she'd accidentally electrocuted herself. "You scared me," she said. "Are you a relative?"

"Yes. I'm his nephew, Mitchel Stein."

"I'm Rose. Sorry if I seemed startled, but we don't get many visitors." She clicked something on her computer. "And none for Mr. Zarkin in three years. Not since his sister passed."

Ray was still in prison back then, doing time for grand theft auto. Phil suffered a minor stroke that sped up his preexisting dementia. Phil was granted a compassionate release—he'd done two dimes for second-degree murder—and his sister set him up in a cheap retirement home in Merced. She died not long after that, but she left her small estate in a trust to pay his bills.

"Was she your mother?" Rose asked.

"My aunt. I'm stuck up in Sacramento for a few weeks on a job, spending my first Hanukkah alone. It's been so depressing. But then it occurred to me that Uncle Phil was close by . . . and that he is also alone. So here I am. It's a real spur-of-the-moment thing. To be honest, I'm a little nervous. I haven't seen him since I was a kid. I'm not sure he'll recognize me."

"He probably won't. He's one of our memory care patients."

"How bad is he?"

"He knows who he is, but not where or when. His passion is Battleship."

"The board game?"

"It's all Mr. Zarkin does, every day, with anyone who will sit with him."

It was the same in prison.

The problem was, Phil always used one of two setups. His battleships were always in the same places. It didn't take many games before his opponents figured that out. After that, he only won if they took pity on him . . . and convicts aren't known for their pity. But Phil would nag them to play, like a dog with a squeaky chew toy, and inevitably someone would give in. There wasn't much else to do in prison if you weren't into weight lifting, butt fucking, or Jesus.

Rose stepped out from behind the desk and looked up at him sadly. She was barely more than five feet tall. "But if someone gets locked out of their room or their car, then he's eager to drop everything to help. He's amazing at opening locks. Sometimes we'll lock doors on purpose just to keep him busy."

"Uncle Phil was a locksmith," Ray said.

"In his mind, he still is."

Ray remembered how Phil would unlock his cell just to amuse himself, then lock it back up whenever the guards came around. That was how Ray knew that Phil hadn't entirely lost his mind.

In fact, Ray wasn't convinced that he'd lost it at all.

Rose led Ray through the lobby, then along a windowed corridor that looked out on the central courtyard, where old people sat staring at a fountain that looked like an overflowing urinal. It was surrounded by peeling garden gnomes, forever waiting to relieve themselves. "You'll be giving George Rosencrantz a welcome break."

"Who is he?"

"Mr. Zarkin's best friend here, and such a kind soul. Mr. Rosencrantz moved in a year ago and has played Battleship with Mr. Zarkin every day since then."

That was what Ray did, too, when they were in prison

together. Ray did it because he liked Phil, but also to protect him from convicts who wanted to know where his
stolen diamonds were hidden.

Phil had been part of a four-man crew that broke into a
big rig that was carrying diamonds and other gems back to
jewelers in LA from a trade show in Las Vegas. The driv-
ers stopped for burgers in Yermo, a hellhole in the Mojave
desert, and left their truck in the parking lot. Phil's crew
was in the middle of breaking in when another trucker
spotted them and one of the guys slit his throat to keep
him quiet. The crew split up their take on the spot. Three
fled to Las Vegas with their shares, and immediately drew
attention to themselves by living large, but Phil returned to
Bakersfield and his locksmithing job, living his quiet life.
Meanwhile, one crew member was arrested, another was
killed in a shoot-out with police, and the third disappeared.
It was never determined which member of the crew killed
the trucker. Hence the second-degree bid.

The only reason Phil got caught was that he gave one of
the stolen diamonds to a stripper he was seeing. Unfortunately, she was also fucking a cop. Phil never revealed where
he'd stashed the rest of his score . . . not to the cops, and not
to any of the convicts, some of whom beat him half to death
trying to make him talk.

Ray also wanted to know where the treasure was, but
he didn't push Phil about it. He figured that the diamonds,
and the hope of one day getting out and retrieving them,
was all that kept the old man sane and alive.

And yet, Phil was here. If he'd gone after the diamonds
after his compassionate release, this is the last place he'd be.

Which meant the treasure was still out there.

"I don't know what they talk about," Rose rambled on, "or how Mr. Rosencrantz can keep playing that same game with Mr. Zarkin over and over."

"Maybe because they are the only Jews here."

"There are a few others . . . so we've set aside a game room for their Hanukkah celebration, though everybody is welcome to participate, and they do, which is sweet," she said, as they approached a row of windowed game rooms. "We have a menorah, but with battery operated candles. Real ones would be too dangerous, especially for the memory care residents."

"Of course," Ray said.

"To celebrate, we're having a Jewish film festival, a different movie every day, culminating with a Hanukkah gelt treasure hunt."

"That's exactly what I'm here for."

A dry-erase board was propped on an easel outside a set of open game room doors and announced that the "Jewish classic" *Fiddler on the Roof* was screening on a loop inside all day. Party streamers made up of glittering paper dreidels, menorahs and Stars of David stretched across the game room's ceiling. Three old ladies and a dozing old man, who was alternating between farting and snoring, sat in armchairs facing a big-screen TV, watching a bunch of poor villagers dancing and singing about tradition. There were two card tables, one with a menorah as the centerpiece, the base surrounded by fake snow. Ray wasn't Jewish, but he didn't think snow had anything to do with Hanukkah.

And at the other table, Phil sat with a blue plastic Battleship tablet open in front of him like a laptop computer. Phil was scarecrow thin, dry strands of gray hair dotting his scabby, bald head like patches of hay glued into place. The left side of his face drooped, making him look to Ray like a wax figure of Don Rickles melting under a heat lamp. But Phil's right eye was bright blue, sharp, and laser focused on his game board, where white plastic pieces in peg holes represented misses, and red pieces represented hits.

"B-three," Phil said, his voice raspy, saliva dripping from the left, drooping side of his mouth.

Sitting across from Phil, with a matching tablet, was George Rosencrantz. He was round-faced, big-cheeked, and heavy-set, his sagging man boobs resting like bags of onions atop his bulging belly, which stretched his orange golf shirt nearly to the breaking point.

"Miss," George said. "A-seven."

"Hit," Phil said, slamming his tablet closed. "You sunk my last battleship."

"It was a lucky guess," George said.

Rose spoke up. "Mr. Zarkin, look who came to see you."

Ray held out his arms. "It's me, Uncle Phil, your nephew Mitch."

Phil stared at him with his one good eye, but didn't react. George twisted around in his seat to study the new arrival.

"You remember me." Ray set his grocery bag down on the table and crouched in front of Phil. "We used to go fishing together at Diamond Lake."

"You can't catch with your line in the boat," Phil said.

"That's right, that's what you always used to say. It's become my motto in life." Ray turned to face Phil's friend. "You must be George Rosencrantz. It's a pleasure to meet you. Rose tells me you spend a lot of time with Uncle Phil."

"I do. We talk a lot."

"About what?'

"His ex-wife. His dead sister. Difficult locks he's opened. The 1972 Oldsmobile Delta 88 he thinks he's still driving to work every day. But you know what he's never mentioned? A nephew."

"That breaks my heart," Ray said, lowering his head sadly.

Rose put her hand on George's shoulder. "We should leave these two alone to catch up."

But George didn't make a move to go. "Nobody ever calls or visits him, but now here you are, out of the blue."

"It's Hanukkah. What better time is there? Thank you for being so attentive to my uncle, but I'll be keeping him company for the next few days. You've earned a break."

In other words, fuck off.

Ray turned his back to George and began unpacking his grocery bag. "Look what I have for you. All your Hanukkah favorites."

George took the hint and got up, Rose helping him to his feet. Phil watched him go and waved at him with his good hand. "Bye, Clete."

"It's GEORGE," his friend said, raising his voice. "How many times do I have to tell you?"

As soon as Rose and George were gone, Ray slid the empty chair closer to Phil and sat down. "How are you holding up?"

"I don't have a nephew. But I know who you are."

"Who am I?"

Phil stared at him with his good eye. "Dave Barer, the junkyard man. You never have the key to anything."

Ray lowered his voice, and leaned close to Phil. "You

may have everybody else here fooled, but I'll bet you're only half as senile as you pretend to be."

"What do you want me to unlock for you?"

"A box of diamonds."

"Where is it?"

Ray smiled. "You tell me."

Phil leaned closer to Ray and whispered: "Want to play Battleship?"

"Sure," Ray said.

RAY STAYED FOR HOURS, eating Matzos and avoiding the gefilte fish, which Phil plucked out of the jar with his fingers, getting fish juice all over his game board.

Phil hid his battleships in the same spots on the board that he did back when they were both in prison. But Ray enjoyed himself anyway. It was amazing how many stories Phil had about opening locks. Ray had heard them all before, but he didn't mind the reruns. They were entertaining. The only stop in game play came when Phil sang "If I Were a Rich Man" along with Tevye in *Fiddler on the Roof.*

It was nearing four o'clock, dinner time at the Peachtree, so Ray decided to come straight at Phil.

"You may have forgotten where you are, what you do, or even what year it is. But here's what I think: you'll forget how to breathe, how to shit and how to brush your teeth before you forget where you hid your diamonds. Problem is, you can't get to them, not in the shape you're in, which must be damn frustrating for you. What you need is someone to get them for you. I'll do it, and split the take with you. But I know what you're wondering."

"Where's your destroyer?" Phil said. "H-seven."

"Wrong. You're wondering why you should trust me to come back and give you anything. D-three."

"Hit. You're going to sink me. I-seven."

"Miss. Maybe I *will* rip you off. But the way it's going, you're never going to see the diamonds again anyway, so what have you got to lose by taking the risk and telling me where to find them?"

Phil tipped his head at him. "Your move."

"I-eight."

"You sunk my submarine. You're a shrewd player."

"Yes, I am."

Phil closed his tablet and studied Ray. "Today isn't the first time we've played together."

"No, it's not."

For a moment, Ray thought he saw a glimmer of actual recognition in the blazing blue eye . . . and then it was gone.

"It's dinner time and I don't want to lose my reservation at Mr. Steak." Phil got up, reached for his walker, and shuffled with Ray toward the dining room, where walkers were lined up outside the doors like parked cars.

"Give my proposal some thought," Ray said, stopping at the entrance to the dining room. "I'll be back tomorrow."

Phil didn't acknowledge the comment. He shuffled into the dining room, where George had saved him an empty seat at a big round table with half a dozen other residents.

George glowered at Ray, who smiled back at him and then turned to go, nearly running into Rose.

"See you tomorrow," Ray said.

"Don't you want to stay for the lighting of the candle?"

"It's battery operated. You flick a switch."

"It's the thought that counts," she said.

"Yes, it is, and you've been so thoughtful," he said, taking both of her hands in his. "I appreciate it and I know, deep down, that Uncle Phil does, too. I can tell already that you are the beating heart of this place."

She blushed at the compliment and Ray left.

RAY DROVE UP TO the UC Merced campus, which was on the outskirts of town in the middle of open farmland and looked as if it had been built yesterday by the same guys who did the Hampton Inn and the Peachtree Meadows.

He walked around the place for an hour or so, just to get a feel for it, then stopped by the student store, where he bought a UC Merced baseball cap and a "Go Bobcats!" sweatshirt. On the way out, he put the cap on his head and asked a young woman who was passing by if he could take a selfie with her. She said yes without bothering to ask why he wanted it, so he didn't have to use the story he'd worked out about scouting campuses for his daughter while he was on a business trip. Apparently, it was impolite to ever refuse a selfie. Now he had a photo of himself with a female student who could pass for his daughter and some Merced swag to bolster his visiting-Dad role, just in case anybody asked.

He stopped by a Kentucky Fried Chicken for dinner and looked up "Hanukkah gelt" on his burner phone while he ate. He discovered that "gelt" was gold foil-wrapped chocolate coins, but there seemed to be conflicting stories about what they symbolized. As far as Ray was concerned, they were basically Jewish Easter eggs.

He drove to the Hampton Inn and parked his car in the spot below the window to his room. The light was on behind his drawn curtains, which meant somebody had been inside or was still there.

Interesting.

He put his cap back on, grabbed his UC Merced shopping bags, and went into the hotel, playing the proud father. There was a different young blond girl at the front desk, who smiled at him as he came in, but she didn't have Britney's spark.

Ray gave her a smile, went down the hall to his room, opened the door, and detected a familiar coconut scent the moment he walked in.

He glanced in his bathroom, where somebody had obviously taken a shower, the mirror still steamed from the hot water. He continued on and found Britney sitting up naked in the huge bed, her back against the pillows, the comforter tugged up to waist. She had a yellow highlighter in hand and a textbook open on her lap. She glanced up at him and said, "You took your sweet time."

Ray dropped his bags and tried to look suitably shocked. But mostly he just looked at her breasts, which were perfect, the size and shape every woman wanted but that nature rarely provided. "What are you doing here?"

"Providing our acclaimed turndown service."

"Do you do this for all the guests?"

"Only the ones I want to fuck and who want to fuck me."

"Wanting and doing are two different things."

"You gave me your key."

"That wasn't what I meant when I did it," he said, trying to sound both fatherly and flustered, but he wasn't much of an actor.

"Yes, it was, and there's that." She glanced below his

waist. His hard-on was tenting his pants. It had been a few days since he'd had a woman ... which, when he wasn't in prison, was a very long time.

Ray looked down at himself. "It has a mind of its own."

"I like the way it thinks."

"You should be studying ... but not here in my bed."

"There are some things you can't learn from a textbook, Mitch. Like this chapter on the stages of arousal." She set the textbook aside and turned to face him. "Here's what I want you to help me study."

She whipped off the comforter, revealing her full nakedness, slid to edge of the bed, and sat facing him, her legs apart.

"Start here," Britney took her highlighter and slowly circled her nipples with it until each one was hard. "Then work your way slowly down my body to here ..."

Britney ran her highlighter down her flat stomach to her shaved crotch. She moaned as she gently circled her clitoris with the tip of highlighter. "And let's see how aroused I get. And then ..."

She put her highlighter between her teeth, freeing her hands to unzip his pants and pull out his cock. Then Britney took her highlighter and ran it the length of his erection. "I want you to use this to do it all."

He did.

RAY TOOK BRITNEY IN every way he could think of, but if she felt degraded or used, she didn't show it. In fact, she subtly but firmly positioned their bodies on the bed to choreograph their fucking to her preference.

Perhaps that's why he felt like he was observing the

situation more than experiencing it. Or maybe it was the entire situation, which was a male fantasy out of a bad porn movie. He suspected that despite all of her moaning and writhing, she wasn't enjoying it all that much, and when she announced, "I'm coming, I'm coming" before her wildly exaggerated orgasm, he was sure of it. The only one who actually came was him, and he didn't make a big announcement. He didn't think she needed to be notified.

When it was over, she took another shower, emerged smelling like coconuts again in her Hampton Inn uniform, and gathered up her textbooks. He sat naked with his back against the headboard, his curiosity about why it was bolted to the wall answered now.

She gave him a coy smile. "Thank you for helping me with my homework."

He shook his head and fiddled with his wedding ring. "I should have walked out of the room as soon as I saw you in my bed . . ."

He never turned down a good fuck, but he figured Mitch Stein would be deeply conflicted about it, and he had a role to play. To get the right expression on his face, he wondered if that yellow highlighting on his dick would give him a rash and what it would look like if it did.

"Are you telling me you've never done this before?"

"I'm a married man . . ."

"Meaning you've never cheated on your wife or that you've never fucked her like this?"

"Both," he said.

"Happy Hanukkah."

"You're the same age as my daughter."

Britney wagged a finger at him. "Trust me on this, Mitch,

you don't want to go down that road or you might not be able to get it up for me tomorrow."

"What makes you think I won't regret everything we just did and check out of here?"

"Because you're going to spend the rest of tonight racked with guilt but spend all day tomorrow remembering how many times you made me come." Which was a big fat zero. She smiled at him. "You'll race back here hard enough to cut diamonds. I promise."

She was half-right. He'd definitely have diamonds on his mind. "How can you be so sure?"

"I'm an expert."

She left the room. He stayed in bed and idly wondered what her game was, not that he cared if it meant that he'd be able to get off again while he was in town running his sloppy con.

He took out his burner phone and reread the old articles on the internet about the jewel heist in Yermo as his bed-time story.

RAY GOT UP EARLY the next morning, showered, and discovered that Britney's coconut scent came from the Hampton Inn shampoo. Either she'd stolen some bottles to use at home, or she did all of her showering at the hotel, which gave him something to think about.

He left his room at eight A.M. and checked out the free breakfast, but decided to skip it. The smell of the defrosted scrambled egg mix and precooked bacon strips reminded him too much of prison food. Instead, he drove to the grocery store that he'd visited the day before, picked up a few bagels, a package of smoked salmon, some cream cheese, and few pieces of plastic cutlery and headed to Peachtree Meadows.

He walked into the game room to find Neil Diamond in a yarmulke on the big-screen TV and Phil at a card table with George. The "Jewish classic" of the day was *The Jazz Singer*. Phil's Battleship sets were open on the table, but he was busy rooting through a big salad bowl full of closed padlocks while George watched him.

Ray said, "I don't think that's what Uncle Phil meant when he asked for lox for breakfast."

George replied, "He thinks he's doing business."

Phil opened a padlock with a pick fashioned out of a paper clip, put the lock on the table, and fished another one out of the bowl.

Ray asked, "How are you this morning, Uncle Phil?"

"I wish that damn farmer Russell wouldn't lose the key to every padlock he buys, but I shouldn't complain," Phil said, working a wire into the lock. "His forgetfulness pays my bills. What can I help you with, Norman? Lock yourself out of your car again?"

"I'm not Norman. I'm Mitch. Your nephew." Ray started unpacking the groceries on the table. "Look what I brought you. Bagels, lox, and cream cheese."

"Yummy." Phil pushed the bowl of locks away and reached for a bagel.

George surveyed the goods and shook his head. "No knishes? No latkes?"

"Do you know a place in Merced that makes them?"

"Nope. But if you're working your way down the list of Jew food clichés, those'd be at the top. Don't you think you're laying it on thick, pal?"

"Impossible." Ray opened the cream cheese and gave Phil a plastic fork. "It's Hanukkah. Feasting on these traditional foods is how we celebrate."

"*We?*" George chuckled. "Shit, pal. You look about as Jewish as the Pope. I like the Chai, though, nice touch. At least you didn't go for a yarmulke, that would've been overkill."

Ray gestured to the TV. "It looks good on Neil Diamond."

"Because he's a real fucking Jew."

"He certainly is," Ray said, then looked George in the eye. "A true diamond among diamonds, wouldn't you say? And who doesn't love diamonds?"

George got up slowly, less to be threatening than because he had bad knees, and glared at Ray. "You think you're real cute."

Ray smiled. "I'm absolutely adorable. Shalom, George. Have a nice day."

George walked out and Ray took his abandoned seat across from Phil. "What do you think about that guy, Uncle Phil?"

Phil tapped his head with a finger. "His eggs are scrambled."

"What do you mean?"

Phil answered while he sliced his bagel, put cream cheese on the halves, and then laid some slices of lox on top of them. "I keep finding him in my house, going through my things. Every time I catch him, he looks up at me confused and says he can't understand why someone else's stuff is in his drawers. So, I tell him it's because it's my house, not yours. And he apologizes, says that sometimes he gets lost, trying to get home, since all the houses in our neighborhood look the same. He's right about that. Fucking tract homes. But you know what I think? It's not his house that he's looking for."

"Do you know what it is?"

"Of course I do. It's the secret location of my battle-ships." Phil slid a Battleship set over to him. "Wouldn't you like to find them, too?"

"I certainly would."

"Give it your best shot." Phil took a bite out of his bagel, nodded with appreciation, and began setting up his board.

WHEN RAY GOT BACK to the Hampton Inn around six, Neil Diamond had finally vacated his head and Britney was at the front desk. She beamed when she saw him. "Good evening, Mr. Stein. How was your day?"

He went up to the desk and, even though he was the only other person in the lobby, he lowered his voice and said: "I spent a lot of time thinking about cutting diamonds."

She allowed herself a little sly smile. "So did I."

"You have a great major."

"My high school guidance counselor told me to find a subject I was passionate about and then studying wouldn't be boring, it would be stimulating and exciting. He was so right."

"When does the turndown service start tonight?"

"Pretty soon. You have time for a shower."

Ray went to his room, stripped, and got into the shower. He'd barely had a chance to work up any steam when he heard his door open and close.

A moment later, Britney stepped naked into the shower and started giving him a hand job. "You're not allowed to come now. Only me."

"That doesn't seem fair."

"Trust me. You need to save yourself for later."

"And you don't?"

"I'm just getting warmed up . . ."

Her hand job graduated into a blow job, and then she demanded the same courtesies from him, and she faked a couple of noisy orgasms. He was still hard as they got out of the shower and dried off in the bathroom.

"There's something I've never tried," she said. "And tonight, I want to do it with you."

"I'm up for it."

"You certainly are." She took him by the cock and led him out into the room, where there was a young man sitting naked on the edge of the bed, casually masturbating. He was scrawny, pale, and looked barely old enough to buy beer.

"Who is this?" Ray asked, pretending to be startled. It would take a lot more than a kid jerking off to startle him.

"Brad," she said, pumping Ray's cock in her fist. "My boyfriend."

"What the hell is he doing here?"

Brad held up his hands in a surrendering gesture. "Hey, it's cool, man."

"Not with me it isn't," Ray said.

"Relax." Britney turned to face Ray, still giving him a steady hand job, keeping things interesting. "I want him . . . and I want you . . . to fuck me together."

"I'm not into that."

"You just have to be into me." Britney turned her back to him, bent over, and guided his cock into her from behind. He began to thrust, hard and deep, taking her doggie style, and she bent down and began sucking on Brad.

As things went on, they ended up in several positions. It

all seemed very fake and choreographed to Ray, almost like they were playing an erotic version of Twister with Britney in charge.

This time, though, when Brad and Ray were doing Britney together, Ray from the front and Brad from behind, her moans were real and so was the orgasm that rocked her entire body. Even her ears twitched, which was something Ray had never seen before.

When it was all over, and Britney lay spent between the two sweaty, naked men, she said: "It was everything I dreamed it would be . . . and more. How was it for you?"

Ray, staying in character, said: "I think I'm going to be sick."

Brad spoke up, too. "I've never been with a man before." He reached his hand out to Ray. "But it felt great having you in my mouth and in my—"

"SHUT UP." Ray pulled away from Britney and scrambled out of the bed, fumbling as he got to his feet, a performance he thought was worthy of Academy consideration. "Shut the fuck up. Don't say another word. Get out, both of you."

Britney rolled over to face Ray. "You liked it, Mitch. All of it. I know you did."

Ray pointed to the door. "Out!"

He covered his mouth, dashed into the bathroom, and slammed the door, but not because he was sick.

It was because he'd started laughing.

He suppressed the laughter by sticking a finger down his throat and puking into the toilet. Afterwards, he went to the sink, washed his mouth out with water, and smiled at himself in the mirror.

Does making yourself puke to sell a performance count as method acting?

When he emerged from the bathroom, Brad was gone but Britney was waiting for him. She sat on the edge of his bed, dressed loosely in her Hampton's uniform, but anybody who looked at her, or got a sniff of her, would intuitively know that she'd just been thoroughly fucked.

"I told you to go," he said.

"Do you feel better now?"

"I'll *never* feel better. How could we do this . . . and on *Hanukkah?*" He choked back another laugh, but to her it just sounded like choking.

"You have no reason to be ashamed, Mitch. What we did tonight was a celebration of life, which embraces the true meaning of Hanukkah."

"You think it's butt-fucking? You show me where that is written in the Torah."

"You're also broadening my understanding of human sexuality, so I can help troubled people find acceptance, happiness, and pleasure. That's a very good thing."

"Is that what this was all about? Some kind of twisted school project?"

"Hanukkah isn't over yet." Britney stood up. "This was my night to experience a fantasy, tomorrow will be yours. We can do anything you want . . . *anything.*"

"What I want is for you to go," he said. "I'm checking out in the morning."

"Okay, if that's how you feel." She sighed sadly and walked out.

Ray was curious what Act Three of this porno would

be, and when he thought about it that way, he saw things clearly and he knew exactly what would happen next.

Because Ray Boyd wasn't stupid.

A few minutes after Britney left, Ray got dressed, went out to his car, drove to a 7-Eleven, bought a six-pack of beer, a box of Ding Dongs, and a roll of duct tape, and returned to his room at the Hampton Inn.

THEY CAME BACK AT three A.M.

The room was dark, and Ray was in bed, pretending to be asleep, the sheets pulled up almost over his head.

Brad kicked the bed. "Wake up, old man."

Old Man?

Ray rolled over and saw Brad pointing a gun in his face. "What the hell . . . ?" Ray said.

Britney stepped out from behind Brad, who wore a T-shirt and gym shorts. "Sorry to wake you up, sweetie, but you were so shaken up tonight, we were afraid you'd check out before morning."

Ray sat up slowly, eyes on the gun. "Is this another one of your sick fantasies?"

"You mean like this?" Britney held up her phone, screen out to face him. Ray slid to the edge of the bed to get a closer look at the screen and she began to play a video. It was a movie of them fucking yesterday and their gangbang earlier that night.

The videos were shot from two different angles, which meant that there were two cameras in the room and that it had been edited. It also explained why she was so intent on positioning him. The cameras were hidden in two of the room's air vents and Britney wanted to be sure Ray's face was in every shot.

She said, "It looks to me like this was your fantasy more than mine. I'm sure your wife and daughter will think the same thing."

Brad waved the gun at him. "Everybody at your office will know you're a sicko perv who loves dick."

Britney sighed sadly. "You will lose everything, Mitch."

"Oh my God." Ray covered his mouth again, and turned his head away, trying not to laugh.

Brad poked him in the shoulder with the gun. "Don't you dare puke, or I'll rub your face in it. Look at me, old man."

Ray slowly turned around. "What do you want?"

Britney said, "Money, honey."

"How much?"

She smiled. "Five thousand dollars in cash."

"I don't have that kind of money on me."

Brad snorted. "Nobody does. We know that. Do you think we're stupid?"

Yes.

Britney put her hands on Ray's cheeks to be sure she had his complete attention. "Honey, here's what's going to happen. Tomorrow morning you'll go to the bank, withdraw the cash, and bring it straight back here to me . . . or I'll post the videos."

Ray looked at her. "How can you do this to me?"

She let go of his face and stepped back again. "Education is expensive. You certainly know that with a daughter of your own in college. We don't want to take out student loans. But look at the bright side. It's not like you didn't get anything out of this. You had two hot nights you will never forget."

Brad aimed the gun at Ray's crotch. "You loved my sweet ass, didn't you, old man?"

"Stop calling me old man," Ray suddenly grabbed Brad's gun hand, pulled him close, and punched him in the throat.

Brad involuntarily released his gun and fell forward onto the bed, gurgling like a clogged drain.

Ray picked up the gun and stood up.

Britney scrambled backward and held up her phone, her hand shaking. "Big mistake, Mitch. Put down the gun or I'll post this."

"Or I could shoot the two of you and myself, problem solved."

"You don't want to do that."

"No, I don't, but I *could*, which just goes to show how little you've thought this scheme through." Ray grabbed Brad by the forearm with his free hand, pulled him up, and pushed him into the desk chair, where he sat gagging.

"Stay." Ray went to the dining table, set the gun down, got out the roll of duct tape from his 7-Eleven bag, and tore off a big strip. "How does anybody as stupid as you two get into college?" He put the strip of tape over Brad's mouth and around his head, then looked at Britney. "Give me the phone."

"No way," she said.

Ray took Brad's left hand, placed it on the table, and duct-taped it down. Then he picked up his gun and hammered Brad's index finger with the butt.

Brad's scream of pain was muffled by the tape.

Ray looked calmly at Britney, the gun butt held over Brad's hand. "Give it to me, *honey*, or I'll break every one of his fingers, and when I run out of them, I'll smash his prick."

Brad looked at Britney with wide, pleading eyes . . . and wet himself, pee running out of his gym shorts and down his bare right leg onto the floor.

Ray shook his head. "Look what you made him do."

She handed Ray the phone, but with a glare of fury.

He said, "Go get some towels in the bathroom and start cleaning up this mess while I check out these videos. I don't want my room smelling like Brad piss."

Ray sat down on the edge of the bed, Brad's gun in one hand and her phone in the other, and browsed through her photos with his thumb. The camera roll was filled with videos of her and Brad fucking dads. Or at least Ray assumed that's who the men were. He was sure, though, that every lone married male traveler who checked in with Britney probably got this sex suite. Maybe she even had one upstairs, too.

Britney came out with towels and began to wipe up the piss while Ray continued scrolling through her videos. The phone had the raw footage as well as the edited versions. He went back to the main iPhone screen and saw one of the apps was a password manager, which gave him an idea.

Ray looked up at her. "I thought you two were dumb, but these guys were even dumber. I bet they all paid up." He glanced at Brad, who had tears of shame running down his cheeks. "I can't believe nobody laughed at your gun, Brad. Even you aren't stupid enough to shoot someone in a hotel."

Britney had regained some of her composure, which wasn't easy given that she was cleaning up a puddle of piss. "That's true, but normal people don't think clearly with a gun in their face. But you aren't normal, are you?"

"I'm probably an undiagnosed sociopath, just like you," Ray said. "But here's what's interesting to me, from a human sexuality standpoint. This scam isn't just about the money for you, Britney. You really get off on it, I can see that. Look at your face when Brad and I were both fucking you." He held up the camera so she could see a freeze frame of her tumultuous orgasm, but she kept her back to him.

"What happens now?" she asked.

Ray changed the master password on her phone while he answered her. "You take those stinky towels out of here, go home, and bring me back twenty thousand dollars in cash and a couple of Egg McMuffins for breakfast or I will post these videos to your Facebook, Instagram, and TikTok accounts . . . and smash Brad's dick out of spite."

Brad whimpered. Britney's fury returned.

"Are you out of your mind?" she said. "We don't have that kind of money."

"If each of these suckers paid you five grand, you have a lot more cash than that, even after paying your school expenses . . . and I'm sure it's at home, and not in the bank, where you might have to explain it. And if I'm wrong, and you don't have the cash, oh well, too bad for you."

She pointed at the phone in his hand. "If you post those videos, the world will see you, too."

Ray looked at her and shrugged. "I don't care."

She stared at him and knew he was telling the truth. "Fuck me."

"I'll be glad to after you get back with my money," he said. "But no cameras or Brad this time."

Britney stomped petulantly to the door, but before she opened it, Ray added: "Oh, one more thing. Before you go, bring back a bucket of ice for Brad's hand, and make sure the security videos from tonight are wiped, for your sake and mine."

"You're so thoughtful," she smirked.

She left for a few minutes, came back with a bucket of ice, and left again.

Ray wrapped some ice in a towel, set it on Brad's hand, then opened a beer, took a sip, and began changing Britney's passwords on her social media accounts. When he was done, he took the tape off Brad's mouth, opened the box of Ding Dongs and offered Brad one. "Eat this. You'll feel better."

Brad took it. "Can I have a beer, too?"

"Sure."

While they waited, Ray had a beer and chatted with the kid who, he learned, was a business major at UC Merced and hoped to start a real estate investing business, buying distressed apartment buildings in Bakersfield, fixing them up, and then renting them out. Once the buildings established a strong cash flow, recouping his investment while the property appreciated in value, he'd sell them at a big profit and move on.

Ray thought that might be a good way to invest his own money, which wasn't doing him much good in the door panels of his Crown Vic, but he didn't share his thinking with Brad.

Britney returned a few hours later with the Egg McMuffins, a UC Merced gym bag full of cash, and a grocery bag containing a fresh pair of underwear and jeans for Brad.

As Brad changed his clothes, Britney held her hand out to Ray. "I'd like my iPhone and Brad's gun back."

"I'm keeping them."

"Why?"

"Because I want to," Ray said.

"Asshole."

"But I left you the cameras," he said. "Are you going to keep doing this?"

"Why not? It's a good gig," she said. "We'll just take extra precautions in the future."

Brad looked surprised at that, but he didn't understand Britney like Ray did.

It wasn't about the money for her. She was in it for the sex, and maybe the humiliation of older men. The money was how she rationalized what she had to do to get off.

You should write a paper about that, *Britney.*

"Maybe I'll demand a cut to keep quiet," Ray said.

She shook her head. "You won't do that. You like cash. What am I going to do? FedEx your cut to a mailbox? You don't strike me as a man who has one."

She's right about that.

Brad stuffed his clothes in a trash bag. "Let's go, Britney . . . please."

They went to the door, but before she stepped out, Britney glanced back at Ray with a smirk on her face and lobbed a parting shot: "I faked every orgasm."

"You did?" Ray said. "I must have missed them. I wasn't paying much attention."

"You don't have the slightest idea how to satisfy a woman."

Ray shrugged. "I only care about satisfying myself."

After they left, Ray checked out of the hotel. He put his suitcase in the trunk, dropped the gym bag on the passenger seat, and drove toward Peachtree Meadows. Along the way, the road passed over a creek. He pulled over and when he was sure nobody was watching, he tossed Brad's gun into the water. He didn't want any cops pulling him over and finding a weapon in his possession.

When he got to Peachtree Meadows, he brought the gym bag in with him and headed toward the game room.

Rose intercepted him.

"You're just in time, Mr. Stein," Rose said. She had a whistle around her neck. "The Hanukkah gelt treasure hunt is about to begin."

She handed him a sheet of paper with the floor plan of the senior living center on it. There were dollar signs written in various spots. "What's this?"

"A treasure map."

"Doesn't it defeat the purpose of a treasure hunt if you show everyone where the gelt is?"

"We want everyone to be a winner. The hunt starts in five minutes."

He took the map and walked to the game room, where the "Jewish classic" of the day was *Yentl.* Phil sat by himself at the table with his Battleship set.

"Good morning, Uncle Phil," Ray said. "Where's your friend George?"

"He left when he saw you drive in. He knows you don't like him much."

"Do you?"

Phil shrugged. "He passes the time."

Ray gestured to the dining room, where all the residents were waiting for the hunt to start. "Looking forward to the treasure hunt?"

"I know where it is." He pointed across the room, where Barbra Streisand was on the big flat-screen, unconvincingly dressed as a boy. "There's a bag of gelt behind the TV."

"Would you like me to get it for you?"

Phil met his gaze. "You could just take it and leave."

Ray set the gym bag on the table and unzipped it so Phil could see the stacks of cash inside. "This is a small token of my good faith."

Ray went to the TV, got the tiny bag of gelt, and tossed it to Phil, who caught it with his right hand. His hand-eye coordination was excellent.

Rose blew a whistle and the treasure hunt started. All the old people scrambled with their walkers and canes, looking for treasure.

Phil unwrapped a piece of gelt and ate the chocolate coin. He held out the bag of gelt to Ray and shook it. "Want a piece?"

"Just a taste."

Phil took out a few coins and passed them to him. Then Phil picked up the Peachtree Meadows treasure hunt map, opened his Battlefield tablet, placed the map inside it, closed it again, and handed it to Ray.

"Happy Hanukkah, Mitch."

It took Ray a moment, but then he understood the meaning of what Phil had given him. The Battleship layouts, the two that Phil kept repeating to himself every day for decades, was his map. The numbers were coordinates of some kind. Longitude and latitude? He'd figure it out.

"You, too, Uncle Phil."

RAY GRABBED ANOTHER BAGGIE of gelt that he spotted in a potted plant on his way through the lobby. George was waiting for him in the parking lot, leaning against the Crown Vic.

"Leaving already?" George said. "You just got here."

"I came to say goodbye to Uncle Phil. It's the last day

of Hanukkah and I have to get back to work first thing tomorrow."

"You're missing your chance to find some gelt."

Ray tossed him the bag of gelt. "I think I just found the last of it."

He got in the Crown Vic, started up the engine, and drove off.

RAY WENT TO PAUL'S Diner, got himself a slice of banana cream pie and a cup of coffee, and took out Britney's phone. He deleted the videos featuring his performance, then used Paul's free Wi-Fi to begin posting all of her other blackmail videos to her Facebook, Instagram, YouTube, Twitter, and Tik-Tok accounts. The uploads would take some time, so he tucked her phone into a crease in the vinyl banquette, took out his burner, and began doing some research.

The jewelry heist and the related killing took place in the parking lot of Peggy Sue's Diner in Yermo, California. He found the longitude and latitude of the diner and the coordinates of Phil's former locksmith shop in Bakersfield, figuring the old man wouldn't have gone too far from either spot to hide his treasure.

Then he opened up the Battleship tablets, placed the plastic ships in the same spots in the number-and-letter graph that Phil had done for decades in his two different game setups. Once that was done, he borrowed a pen from his waitress and wrote down the numbers and letters on a napkin.

With all those numbers, and Phil's two Battleship setups in front of him, he tried to figure out how the old man used the game to memorize the coordinates where his treasure was hidden.

It took two hours, three more slices of pie, and four more cups of coffee, before Ray saw a pattern in the Battleship setups that produced a number that corresponded to the general vicinity of Yermo.

He took the longitude and latitude he came up with, plugged it into a search engine, and it matched a spot in the craggy hills above Calico, the ruins of an old silver mining town that had been turned into a tourist trap, a few miles north of Peggy Sue's.

He'd cracked the code.

Ray paid his bill in cash, gave the waitress a generous tip, and purposely left Britney's phone hidden in the banquette seat, as if she might have forgotten it there herself.

He drove to a Home Depot and bought a few shovels, a sledgehammer, a pickax, a crowbar, a hard hat with a lamp attachment, heavy gloves, a few tarps, some metal stakes, and a heavy-duty collapsible four-wheel yard cart to carry all of the tools. He stopped by a Big 5 Sporting Goods store to get fishing line, a canteen, a Maglite, a basic backpack, hiking boots, and a metal detector.

It was probably more supplies than he needed for the job, but he remembered something his grandmother used to tell him: *It never hurts to be overprepared, it always hurts to be underprepared.*

YERMO WASN'T REALLY A town. It was the name given to a bleak rest stop a hundred and fifty miles south of Las Vegas and a good five hours from Merced. It was little more than a smattering of fast-food restaurants and two gas stations, under the shadow of the jagged Calico mountains in the vast Mojave desert.

He arrived too late in the day to start digging, so he checked into the Travelodge, parked his Crown Vic under the window of his room, and went straight to bed.

He woke up at daybreak, went out to his car, and saw that there was now another car in the parking lot: a Chevrolet Impala with a handicap placard hanging from the rearview mirror and a Peachtree sticker on the bumper.

Hello, George.

Either George had finally figured out that the Battleship game was how Phil memorized where his loot was hidden or he'd put some kind of tracker on Ray's Crown Vic. Or maybe he did both, figuring he'd let the young man do the work for him . . . and then take the diamonds from him afterwards.

Either way, George had followed him and was forced to stay here because it was the only hotel in Yermo.

You should have slept in your car, George.

Ray drove along the base of the Calico Mountains before he found an area that suited his needs—a secluded trail head into a forgotten canyon.

He parked, squatted under his car, felt around, and found an Apple AirTag hidden behind the bumper. He left the tracker where it was, opened the trunk, loaded some of his tools and supplies into a yard cart.

Ray hiked into the canyon, wheeling the cart behind him, and was pleased to see it was leaving a nice clear trail of distinctive tire-tread marks that George would have no trouble following. The canyon walls were steep and craggy, eroding in piles of jagged stones that lined both sides of the winding, ascending trail. The only vegetation were cacti and dry chaparral, baking in sunlight that was already scorching.

He continued up until the trail curved around an out-cropping that would hide him from view from below. It was the perfect spot. He used his pickax and shovel to dig a hole about three feet deep, two feet wide, and five feet long.

He dropped a few jagged rocks into the hole, placed a tarp over the top, and then secured it in place with some more stones. He lightly dusted the tarp with dirt until it was invisible.

Ray used the sledgehammer to drive a metal stake into the ground on either side of the trail in front the hidden hole, then he tied a fishing line between them, stretching the line across the trail. He hid the stakes under some dry brush, reviewed his work, wheeled his cart and tools farther down the trail, and then sat back to wait.

The canyon he'd picked was across a dry lake bed, at the foot of the Calicos, too far from the hotel to approach on foot, at least for a guy of George's age. So, unless the old coot had a drone, he'd have to drive out to see what Ray was up to.

And he'd have to park beside the Crown Vic because there was nowhere else to leave the car where it wouldn't be spotted in the open desert.

And since he was out in the open, he couldn't wait there for Ray to show up, because Ray would spot him first.

And he couldn't wait at the hotel, because he couldn't be sure that Ray would come back after he found the diamonds.

The only option old George had was to come in after Ray, see where he was digging, find a hiding place, and hope to ambush him as he came back down the trail with the treasure.

It was only a matter of time now.

TWO HOURS WENT BY before Ray heard the surprised cry and then a wet smack, like a hammer hitting a cantaloupe.

He got up, walked down the trail, and found George at the bottom of the hole, his body twisted at an unnatural angle on top of the tarp, which covered the jagged rocks he'd landed on. But the rocks had done their job. Ray could see some bones sticking out of George's right leg, which was oozing blood.

There was a Glock, with a suppressor, lying in the dirt beside the trail. Ray figured it must've flown out of George's hand as he tripped over the fishing line.

Ray picked up the Glock and squatted in front of the hole, blocking the sun from George's eyes. "How are you doing?"

George looked up at him, blood dribbling out of his nose and mouth. "I think my back is broken."

His voice was weak and cracking, but he was lucky he was conscious and could talk at all.

"It's worse than that," Ray said. "It looks like you broke your leg and your hip too, and there's probably some internal bleeding."

"You've got to help me."

"I will."

"You can have the diamonds."

"That's very generous of you, considering you were going to kill me for them." Ray waved the gun for emphasis.

"They're rightfully mine."

"Because you were part of the crew that stole them the first time. You're the lucky bastard who got away. I looked you up after Phil called you Clete."

"Fucking Google."

Ray nodded in agreement. "It's the death of secrets. What happened to all of your money?"

"I spent it," he said.

"You should have invested some of it. Did you consider rental properties?"

George groaned. "You said you'd help me."

"Okay, you don't have to nag." Ray ejected the clip and emptied all but one bullet into the hole, put the clip back in place, and tossed the gun down to George, within reach of his good arm.

"What's this for?"

"I'm going to bury you now, but if you want, you can shoot yourself first. I left you a bullet."

"You call that help?"

Ray shrugged. "I could've just buried you alive. Now you don't have to suffer. I think that's helpful."

George lifted the gun with a shaking, bloody hand, then looked up at Ray, who had moved, so the sun was now in the man's eyes. He fired the gun in what he guessed was Ray's general direction. The bullet didn't even come close.

Ray sighed. "Okee-dokey," and started shoveling dirt back into the hole.

GEORGE'S IMPALA WAS PARKED beside his car. He peeled the Peachtree sticker off the bumper, removed the license plates with a screwdriver, which he also used to pop the lock on the driver's side door.

He pried the VIN tag off the dashboard, opened the glove box, removed the registration and a tin of Peppermint Altoids, popped the trunk, and found a bunch of suitcases and the UC Merced gym bag. Ray unzipped the bag. It was filled with cash.

You old bastard.

He tossed a mint in his mouth, hot-wired the old Impala, and drove it into a ditch about a hundred yards away that was surrounded by brush, creosote, and boulders. It might be years before anybody discovered the car. All he needed was a few hours.

It was time to get his diamonds.

RAY ARRIVED IN MERCED after nightfall and checked into the Motel 7 on E. Childs Avenue. From the front office, he could see police cars in the Hampton Inn's parking lot. He asked the gangly clerk what happened, and the man laughed, his huge Adam's apple moving like a trapped animal trying to escape from his throat.

"The cops give us shit about tweakers and whores using our rooms, but it's nothing compared to what goes on in the classy joints. This happened yesterday." He reached under the counter and handed Ray a copy of the *Merced Sun-Star.*

The big story on the front page was about a murder-suicide at the Hampton Inn. A San Francisco man drove to Merced, gunned down Britney and her boyfriend, Brad, and then shot himself. The killings happened in the immediate wake of the release of secretly recorded videos of the couple having sex with various men, including the killer, at the hotel over the last two years.

The clerk said, "She blackmailed the men they fucked together. They must've made a fortune. Now the cops are tearing every single room apart, looking for more cameras."

Ray noticed a grin on the clerk's face. "Are you thinking about trying it yourself as an additional revenue stream?"

The clerk waved off the suggestion. "Our guests wouldn't care if they were filmed fucking a goat."

THE NEXT MORNING, RAY checked out of the Motel 7, drove to Peachtree Meadows, and strode into the lobby carrying the UC Merced gym bag full of sex cash.

Rose stepped out from behind the front desk to greet him. "Mr. Stein, I didn't expect to see you back again so soon."

"My job in Sacramento is over and I'm driving home. I wanted to see Uncle Phil one more time before I go."

"I'm glad, because you're a good influence."

"Nobody's ever told me that before."

"He's a new man. He's been participating in all of the community activities. Every woman in the place has her eye on him now."

"Even you?"

"I go for younger men," she said.

"How much younger?"

"About your age," she said and gave his forearm a playful pinch.

"Don't tempt me." Ray grinned. "Where can I find him?"

"He's in his room," she said, pointing to a corridor that branched off the lobby. "One-oh-six, right down there."

"Thanks," Ray said, and followed her directions. He knocked on the door. "Uncle Phil? It's Mitch, your nephew."

Phil opened the door and gave him a big smile. "I wasn't sure I'd ever see you again."

"Honestly, I wasn't, either."

Phil stepped aside. "Come in."

Ray walked past him into a studio apartment the size and shape of a hotel room, except that it had a refrigerator, sink, and a small microwave along one wall of the combination living room/bedroom. It was the Four Seasons of prison cells.

Phil closed the door and gestured to a small dinette table with two chairs. "Take a seat. I see you found my missing bag. How is George?"

"He's a buried memory." Ray set the bag on the table, unzipped it, and removed the rusted lockbox that was resting on the pile of cash. The box was the size of a countertop toaster oven and had an elaborate lock. He'd found it by plugging the longitude and latitude into a GPS app, which led him to an old mining cave. An hour of digging, he found his fortune. He set the box down in front of Phil. "I'm hoping you might be able to open this for me."

"I'd be delighted." Phil reached into his pocket, removed a slim leather case, and unzipped it to reveal a set of picks. He selected one, worked it gently into the lock, and the box opened with an audible click.

Ray lifted the lid to expose dozens of glittering diamonds on a red velvet tray. He removed the tray. Underneath it was another tray of diamonds and assorted gemstones, and below that, there was one more.

"This is the best Hanukkah ever," Phil said.

"Do you still know anybody who can fence these?"

"I have some friends in San Francisco."

"In Chinatown?"

Phil nodded. "It's a family business. They have a restaurant, too."

"How's the food?"

"The egg foo young is amazing."

"If we leave now, we can be there for lunch," Ray said. "Up for a road trip?"

Phil studied him for a long moment. "Will I be coming back, Ray?"

"Do you want to?"

"Back here, to this place? No. What I meant was, after we exchange the diamonds for cash, will you kill me and take it all?"

Ray shrugged. "I don't know yet. Let's see what happens after your Yakuza friends decide to save money and kill us for the diamonds."

Phil put the trays back into the lockbox and closed it. "I can live with that."

"We'll see," Ray said.

NIKKI DOLSON

NIKKI DOLSON is the author of the novel *All Things Violent* and the story collection *Love and Other Criminal Behavior*. Her stories have appeared or are forthcoming in *Southwest Review*, *Best American Mystery and Suspense*, *Vautrin*, *Tri-Quarterly*, *Tough*, and other publications.

COME LET US KISS AND PART

Nikki Dolson

Farah was down to her last usable blade when she dropped her box cutter and broke its tip. She still had half a pallet of paper products to unsheathe from cardboard and plastic wrap and she refused to do it by hand. She'd lost most of a nail the week before doing that and still had that finger bandaged. She swore, irritated at her clumsiness.

"Break it?" Joe asked. He was pulling his own pallet of product past her location in aisle six.

"Yeah," she muttered and headed off to the back office through the double doors that separated the employee area from the public where they stashed a box of cutter blades. But when she yanked the drawer open, there weren't any blades to be found. She stuck her head back out. "Joe, where are the blades?"

He stomped into the back office and blinked at her. She gave him a minute. It wasn't midnight yet and it always took him a couple of hours to really wake up. Graveyard was the worst shift to work even if it did come with better pay.

"Terry took 'em all. Said something about theft. If you want a new one, you gotta get it from him." He shrugged and loped back out onto the grocery floor.

She kicked the wall with her steel-toed boot. Terry was the second assistant manager and full-fledged kiss ass. Which was hilarious because some folks said that Terry was breaking company rules by carrying a gun in the store, not that Farah had ever seen it. Store gossip had it that he'd been demoted, transferred to their store and onto the night-shift as punishment because he'd had a habit of leaving the safe open at his old store—then they were robbed. Store robberies happened at least a couple times a year to grocery stores across Las Vegas. It happened so often management generally weren't held responsible so Terry's fuckup must've cost them a lot. Now he found every reason to cut costs and disciplined everyone for the smallest infractions. Farah was sure he'd claim night crew went through too many blades and must be stealing them. Anything to make himself look better.

As Farah stepped out onto the floor "8 Days (Of Hanuk-kah)" began to play through the overhead speakers. Out of habit she sang along with the singers, who sounded like a sixties girl group. From mid-October through New Year's Day, Christmas music played constantly. She and the other employees would eventually succumb to the holiday music sickness: involuntary singing. They sang during their shifts and hummed song fragments at home. The yearly interlude of Hanukkah songs was always a nice break even if that play-list hadn't changed in years. For the next couple of weeks, accompanied by a playlist of mostly instrumental Hanukkah songs, Farah and the rest of night crew would be straighten-ing and filling end displays of matzo crackers, potato pancake mix, concord grape juice, and at the registers mesh bags of gold foil-wrapped chocolate replaced gum and name brand chocolate bars. Even though 90 percent of the Hanukkah stock wouldn't sell because, as Farah had heard many a customer complain, these things were mainly for Passover, not Hanukkah. What kind of grocery store doesn't know that? they said as they turned their carts away from her and told their oldest child to grab a box of potato pancake mix before they headed to the checkout. Every year was the same in this store. Nothing had changed for Farah in years.

She made her way upfront, noting the few customers in the store as she went. Two quick knocks on the door that led to the upstairs office brought the sound of Terry's heavy footsteps. She stepped aside just as the door swung open.

Terry leaned out at her. His face was pale, round and soft. A back-to-front comb-over of brown hair lay plastered across his head in an attempt to hide a growing bald spot. "What?"

"I need a new blade." She held up her cutter.

He hmphed and popped his gum in her face. "Fine." He pushed the door wider and nodded at her to come in. She took in a breath and stepped on first stair. The heat of him as she slid past made her skin crawl. The second stair creaked loudly when she stepped on it and again as Terry followed her up. She felt his eyes on her ass as she climbed the stairs. There was nothing to see on her. She made sure she was shapeless in her baggy work pants and too-big sweatshirt that hung past her ass. She stood by the other manager's desk and waited for Terry to slowly make his way up.

"Have a seat," he said. The armless chair squeaked and groaned as he sat down and started looking through paperwork on his desk.

"I'm okay. I just need the blade."

"Do you like night crew?"

She shrugged. "It pays for half an apartment."

He chuckled. "Well, the management program is coming up again. I could put your name in, if you wanted."

"You would?" The management program would mean a raise and better hours. More money meant she and roommate Chris could find a bigger apartment. One with two bathrooms so they didn't have to fight over the one when they were both getting ready to go out.

"Sure. You're twenty-one now, right? You've got the time in. Just gotta fill out the paperwork."

"That would be great."

He turned away from her, patting the top of his desk, lifting a clipboard, a folder. A *Sports Illustrated* with OJ Simpson on the cover slipped to the floor. Everyone was talking about his trial.

"You ever see Mike anymore?" Terry asked.

"Mike who?"

"Mike Sutton." He turned to face her. "You two were high school sweethearts before he went to prison, right?"

Farah looked down at her shoes. People still talked about the robbery and the guys who did it. "I see him around sometimes. We were together a long time ago."

"He ever tell you what happened that night?"

She sighed. She'd been asked this so many times. "No and I haven't asked."

"Yeah but for a pretty girl like you, he's gonna want to impress, right? He hasn't been bragging? Nothing?"

"We don't really talk." She was shifting from foot to foot now.

"Well, when you see him again you tell him I said hey and he should give me a call."

"Sure," she said. Terry just smiled and nodded like he was the Las Vegas Stars bobblehead on the dash of her mom's car. "Can I get a blade now?"

"Oh, shit. Yeah." He pulled open a drawer and handed her a box of the cardboard-wrapped blades. She slid one out and fitted it into her handle. "And the program paperwork?"

He snorted and opened a different drawer and pulled out a folded application. "Fill out all four pages. Get it back to me."

Farah looked over the pages, then said, "Why are you offering to help me?"

He shrugged. "Maybe I want you to be my replacement."

"Are you going somewhere?"

"I fucking hope so. I need out of this tiny ass store. There's no future here."

The store was half the usual size but it had been around forever and the customers were faithful. It was the only store she'd ever worked at though so maybe there was a better future out there. She didn't know.

"Hoping to go back to your old store?" she said.

He stood up and patted at his head. "Nah, I have bigger dreams. Now go get back to work."

THE NEXT MONDAY WAS the first day of Hanukkah and the store was packed. Management had menorahs painted across the store windows. Over the automatic doors hung a banner with HAPPY HANUKKAH in blue lettering against a white background. Tiny blue and silver dreidels spun on hand-painted sale signs for fresh challah bread and two-for-one whole chicken roasters. Farah had swapped shifts so she could meet Chris at the pool hall that night. She rang up the last of the customers in her line, counted down her drawer, then changed into a sweater and jeans and walked out into a frigid night. The parking lot was mostly empty. The only cars belonged to the night crew and the people at the pool hall. Joe was out there before his shift saying goodbye to his boyfriend, Nate. Joe nodded at her and she smiled then looked away when Nate turned Joe's face to his own and they sunk into a kiss. The winter cold made her walk quick across the pavement. She thought of summer heat. Summer was for kissing on hot nights in parking lots. Wearing the least amount of clothes possible. For dancing under a stretch of night sky unencumbered by responsibilities or worries. She missed summer.

Farah stepped into the pool hall and for a moment she stood at the door reveling in the heat. Then she saw Chris waving wildly at her at from a back table. She scanned the room as she walked through and saw Mike Sutton hunched over his beer surrounded by guys she didn't know. He raised his beer in her direction and she gave him a quick smile. She'd known he'd be here. Half her reason for going out tonight was to talk to him. Terry was adamant that she tell Mike to call him before he'd turn in her paperwork.

Farah dropped her purse on the little high-top table in the corner and grabbed the beer from Chris's hand. "Are we playing or hustling?"

Chris toyed with the choker around her neck, eyeing a couple guys the next table over. "Maybe both? I'm going to be short on rent unless I make a little money real quick."

Farah grabbed a cue stick and chalked it. Chris racked the balls. "How short?"

"A hundred. Maybe more. Everyone is getting teeny tiny cheap tattoos this month."

"I can cover it."

Chris turned wide eyes on her. "Oh, did you hit a jackpot on your break last night?"

"No, but I can tap my savings for it."

Chris gave her a look.

"It's fine," Farah said. "I'm probably getting into the management program so there's a raise coming soon."

"Probably?" Chris's perfectly arched eyebrow lifted.

Farah nodded. "Definitely."

"You're getting promoted!" Chris exclaimed. They clinked beer bottles. This attracted the attention of the guys at the next table. Chris stared and licked her lips. Farah nudged her. "Stop looking for trouble and get your stick."

"I'm trying to get my stick."

"Oh my god." Farah rolled her eyes. Sometimes she hated how tiny her world was. She ate at the Macayo's across the street from the grocery store she shopped in and worked at. Now she was hanging out in the pool hall with her friends. Her life was lived in five square miles. But on nights like this with Chris ready to play and cause trouble, Farah didn't hate it at all.

Someone tapped Farah on her shoulder. Startled, she spun around and found herself face-to-face with Mike Sutton. "Hey, you," she said, half laughing.

"I didn't mean to scare you. I was just—"

"Lurking?"

"Sorry," he said. "I remember you smoked back in the day so I thought you might have a light."

She dug into her purse. "All those guys over there and you pass them up to ask me?"

"You're the only person who looks at me and doesn't seem like you're already planning your escape from the conversation."

He smiled and there was the boy she had loved all that time ago. His face had been soft and round back then. He looked so skinny to her now. Hollowed out.

"You're so thin. Your mom not making you clean your plate?" She remembered too late that his mother had died while he'd been in jail. She scrambled to correct. "I forgot. I'm sorry."

"It's okay. Can't ask you or anybody to keep up with all my troubles."

Her hand finally closed around the lighter and she handed it over. He lit his cigarette and drew in his first puff. He exhaled smoke and settled next to her, both of them leaning against pool table's railing. She glanced over her shoulder to see Chris moving in on the guys at the other table. Chris didn't need her to hustle those guys. She was too good a player and they looked like they were drunk enough to bet on every ball she lined up. She would come up with rent money before the night was over.

He blew smoke off to the side. "How are you though? Good things happening?"

She started to tell him about the program but then she remembered Terry. "Do you know Terry? Assistant manager at the grocery store?" He shook his head. "He asked me to tell you to call him."

He blew smoke at the ceiling. "I wonder if I do know him."

"Honestly, I don't think you do. He asked me if you talked

about what happened. If you bragged to me to impress me."
She said this last bit in a whisper.

Mike laughed and smoke curled around his mouth.
"He's one of those guys. Some folks think I have the money
hidden somewhere."

"They do?"

"Yeah. The cops never found anything but a couple
thousand. Everyone assumes there's a pot of gold buried
somewhere."

"That would be something." She laughed and toed the
carpet. "Can I ask, why did you do it?"

"I don't know. I was bored and it seemed exciting. Easy.
Superbowl weekend. It was going to be dead that night with
everyone at home watching the game. Only a couple people
on shift. Easy money and all I had to do was drive. The plan
was for them to hop in my car and I'd drive them to another
car and we'd all escape. Police would be looking for three
guys in a Honda CRV but it would just be me. They'd be off
in other cars going different directions. Home free."

"What happened?"

"I dropped them off and drove around as planned.
I knew my uncle would still be up drinking and raging,
my mom right there with him, so I didn't go home. Didn't
want to give him a target. You were at some girl's birthday
party so I just cruised around. Then you called my beeper.
I pulled over to use a pay phone. I got as far as picking up
the receiver and police rolled up on me. Lights going. They
asked me to step away from the phone. Asked me where I
was going. What I'd been doing. I told them just driving.
They wanted to look in the car. I let them. I thought I was
clean."

"But they found that glove."

"Heard about the glove, huh?"

"You made the papers and the evening news." It had been everywhere for weeks. Kids at school asking her questions. The police showing up at her mom's place wanting to know what Farah knew. Which had been nothing. Not that anyone believed her.

"We only made the news because they tried to tie us to some other robberies in town. They caught Ty because he was driving a stolen car, the dumbass. They found a glove on him that matched the glove in my car. Ty broke down and told them this was the only job he'd been involved in. He'd only asked me for a ride, which both helped and hurt me. I got off easy though and we both did better than Freddie."

"They killed him," she said.

"Nah, he killed himself. He had done a couple years for boosting a car. He swore he'd never go back in. Can't say I blame him."

"They caught you because you were going to call me." She felt bad about it even though it was him who'd done something stupid and paid the price for it. She had to live with the gossip but he'd gone to prison.

"Not your fault." He wrapped a big hand around her forearm and gently squeezed. She remembered other nights he'd touched her. Nights on the hood of his car watching the night sky and talking about high school drama, family drama, and their dreams of adulthood.

Surprising them both, she asked, "Do you want to hang out sometime?"

He stared at her. "Uh, sure."

"I mean, we're friends. Friends hang out."

"Yeah, they do."

Not long after Chris ran past them and out the front door. She'd taken a few dollars too many from one of the guys and he was pissed off and drunk. His buddy had to hold him back. Farah said goodbye to Mike and the room-mates headed home, each of them riding a high from the night. They paid the rent in full.

THEY MET UP THE next night. Mike didn't want to come up to Farah's apartment. He didn't want to see Chris again or anyone else for that matter. Which didn't make sense to her. "What about the guys you were with the other day?" she asked. They were parked in the Jack in the Box parking lot, eating sandwiches and fries and smoking in the front seat of his newly acquired used Dodge station wagon.

"They aren't my friends. They bought the beer and I spun them a story." He passed the joint to her.

"I hope you didn't tell them all your good stories."

"Why not?"

"That beer isn't worth good stories."

They laughed, ate their burgers, and smoked. Then he drove her out of the city proper into the lightly bulldozed desert, acres of land stripped of vegetation, where sub-divisions were going to happen one day. On the radio a children's choir was singing "I Have a Little Dreidel" and when it ended, TLC's "Red Light Special" began. Mike shut the radio off. He cracked the windows and turned up the heater. The cold air made her shiver but her feet were almost too warm. When the smell of manure hit her, she choked and coughed. "Oh my god, where are we going?"

"Out where no one will bother us. No kids come out here

to make out and have awkward car sex." She looked at him. "Don't worry. I just want to sit out under the stars like we used to."

They pulled off the paved road into an empty, uncleared lot. The mountains loomed large against the backdrop of dark sky. There was snow on all the peaks now. The wind shifted direction and the smell died down. Faintly, she heard the sounds of pigs, oinking and grunting in the night. "You took me out to the pig farm?"

He shrugged. "It's nice out this way, once you get over the smell."

"When did you start coming out here?" she asked.

"A guy I did time with has a brother who works there. He tried to get me a job but it didn't work out. He lets me hang though. He's a bad card player. I can usually make enough off him to buy me a couple of cartons of cigarettes every week."

"Nice work if you can get it."

"What do you want to do? Run a register for the rest of your days?"

"Maybe. That doesn't sound so bad some days. I am going to finish college. Just saving up."

"Nah, you should leave town. See the world."

"Why don't you do that?" she said.

"Oh, I will. I just waiting."

"Waiting for what?'

"An opportunity has come my way."

He wouldn't meet her eyes then. She wondered if he could be stupid enough to break the law again. She sat up, ready to lay into him, but he met her as she moved, a hand on the back of neck pulling her to him and into a kiss. The hand was only gentle pressure. So gentle that later when she replayed the kiss in her mind she thought that she initiated it. That she had pulled him toward her. They kissed under a sliver of moon, fogging up his windows, and listening to pigs snort and grunt in their pens.

When he dropped her off, she kept leaning back in to kiss him goodbye. His smile grew with each kiss. In between kisses she asked if he'd talked to Terry yet.

"I think I'm going to blow him off," Mike said. His hand held her face close to his. "I'm very busy with this old friend of mine."

"Oh yeah? This old friend hot?"

"Nah but she cute as hell."

Farah pulled away to swat at his arm. He caught her wrist and pulled her close again.

"You're crazy beautiful." His voice was low and sweet.

She said, "See you tomorrow? You can stay."

"Maybe." He looked away.

She turned his face back to hers. "Chris will be gone."

His eyes lit up then. "I'll bring movies."

THE NEXT NIGHT ARRIVED and Farah ushered Chris out of the house. "But I just want to say hi to him."

"He's not ready."

"Is he a mouse or a man?"

"Get out."

Chris cackled, grabbed her leather jacket, and swung out of the apartment in all black except for the glow in the dark laces in Doc Martens. Pizza arrived in the half hour between her roommate's exit and Mike's knock at the apartment door.

She gave him the tour of all four rooms. "This is it. Five hundred square feet for two people and all their shoes."

They sat on the couch with slices of pizza and a beer each. They ate and pretended to watch the movie he brought. They lasted all of thirty minutes before they were on each other. She pulled him off the couch and into the bedroom. Then it was all teeth and lips and hands on skin, pulling, pushing, grasping, rubbing and it was the best time two naked people in twin size bed could have. Later, Chris came home and smacked on Farah's bedroom door, yelling, "I'm here, fuck quietly."

They laughed. He was curled around her, his head on her shoulder, his arm draped across her chest. He tilted her face to the window and kissed her neck. He whispered into her ear, "Where would you go if money was no problem?"

She stared through the slats of the blinds at the streetlight against the velvet blue night sky. "First stop, New York. There's an exhibit of Gustav Klimt I'd love to see."

"Who the fuck is Gustav?"

"A painter. He has this painting called *The Kiss*. It's this man and woman wrapped up in a quilt, or maybe it's a cloak. Not that it matters. But she is looking up at him and he is looking down at her, his hand cradling her face and . . ." Farah trailed off and sighed. "I just want to see it up close. I've only seen it in books. I want to see the paint. I want to see the light on the canvas. It's beautiful on the page, can you imagine how stunning it must be in person?"

"Paintings, huh? You like art?"

"I like everything. I haven't been anywhere or seen anything. Just Vegas and the desert and Mt. Charleston." She shrugged.

He lifted himself up off her for a moment but then settled back down two inches closer so now his face was pressed into her neck and when he spoke she felt his words more than heard them. He told her about a job in the Oklahoma Panhandle. He just needed enough money to get there. A couple of grand to get him over the hump until his first check. If he could get there, his buddy had a job for him. Guaranteed. When she tensed at the idea of him leaving her, again, when she'd just gotten him back, had just made peace with the idea of him in her life, he soothed her with three little words: Come with me.

"How will you get the money? I don't have that much."

"No, baby. I don't want your money. I'll get my own. Don't worry."

"But how?" Instantly worried, Farah tried to sit up, but he settled his hand on her cheek, his thumb stilling her lips. He looked into her eyes. "Don't worry. I'm not going back to jail." And she believed him.

THREE NIGHTS LATER, ON a busy Friday night that saw Farah at the register more than in the aisles helping Joe restock the place, she answered a call while in the check stand ringing up a customer's late-night restock of vodka. "Lucky's," she said.

"I thought you were off tonight."

"Fifty sixteen," she said to the customer. To Mike she said, "Someone called off. What's up?"

The customer handed her three twenties and slipped her a frown too. She smiled a fuck you back at him and gave him change.

"Can you go on break in ten?"

"Doubtful." She thought of the empty shelves where the soup belonged. The store had had a two-for-one sale that had wiped them out.

"I'll be out back. Come find me." He made her promise to meet him. She would do it. Of course she would. She was tired and her feet hurt and being at work was not where she wanted to be that night and Terry, who was up in his office doing a crossword or watching TV or something unhelpful, said he didn't know when the program start date was and for her to be patient. Terry, who had spent half the night humming to himself. Like he was the one getting a chance at a promotion. Fucking Terry. She called up to the office while she wiped down her check stand.

"I need a break," she said.

"I'll be there in a bit."

"I want one now. There are only a couple people here."

"Fuck. All right, I'll be down."

Five minutes later, Terry appeared, sweaty and wrinkled like he was every night they worked together but nearly bouncing with every step, too.

"Why are you so happy?" she asked.

"I'm not. It's just not a bad night."

"Half the shelves are empty." He shrugged and laughed. She rolled her eyes. "I'll be back in ten."

"Don't be late and thanks for giving him my message."

"What?"

"Mike. I appreciate it. I mean, who knows if you'll get into the program but I appreciate you doing me the favor."

She started to speak but he tapped his wristwatch. "Get going." So she weaved her way toward the back through the aisles. A woman still in her casino uniform rolled past her with an overloaded cart. Terry would be busy with her the entire length of Farah's break. In the back office she found Joe having his dinner of ramen while smoking and drinking coffee. She sorted through the timecards on the wall to find her own and clocked out.

"Going home?" Joe asked.

"Just going on break. There's only one customer so he'll be fine for a few minutes."

"I'll head out in a couple."

The night air had a bite to it but it wasn't too cold to wait a few minutes. Farah shoved her hands into her pockets, wishing she'd remembered to grab her sweatshirt. The long-sleeve shirt under her uniform white button-down and jeans weren't quite up to the weather but Mike would be there soon. They could sit close together in his front seat and let the car's heater keep them warm and if that didn't work she could slip onto his lap and they could make their own heat. Farah smiled at that thought. Mike was back in the world again and they were a couple. Her personal life was in a good place. Maybe she would go with him. Chris would come. She was always up for a change. But first, just to satisfy her curiosity, she would call the regional manager to see if her application for the management program had been accepted. If it wasn't there, then she knew that Terry was a fucking liar. But in her gut, Farah already knew. He had used her to get to Mike for some reason. Maybe to get Mike to reveal something the police hadn't known about the robbery or the money or maybe there was someone else in on it. Anything would do for Terry. He just wanted to look good.

She was rocking in place and humming softly. The minutes ticked by and she started to wonder if Mike would show at all. The store phone began to ring. She knew Terry would pick it up and eventually the ringing did stop. She waited a few more minutes then called it. Mike must've got busy doing something. She sighed. She would call him later to find out what was so important he stood her up. She clocked back in. The phone started ringing again. She ignored it. Joe was gone now. His cigarette, balanced on the edge of the Styrofoam ramen cup, had burned down to the filter and the cup itself was smoking more than the cigarette. She pushed the cigarette into the remnants of the ramen. She plastered on a friendly customer smile and swung out the doors singing softly, "Dreidel, dreidel, dreidel, I made it out of clay."

Back out on the store floor, the ringing phone was louder. Then she realized there was no music playing. If the music had stopped it was because the tape had ended and Terry hadn't turned it over yet. Which had happened before on busy nights when all three of them had to work registers, the tape would end but they didn't notice until after the rush. Their job was to smile as they slid groceries over the scanner and make sure their customers had a pleasant trip to their grocery store. They bagged and made small talk. They reviewed coupons and discussed sales upcoming and missed. But never once had the phone kept ringing. Ever. Terry would never let it ring so long. Farah had seen him take it off the hook so if anyone from corporate called they would think they were just busy on calls. Sometimes when there were sales or highly coveted oven safe dishes available with the purchase of four turkeys or the redemption of a fully stamped coupon book, the calls would come in all day and night. They could be busy on multiple registers but never would Terry just let the phone ring on and on and on.

Farah made her way to the front, glancing around. She saw no one, not even Joe in some aisle lining up bags of chips or rows of canned whatever. Maybe he was ringing customers too. Farah walked faster. Never had the store felt so big as it did in that moment. She squeezed past pallets of baby formula, another of canned fruit and soups. Still the phone rang on, then there was the scream. Sharp and piercing. Then nothing but the phone *ringing ringing ringing*. Farah crept closer. Something made her slow down. Something made her afraid.

"Look, man, you don't need to do this." It was Joe. Farah peeked around the end display of two-liter sodas. Joe was in the check stand with his hands up. A man in a black hoodie, a black ski mask over his face, was pointing a gun at Joe. Farah crouched, worried she'd been seen. She saw the woman in the casino uniform on the floor next to the check stand with both hands pressed tight against her mouth like she was trying to hold in another scream. The woman's eyes were wide with fear. Farah held a finger to her lips. There was nothing Farah could do to help the woman without revealing herself. Farah turned to head back down the aisle. She could call for help from the back office.

"Stop right there." Farah froze. "Turn around."

She thought about running. She could probably make it to the end of the aisle before the gun went off. Maybe he'd miss. But what would he do to the others because she ran? She lifted her hands up and turned to face the man with the gun, but this wasn't the same guy. He stood a little taller. He was in a black mask and a black hooded sweatshirt, too, but he wore a satiny black jacket over it. He stood between the registers, pointing a gun at her. Where had he'd been hiding?

"Come here." He gestured with his gloved hand for her to move forward. When she was close enough, he grabbed her by the elbow and shoved the gun into her stomach. "Anyone else here?" Their faces were inches apart. Farah shook her head. Tears welled up, blurring her vision. He shoved her toward Joe's register. The woman on the floor let out another scream. "Just get up, honey, and move to the front of the register, okay?" the man said. "You're fine. You both are. For now." The woman started sobbing as she crawled forward. Farah looked over at Joe and saw Terry just beyond him at the next check stand. His face was expressionless. His forehead was shiny under the fluorescent lights.

The man with the gun on Joe seemed to startle at her appearance. He took a step backwards, shifting the gun to his other hand. Joe turned and seeing her said, "Just be cool, Farah."

The man in the jacket placed a hand on her shoulder and pushed down until she was seated next to the crying woman. "Yeah, everybody, be cool. Now, Mr. Manager, let's go get this money. We don't got all night."

Terry shook his head. "Safe is locked."

"Bullshit, you gotta count drawers and shit tonight. I know how this works. Take my guy with you and open the safe." He moved to stand over the women, keeping Joe always in his sight.

Terry walked out from behind the check stand and the other thief in the black mask looked down at Farah and she knew those eyes. She had to look away. She didn't want to say something that would reveal what she knew. She turned her body toward the woman next to her. The phone had finally stopped ringing. She heard the sticky sound of rubber-soled shoes on the linoleum. She heard the swish of the door to the upstairs office as it slid across the floor. There was the creak of the second stair as Terry put his weight on it. Farah glanced up at the man in the jacket. Nothing about him seemed familiar. Maybe he was the friend from the pig farm. Would they do it together? Is that why Mike called her to the back of the store? So she wouldn't be here when it happened?

There was a yell and gunshot exploded into the silence of the room. The door to the upstairs flew open and smacked against the wall. Farah turned, saw Mike falling to the floor, and Terry stepping over him with a small black gun in his hand.

The man in the jacket yelled "Fuck!" and Farah watched him raise his gun and fire. Someone screamed. The woman next to her was screaming and crawling away.

Another gunshot. Farah crawled toward Mike. She couldn't look away from him. He yanked off his mask. His body twisted around until he was on his belly, his hands against his stomach, and he looked right at Farah. It was like that night in the pool hall. That night in his car. That night in her bed when his body curled around hers, warm and solid. Like every time he had ever looked at her and she had seen something—tenderness, hope, desire—whatever it was that had made her heart lurch in her chest.

His mouth formed her name. His bloody hand extended toward her. She crawled closer. Terry went down in front of her, clutching his chest. She jerked back. His dingy white shirt bloomed red with blood. She looked over him to see Mike but now his eyes were closed. Farah was sure Mike was dying and now she was screaming too. Joe ran to her and pulled her away, down past the check stand. The man in the jacket ran out of the store. Farah strained against Joe's grip on her. She was screaming for Mike and Joe was saying, "Don't look, Farah. Don't look. You can't help him now."

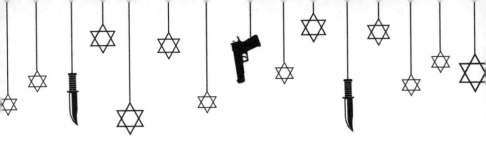

© JERRY BARKSDALE

J.R.
ANGELELLA

J.R. Angelella is the author of the irreverent and twisted coming-of-age novel *Zombie* (Soho Press, 2012). His short fiction has appeared in various journals, including *Hunger Mountain, Sou'wester, The Literary Review, Coachella Review,* and *Southampton Review.* His original screenplays have won numerous awards, most recently at the Houston Comedy Film Festival (2020) and Baltimore Next Media Web Fest (2022). He teaches creative writing at the University of Maryland College Park, where he directs Jiménez-Porter Writers' House, a literary center for the study of creative writing across cultures and languages. He also serves as screenwriting faculty in the Electronic Media & Film department at Towson University. J.R. received an MFA in Creative Writing & Literature from Bennington College. He lives in Baltimore with his wife, Kate, and two kids, Geno and Lily. Visit his website: www.jrangelella.com.

MI SHEBEIRACH

J.R. Angelella

For Gabe Hudson

Molly Blaze stood in the middle of the TD Bank, hands in the shape of guns, aimed at the other customers, the heel of her Chuck smashed into the neck of Gershom Fox, an old Orthodox Jew, her target, his damn briefcase, the thing she was commissioned to steal, handcuffed to his wrist. Oh, and this was not the plan. She was never meant to be in this bank. She was a driver, not a thief, despite looking like one. Dressed in all black. Hoodie. Jeans. Chucks. Hair in a ponytail. She should never have said yes to the job. And yet here she was, looking like a fool.

Gershom didn't so much as blink under her Chuck.

"Give me the fucking briefcase," she said.

"Faith makes miracles possible," he said.

Molly stabbed her heel harder into his neck. The cell phone in her pocket buzzed. It was her husband, Ritch; she knew it. Withdrawal was settling in by now. He needed her home. But unfortunately, he would have to wait.

A construction worker in a bright yellow vest approached Molly, unafraid of her finger guns, his weekly pay in his hand. His mustache was stained from decades of cigarette

smoke. It was lunchtime on a Friday afternoon and he just
wanted to cash his check.

"Take it easy, lady," he said. "Let the old man up. This is
hard to watch."

Even though he was right, she didn't like to be called *lady*.

"Stay the fuck back," she said.

Molly knew she looked ridiculous—finger guns, really?
Not to mention that to the casual passerby, she was in the
full commission of a hate crime, stepping on the neck of an
old Orthodox Jew, even if she was just doing her job.

The construction worker folded the check into his pocket.
His hands turned to fists, like a boxer charging the center
of the ring after the bell.

She had control of nothing, but tricked herself into
believing she was God.

"If you touch me, I will end you," she said.

"The fuck you will," he said, menthol cigarettes and sugar-
free Red Bull on his breath.

Molly felt bad for the dude. He didn't know what was
about to happen to him.

"Stay back," she said. "Don't do this."

But he didn't stay back.

Molly eased up on Gershom's neck. He immediately
snaked free, just when the construction worker lunged at
Molly. But she didn't run or brace for impact. She wasn't
afraid of this fuck. She wasn't afraid of anything except losing Ritch. Instead, she held her ground because she had a
fucking job to do.

The two collided and collapsed hard to the marble floor.
The weight of the man crushed Molly, but she anticipated this.
A man of his size at the end of a long day, at the ass end of a

long week, working construction, he was not going to take the fall well. And she was right. Molly absorbed the impact and used the momentum of their bodies to roll up on top of him.

"Stay the fuck down," she said. "Don't fight."

But he swung on her.

"Mistake," she said.

She blocked the weak punch with her elbow, then slammed the palm of her hand into his chin, cracking his head into the marble, knocking him out. She patted his chest. A half-hearted apology.

Her cell phone buzzed in her pocket again. Ritch had terrible timing.

A Baltimore County police officer crashed through the front doors of the bank. He had a real gun and shouted for her to get down. To put her hands up.

It was cute.

She unclipped the fake leather ropes from a gold pole near the island where old people handwrite their deposit slips. Molly wound the pole back and swung it at the cop as he entered, smashing the base into his hand, knocking his Glock across the room. The cop dropped, curled into his hand, writhing in pain on the floor.

Bank employees cowered.

Two businesspeople, a man and a woman in suits, lay face down.

Molly walked over to the real gun and picked it up.

God, she felt stupid. There were only two rules. And she had broken them both. First, never get out of the car, and second, never *ever* carry a gun. Guns got people killed. And getting out of the car got people arrested. But she did get out of the car. And now she had a gun.

Gershom stood by the island of deposit slips, staring her down.

"Give me the briefcase," she said through grit teeth.

"You really have made a mess of things," he said. "But it's not too late to fix it."

Molly aimed the gun at him. She didn't want to shoot him. She didn't even know him. But when it came to Ritch, she was willing to do whatever it took.

Sirens approached, the Baltimore County cavalry on its way.

"If you're going to do it, you better do it now," he said.

She froze.

"You should never have said yes to that weasel-pimp Slavi," he said.

Molly grabbed Gershom by the elbow and ushered his ass away from the front of the bank to the exit in the back where she had parked her getaway car—a 1987 Buick Regal Limited T-Type Turbo—and pushed him inside. She wiped the gun clean of prints, tossed it in a dumpster, and revved the engine, peeling out toward the highway. All Molly could think about was that Gershom was right—she never should have said yes to Slavi.

THIS WHOLE DISMAL MESS started a week prior when Molly arrived for a meeting at one of Slavi Slavov's fake businesses, Direct Care & Modern Medical Supply Company, a narcotic rehabilitation center and medical supply chain nestled in a Pikesville strip mall, a northwest suburb of Baltimore City. She arrived early as instructed. Eight on the dot. The county school buses had just started pickups. She rang the buzzer and banged on the door, but no one answered. There were blackout curtains in the windows, so other than the sign above the building's entrance, there was no indication any kind of business existed whatsoever.

She leaned against the doorframe while she waited for him to let her in.

"Come on," Molly said, pounding the door. She knew he was inside. His bright yellow Hummer was parked out front.

It was Monday and Slavi was always hungover on Mondays. A heavy lock finally turned, and the door popped open. A pale face peeked out wearing wraparound sunglasses, like a juiced-up baseball player from the '90s.

"Wipe your feet. I just had the floors cleaned," he said.

His Ukrainian accent was thick, but Molly had trained her ear to understand him, or at least take a guess at what he was saying based on the syllables of his speech. Context was sometimes easier than the words themselves.

Molly pushed on the door and stepped inside.

Slavi Slavov had established himself as the next generation of criminals in the DelMarVa area. The son of poor Jewish immigrants from Ukraine, Slavi spent his weeks in Delaware, Maryland, and Virginia, buying real estate, operating legitimate businesses out of the buildings on his properties, and funneling his gambling and gun-running money through their books. Then he'd spend his weekends in Manhattan and Brooklyn clubbing.

Dressed in a white tank top, white boxers, and white knee socks with a gold rope around his neck, Slavi snaked through the empty space, like a dad making his way to his den to read the newspaper. Molly trailed after him, fighting the chemical fumes; the space reeked of ammonia. Three men in full-body coveralls and N95 masks moved about in the back of the store, loading and unloading a truck. Slavi stopped to watch them, before noticing Molly covering her nose with the crook of her elbow.

"You have problem with the smell?"

"Can you open a window?" Molly choked.

"Windows are for pussies." Slavi resumed his route to an office. "Don't mind the men in the back. They are taking out trash for me."

Molly smashed her eyes with her palms, trying to wipe away the burn.

Slavi shook his head. "No. No. Men don't cry, Molly. I can't have a man who cries working for me." He stood behind a clutter-free desk, before throwing a N95 mask to Molly, who strapped it over her face.

"I'm not a man," Molly said.

"Some people think sensitive emotions makes you a man. I think maybe we get you big, strong muscles and that make you a man. Would you like big, strong muscles, Molly?"

"I think emotions just make you human."

"My ex-wife says this too. And is why she's my ex-wife." He paused, shifting gears. The bullshitting was done. "You do good work," he said. "It is a shame to see you go."

"Thank you." Molly hated working for him and couldn't wait to be done with this last run. "I have appreciated our time together."

"What do you say you do not leave me, and you work for me only? No one else. We're doing bigger things soon. We have you work with my friends. You make some real money. For you and Ritch. Make life easy."

Molly wanted to be as far away from Slavi as possible. "I appreciate the offer. But I no longer need your assistance."

He looked surprised. "No longer need my assistance? Okay then. I'm happy for you. This makes me disappointed." He dug through a drawer in his desk and pulled out a cell phone and handed it to her. On it a picture of an old man dressed in all black, wearing a shtreimel, an Eastern European fur hat, and holding a black briefcase in his hand.

For the last year, Molly had been Slavi's courier. Not by choice. By necessity. Her husband had been injured and needed medical care she couldn't afford, so she turned to Slavi for help and had been in service to him ever since. At least until this last job, when she was going to finally get her husband real help.

As his courier, she never had to get out of the car. The Slavi jobs were easy. He would give her a cell phone with an address. She would drive to the location and call the only number in the phone. Someone would answer. She would tell them she was outside, and they would bring something out to her. She would pop her trunk. They would put it in. They would go back inside. She would drive away, throwing the cell phone away in the dumpster outside a fast-food restaurant on the way back to the loading dock of Direct Care & Modern Medical Supply Company where Slavi's men would retrieve whatever was in her trunk and Molly would drive away. She was never paid for any of these jobs. But it was an easy job to do for what she did get from him.

Molly examined the photo. "Who is this?" She had never been given a photo with a phone before. Only a number and an address.

"This is Gershom Fox. He has a briefcase. And I want you to get it for me."

She checked the phone. There was no number preset in it.

He watched her. "Yes," he confirmed. "There is no one to call. I want you to know what he looks like, so you can find him. And bring back my briefcase."

"What's in the briefcase?" Molly didn't want to know but couldn't stop herself from asking.

Slavi clicked his tongue twice, wagging his finger at her. "You just worry about bringing it back to me." Slavi moved behind his desk, revealing a menorah with no candles on it at the corner. "Gershom owns the Chinese restaurant Jumbo Seafood. Not too far from here. They close early on Fridays for Shabbat and stay closed through Sunday for the Sabbath. To make things more interesting, this Friday is the first night of Hanukah. He will be preoccupied and will never see you coming. You have all week. But I need the briefcase by Friday."

Molly didn't know anything about Hanukah but couldn't be bothered to listen to Slavi blow on about it, so she nodded. "I know of this place." Molly and Ritch loved Jumbo Seafood's beef with broccoli and shrimp fried rice. Best Chinese food in Baltimore. "Gershom isn't going to give me this briefcase, is he? I am going to have to take it from him, aren't I?"

Slavi smiled but did not answer. "My children sing this song. I don't know what it is, but there is a part in the song where they shout: *chicken wing, chicken wing, hot dog and baloney, chicken and macaroni, chillin' with my homies!* It brings them a lot of joy to say these stupid things. Makes them smile." He zeroed in on her. "Make me smile, Molly Blaze. Make everything *chicken and macaroni.*"

"I'll see you when it's done." Molly had attitude in her voice.

And as she turned to leave, Slavi snapped his fingers, drawing her to look back. He held up a bottle of pills. Shook them. "Don't forget about my assistance you no longer need."

She hated herself for being in this situation, but she had no choice. Ritch would need them come Friday, but after this week she was done doing things this way.

"Molly Blaze," he said, placing them at the corner of the desk. "I am not the bad man here. It is your husband. Your husband is the bad man here."

MOLLY'S HUSBAND, RITCH, WANTED to kill himself.

It all started two years ago when he hurt his back working at The Hooch House, a craft beer and artisanal wine shop in Hampden, a once-hipster neighborhood of Baltimore that had turned real yuppy real fast. They were saving up money to buy a house outside of the city. To help stash cash, Ritch worked as a mechanic for a Toyota dealership during the week, and as an assistant manager in the wine and beer shop on weekends.

The beer truck delivery had been delayed two days and didn't arrive until Saturday morning. It was July Fourth weekend, so the order was three times the normal size. And he was there to receive it, stacking three hundred cases of shitty American beer in a mountain display in the back of the store. Later in the day, some drunk yuppy dropped one of the cases of beer and left it to leak across the floor without telling anyone or cleaning it up. Ritch didn't see it. And on his way back from a lunch break, he took the turn, slipped, and fell hard.

According to his MRI, his lower lumbar was fucked with herniated discs.

Workers' compensation eventually ran out. So did his physical therapy sessions that were covered by Toyota's insurance. Two surgeries, a fused lower lumbar spine and three bulging discs later, he was in more pain than ever before and was fired from both jobs, first The Hooch House, then the dealership.

Molly felt responsible for Ritch and his situation. He didn't need to work two jobs. Hell, he didn't need to work any jobs. She made more than enough as a getaway driver. But he didn't know that. Well, he did, and he didn't. He knew what she did. And he loved what she did. He was excited by it. But he was also prideful and wanted to pull his own weight. To feel like he was contributing. Like he was taking care of his wife, not the other way around.

"This is what men do, Moll," he'd say. "So let me do it."

And so Molly let him get a job as a mechanic and later as the assistant manager in the beer and wine shop, even though the money he made barely covered rent and groceries, let alone savings for a house.

But the problem wasn't the surgeries or the injuries.

The real problem was the pills.

Ritch chewed sixteen pain pills a day. Eight in the mornings. Eight in the evenings. He didn't care what kind, so long as it killed the pain. Codeine. Hydrocodone. Hydromorphone. Demerol. Morphine. Oxycodone. Hell, he'd even eat a Fentanyl lozenge, although he preferred the lollipops. He would take anything except Tramadol. "Tramadol can suck my dick," he'd said to a doctor once who tried to prescribe him a lesser narcotic. He had burned through so many pain clinics and back specialists, hypnotists and Eastern medicine gurus, psychiatrists and psychologists and gotten himself blacklisted from most primary care physicians as a pillhead.

And so it was on Molly to keep him out of pain. To keep him afloat. To keep things moving. Because it was all her fault really. So, she did. Hunted down 120 pain pills a week.

She doctor-shopped and when that ran its course, she turned to the streets and burned through her savings buying clean pills wholesale off dealers she knew through professional connections who weren't fucking with their supply. She tried to taper him down once and he ripped all the doors off the hinges in the apartment. She tried to dole out the pills in a different schedule and he locked himself in the bathroom for days, doling them out himself, afraid she was gonna take them from him, until he ran out. She tried everything she could think of. But none of it worked. His body was addicted, and she had no choice. And when the money ran out and she couldn't cover the price of legit shit anymore, and there were no more avenues to navigate, Ritch told her he wanted to kill himself. To end the pain.

Molly woke and listened to life passing by outside her bedroom window one morning. It was a Sunday. Easter, no less. Families probably dressed in their most pastel and frilly best, on their way to church or brunch or Grandma's or egg hunt. She opened her eyes and could see through the crack in the curtain that the sun was high, and the sky was blue. The birds chirped away. She finally rolled over to find an empty bed, the sheets twisted and soaked through with sweat next to her. She moved through the kitchen and hallway, checking the bathroom along the way, but Ritch was nowhere. She finally found him in the living room. Sitting on the floor. He was naked, his wet clothes in a pile next to him. Her gun box dug out of the closet and its contents spilled across the couch behind Ritch. He held her 9mm in his hand which rested on his lap. Tears poured down his cheeks, but he didn't make a sound.

"Ritch," she said.

He looked up, embarrassed for her to see him like this, but not surprised.

"What are you doing?" she said.

"This is no way to live."

She walked slow toward him, like she was trying to lure a stray cat.

"I love you, Moll," he said.

She got down on all fours and crawled to him, careful not to spook him.

"I'm sorry," he said.

She stopped. "Ritch." She wasn't close enough to knock the gun away. "Don't."

He opened his mouth. He jammed the nose of the 9mm to the back of his throat. And pulled the trigger. But the gun didn't fire.

Molly scampered to him. Took the gun from his mouth and hand. Curled around him. Held him close. And let him sob.

She didn't keep loaded magazines in the gun box. She kept the rounds in the pantry in the kitchen in an old cookie tin. She was careful when it came to dangerous things. It's what made her great at her job as a wheelwoman.

"I'm gonna figure this out," she said. "Everything is going to be okay."

To save his life, Molly turned to Slavi. In exchange for

a bottle of 120 pain pills every Friday, she would be his courier.

MOLLY KNEW SLAVI THROUGH professional contacts, the criminal grapevine. He was seen as a new, no-nonsense, up-and-coming front man in Baltimore. He was affiliated with bad dudes in Brooklyn and had made a name for himself by being a great money launderer. People paid him to clean their money. And from there, the rest followed—guns, gambling, drugs. On paper, he owned a lot of businesses, but no actual business ever existed, which she learned when she first arrived at Direct Care & Modern Medical Supply Company.

The first time she met him, she knocked. Then buzzed. Then knocked again. She knew he was there because his obnoxious yellow Hummer was parked outside. Finally, he opened the door. White tank top. White boxers. Gold chain. Wraparound sunglasses. What would go on to become a regular Monday outfit for him.

"Molly Blaze," he said. "It is a pleasure to finally meet you. Come in." He stepped aside, welcoming her in. "I'm sorry we're meeting under these circumstances, but I am excited to have you working for me. I think we will do many great things together."

Molly had been a getaway driver for ten years and never worked long-term for someone. She never had a boss. She was always in control of herself and her car and her jobs. But not anymore.

"This way," Slavi said, closing the door and walking toward the back of the space.

What should have been a retail space was completely empty. Not so much as a phone on the floor. A horrible chemical smell permeated the space. Molly's eyes cried fast, burning. She followed him to his office, where he handed her a cell phone. In it was only one number associated with an address.

"You go to that address. You call that number. You get a package. You drive it back here."

"When do I get paid?"

Slavi opened his drawer and pulled out a pill bottle, placing it at the corner of his desk. "Here are your pills. Which you can take. When you return. With my package."

"Okay," she said, and went to leave, when he snapped his fingers for her to stop. She looked back at him, sitting in his chair, reading a piece of paper.

"If you wrote something and someone said what you wrote was *impossibly dense*, what does this mean?"

Molly had no idea what he was talking about, and her facial expression must have communicated this clearly, because he popped up out of his chair and approached her, holding the paper out for her to see for herself.

"Look. Read. Right here." His finger tapped the paper. He pushed the paper to her face. "I take poetry writing class. I write poems. We had workshop yesterday and someone in class wrote this on my poem. *Impossibly dense*. This fuck."

The poem was short, just a few lines, and the feedback at the bottom of the page said: *this poem is not only confused, but confusing. Impossibly dense. Lacks depth. Lacks emotion.*

"I have no idea what makes a good poem good or a bad poem bad," she said.

"Yes, but this poem, is it *impossibly dense*? What does it mean, this comment?"

"I couldn't tell you." Molly felt her chest tighten.

"I want you to read this poem to me. I want to hear these

words. From someone not me. Maybe I need to hear my words from someone else. Start at the top. I am excited to hear this. Thank you, Molly Blaze." Slavi eased himself onto a leather couch next to his desk, crossing his legs. "Come. Step away from the door. Stand in front of me. Project your voice. Be clear. I want to hear all of my words."

She moved farther into the room, stood across from Slavi and cleared her throat. She read the title first. "'These Hands.'" Molly looked to Slavi, who waved her to continue. Molly obliged, reading slow and enunciating more than she ever had before in her life.

> *Her ignorance breeds feral fallibility*
> *the moral sacrifice of his broken doves*
> *her poison sun burns with tiger teeth*
> *the blood of his bastard in the night*
> *her vendetta curls against black, veiny waves*
> *the end of his dead days pulverize concrete*

Molly had no idea what the hell she just read. Slavi uncrossed his legs, only to re-cross them in the opposite direction. He closed his eyes and spoke toward the ceiling.

"Do you think I'm depressed?"

Molly handed the paper back to him. "No," she said, carefully, looking at the pill bottle on the table, thinking about Ritch back home, withdrawal setting in.

"I title it 'These Hands.'" He raised his hands, first elevating the left. "Her." Then elevating his right hand. "His." He makes fists. "It's poem about these. You see how each line goes *hers*, then *his*, then *hers*, then *his*, then *hers*, then *his*. Three times it does this." Slavi recognized her inability to help him with his poetry and waved her on. "You go. We will discuss later."

When Molly stepped outside the office, she saw a pile of industrial black trash bags in the back loading dock. They were fat, resting by the dock door, tied off, ready to be taken out. All except one. Still open. The bag had tipped over. Bloody towels inside.

"What do you see?" Slavi said, although it didn't sound like a question. He placed his hands at her back and gently pushed her. "Go. See what it is."

Molly moved across the room through a door to the back loading dock. And as she turned, there on the floor, hog-tied with duct tape, bloodied and pleading, was a man. The man writhed on the floor with the terrified eyes of a child.

Slavi leaned close to Molly's ear.

"I didn't like what he said about my poem."

Molly held her breath.

Then Slavi laughed, genuinely. "I'm kidding, Molly Blaze! Look at your face. Oh, my goodness! You think this of me? It's just a poem! I would never." Slavi kissed the top of Molly's head. "This is something else. This motherfuck stole from me. This is nothing you should be concerned about." He paused. "You go now." Slapped Molly on the back. "Go get my package."

And she did. And when she returned a few hours later, the hog-tied man was gone, the blood was cleaned up, and Slavi handed her the pills.

MOLLY SPENT THE WEEK watching Gershom Fox. She learned his schedule, which was easy since all he did was operate out of the restaurant, and tracked his security levels, which were none. He was always alone and the briefcase in his hand. Friday came, and finally she was ready to make contact.

Jumbo Seafood was a fixture in Pikesville, nestled unironically between a dry cleaners and emergency veterinary medicine office. Molly parked outside with the rest of the midday crowd. Mostly older. All Jewish. Shuffling in and out. Takeaway in their hands.

Molly checked her phone. No messages. Only missed calls. She typed Ritch a text message, checking on him, asking if he needed anything other than his weekly pills. She waited a minute. No response. He was likely asleep. She put her phone in her jeans pocket and pulled out Slavi's phone, looking at Gershom Fox's photo again. He had kind eyes. She locked the screen and dropped the phone in the passenger seat and when she looked up, there he was.

Gershom Fox stood at the hood of her car, staring at her, like he was expecting her. He looked just like his photo. Old, but kind. Black suit. Two long payos curling down the sides of his face from under a fur hat. And then the briefcase. Loose in his hand. Not (yet) handcuffed. She didn't have a plan but didn't have a choice. It was time.

Molly exited the car, careful not to cause a scene, and waited by her side mirror for him to speak first. He didn't. He didn't speak at all. He didn't so much as blink. Finally, Molly moved around to the front of the car and faced Gershom. She was half a head taller than him. She could rip that briefcase from his hand so easy. But she couldn't bring herself to do it. Maybe it was his eyes.

The phone in her pocket buzzed. It was Ritch. But she didn't have time for that right now.

Gershom checked his watch. Then finally spoke. "You look tired, my dear. When is the last time someone cooked you a meal?"

Molly was shocked by the kindness and felt a wall of emotion crack in her chest.

"Let's get you a plate of food. We can sit. And talk. About why you are here."

Molly was taken aback. She wasn't expecting to be fed by him. Before she knew it, she nodded.

"Good," he said. "This way."

He walked to the door, held it open for her, and followed her inside.

The restaurant was very red. Red walls. Red booths and chairs. Red fringe hung from red lamp shades. An older Jewish couple finished their lunch and took their leftovers with them. They stopped Gershom on their way out and the three prattled away in Yiddish. Gershom clearly referenced Molly, pointing to her at one point, and the couple examined her, but not with judgement. With empathy. And as the couple made their way past her, the older woman grabbed Molly's hand and held it and said, "I'll say a Mi Shebeirach for you, sweetie."

Molly had no idea what the old woman had said, and before she even thought to ask, the couple was gone. Gershom had moved farther into the room, and whispered something to one of the waiters before sliding into a booth, setting the briefcase on the floor at his feet. Molly followed and slid in across from him.

"I know you know who I am," he said, "so I think it only fair I know who you are."

"You can call me Molly Blaze."

"No, no. Not that silliness. Your God-given name."

She hesitated. Then was honest. "Molly Bevilacqua."

"It's a pleasure to meet you, Ms. Bevilacqua."

"Mrs."

He looked pleasantly surprised. "Mrs. Bevilacqua."

Three plates hit the table next—vegetable spring rolls, beef with broccoli, and a bowl of rice. Gershom built a plate in front of him, before sliding it to Molly.

"Eat," he said. "Please."

Molly dug in. She didn't realize how starving she was. Her nerves and anxiety from both working for Slavi and caring for Ritch had zapped her of hunger. Food was the next to last thing she thought about, the last being her own happiness. They ate together in silence. Eventually, he exhaled a long breath, reveling in the food.

"Very good," he said of the food, more to himself than to Molly.

"What does Mi Shebeirach mean?" Molly asked.

"It's a prayer of healing."

"Did you tell that couple earlier that I needed prayer?"

"I told them you needed healing."

"I don't."

"Then why are you here?"

Molly didn't respond.

"Do you pray?" he asked.

"Never."

Gershom shook his head. "You should. Shame is a cancer. Don't hide from it. Expose it."

"I'm not sick. I don't need healing."

"Then you don't need prayer." He shoveled more food into his mouth and stopped speaking. The silence bothered

Molly. She looked to the kitchen, expecting Jewish men with guns to storm the table. But they never came. No one came.

"Where is everyone?" she asked.

"We're closed," he said. "I've sent them home. It's just you and me."

Her phone buzzed again. She pulled it out and looked. Ritch was calling. Not texting. It must be an emergency, she thought. They agreed to never call unless there was a problem.

"You can answer it," he said. "From your face, it looks important."

She sent the call to voicemail. "It's not. It can wait."

Gershom examined her a moment. Really investigated her face. Then leaned forward, his elbows on the table. "Your husband. *He* is sick. *He* is the one who needs healing. And *you* are suffering for it. I see this now." He leaned back, closed his eyes, and spoke a prayer in Yiddish.

"Was that the Mi Shebeirach?" she asked.

Gershom spoke the prayer in English, plainly, for her. "*He who blessed our fathers Abraham, Isaac and Jacob, Moses and Aaron, David and Solomon, may he heal this young woman who sits before me and her husband who is ill. May the Holy One have mercy and speedily restore both him and her to perfect health, both spiritual and physical; and let us say, Amen.*" Then he pinched another spring roll off the plate and ripped a hunk off. "A prayer of healing."

Tears hit her eyes. The kindness of the moment broke her. Her world had been so hard for so long that she had forgotten what it felt like to receive kindness.

Her phone buzzed again. A text came through.

It was Ritch and all it said was, "I'm dying."

She pulled focus. "Give me your briefcase," she said.

"I was wondering when you were going to get around to that."

"I don't want to hurt you."

"I don't think you will. I don't see a killer in you."

"I need it, Gershom. Please. Just give it to me." She sounded desperate and she hated it.

"Why do you need it?" He waited. "There must be a reason." She didn't respond. "Mr. Slavov needs my briefcase. Which he will never get. But you need something else."

Tears still broke from her eyes. Gershom's kindness hurt. But she pushed through the pain in her heart, and whispered, "I don't have a choice. Please. Just give me your briefcase."

Gershom wiped his mouth with his napkin, setting it next to his plate. He checked his watch again before grabbing his briefcase from the floor and setting it on the table. He took a key from his pocket and unlocked it, popped the gold latches, and retrieved a pair of handcuffs from inside. Then closed the top, locked the latches, and snapped one cuff to the handle and the other to his wrist.

"What did you just do?" she asked, laughing out of shock.

"It is Friday. The sun is setting. And the first night of Hanukkah. I must be getting home." He exited the booth and moved next to Molly. "You are a nice young woman. I am sorry you are in so much pain. Thank you for sitting with me. And eating with me. Of all the people Mr. Slavov has sent, you are the only one I have fed. I hope God heals you and your husband." Gershom walked to the front door.

Molly slid out of the booth fast, knocking her plate off the table. It crashed to the floor. Food and glass shattered and rolled. Gershom stopped, his hand on the door, ready to leave.

"Gershom," she said, no longer crying, no longer caring.

"I must go the bank before they close," he said, but in a way that sounded unsurprised by what she was about to say. "We both know you will follow me. Let's not make a scene."

"I'm sorry," she said. "For the mess."

"There is no mess, Mrs. Bevilacqua. Only solutions."

Molly approached him. "If you want to help me, I need you to give me that briefcase."

"Giving you this briefcase is not helping you," he said. "Submit to God. That will help you. Have faith in miracles. That will help you."

"If you don't give it to me," she said, "I will be forced to take it. By any means necessary."

"Yes," he said. "I am aware of what happens next."

And then he left for TD Bank.

MOLLY BLAZE'S GETAWAY CAR—A funeral black, 1987 Buick Regal Limited T–Type Turbo with chrome bumpers and trim—topped off at 110 mph on the highway. The cops gave chase, but their state-funded vehicles were no match for Molly's beast. She exited the ramp and snaked through neighborhoods, heading toward Direct Care & Modern Medical Supply Company. Gershom sat still in the passenger seat with the briefcase in his lap, finally turning to her.

"I am not a foolish man. I know what you need to do. I get that my actions have consequences. But I would like to make a request. My family is waiting for me. To light the first candle. I know this is the end. Slavi will never let me go. And that is okay. I'm prepared for that. But please. Take me home. Let me light the candle. Kiss my kids. Tell my wife I love her. And then we can go. I know your husband needs you and you're just caring for him."

Molly didn't hear his words, she felt them in her bones. She was a driver. Her emotions kept her sharp and focused but were also a liability in other contexts. Like this. There was no world in which she could tell him no.

She pulled the car to the side of the road. She wasn't mad at him. She was mad at herself. The weight of her decisions sinking into her chest. "Where do you live?"

"Bless you, my dear," he said. "We're close."

Molly moved through quiet communities until she reached Gershom's house, the last house on the left of a cul-de-sac. And immediately she knew she had made a mistake. Parked outside, leaning against an obnoxious bright yellow Hummer, was Slavi Slavov.

Molly lost words. Her gut gave out. Her phone buzzed constantly, Ritch circling the drain. And she couldn't be farther from helping anyone, let alone him.

"Just breathe, my dear," Gershom said. "I had a feeling he would be here. We think a lot alike, he and I."

Molly eased into the spot next to Slavi, and Gershom patted her hand still holding the wheel.

"It's going to be okay," he said. "I promise." Gershom exited the car and greeted Slavi. "Mr. Slavov. We were just on our way to meet you."

Molly slipped her hand to the floor and popped the trunk.

"Get out of the car," Slavi shouted at Molly. "I knew you were weak. People said you were tough, but I knew. I always knew. But this is okay. I am a man, and I am here."

Molly exited the car and moved to the back of the Buick. She wasn't hurt or offended by Slavi's words. Or even angered by them. She knew he was a scared little boy playing a clichéd role he constructed from American movies. But she also knew he was disconnected from how people moved through the world. He lacked empathy, and this scared her. He could never be trusted.

"She's done nothing wrong," Gershom said.

Slavi shushed him, then spoke in Yiddish. Gershom responded in kind. It sounded heated before they returned to English.

Molly lifted her trunk a bit and popped the top of the cookie tin.

"I'm tired of the fucking games, old man," Slavi said, "Give me the briefcase. Last chance."

"I will say hi to God for you," Gershom said, squaring his body on Slavi, not backing down one iota.

"I knew this would be your response." Slavi opened the door to his Hummer and retrieved a large pair of bolt cutters. Slavi grabbed Gershom and slammed him to the pavement without any resistance.

Molly stepped out from behind the Buick, her hand behind her back. In a nearby window, Gershom's children and wife watched, in horror, hysterical. His wife was on the phone. The cops maybe. She hung up and ushered her kids further into the house away from the carnage.

Molly always knew it would end like this, breaking her rules. Getting out of her car. Grabbing a gun. She felt she had been running for her life for so long. For her husband. For herself. And she just wanted it all to end. And this was it.

Slavi smashed his designer boot into Gershom's neck and jammed the bolt cutter to Gershom's wrist. "Let this be a lesson to your people. Not to fuck with Slavi." He opened the blades of the bolt cutter wide and set them at the base of Gershom's wrist.

A voice came from behind him.

"Yo, Slavi."

It was Molly.

He looked up at her.

She raised her hand. In it, her 9mm. Fully loaded. The one she had planned to get rid of after Ritch's attempted suicide. And unloaded it into Slavi's chest. His body blew back off his feet, dropping him to the sidewalk.

The echo from the gunshots hadn't even faded when cars rushed the complex, ripping toward Gershom's house. But they were not cops. They were more Orthodox Jews. Men. Some in shtreimels. Some in yarmulkas. Dressed in white shirts and black suits.

Shouting in Yiddish, they dragged Slavi's body from the sidewalk to the Hummer and threw it in the back. They stripped Gershom of his jacket and wiped down his face with bottled water and paper towels. They moved with intention, looking to Gershom for guidance, and he gave it. He was calm and collected. He hugged each man, cupping the backs of their necks, pulling them close, speaking what Molly thought sounded like little prayers into their souls.

With a father's kindness, Gershom took the 9mm from Molly's hand and nodded as if to let her know everything was going to be okay. He handed it to one of his men, who took it before he hopped in the Hummer and drove it off.

"May I have your keys?" he asked.

"No," she said.

"I promise you'll get it back."

Molly hesitated.

"You saved my life, Mrs. Bevilacqua. Now let me save yours."
She handed him the key. "Not a scratch."

He laughed. "Thank you, my dear." Gershom tossed it to a younger man. "Not a scratch," he instructed, before the younger man got in and drove the Buick away.

And just as quick as they had popped up, the Jewish cavalry was gone—no bodies, no cars, no blood, no sign of nothing. For a moment there was silence. Just the two of them, Molly and Gershom, out in front of his house. It was a perfect moment and one that Molly would not soon forget. Then police sirens approached.

"We must go inside now," Gershom said. "We can hide many things, but not the sound of gunshots."

"I don't know what to do anymore," she said. "I think I've run out of road." Slavi was dead. Her connection gone. Her husband suffering. The police on their way. "I don't think I can go on." She didn't cry. But she was drowning. "I'm tired, Mr. Fox. I have no plans. Never really did. Not when I decided to leave Slavi. Not with you. Not now."

"Mrs. Bevilacqua, I would very much like it if you would consider working for me. The terms of which would be set by you. My only stipulation is I pay you in cash. And I know people who can help your husband." He held out his hand. "I want to help you just as you have helped me."

Without hesitation, she received it. "I'm sorry I stepped on your neck," she said.

"Remember the past. Live in the present. Trust the future." Gershom held the door for her, and she entered.

Inside, she was welcomed by his family. Five children—four young boys and one teen girl who hugged and kissed Molly.

"You saved my husband," Gershom's wife said, pulling

her into the kitchen. She yanked a loose-fitting long sleeve sage-green dress over Molly's head that hit her ankles. Then removed the hair tie from Molly's ponytail and placed a long, black wig on her head. "This will make it so you're one of us. They will never know." Gershom's wife held Molly's face in her hands with tears in her eyes. "Thank you."

Molly lost her words again.

Then thought of Ritch.

The family sat in silence at a table in a dark dining room as red and blue lights whipped outside. There was a knock at the door. Gershom didn't stand. Instead, he held his hands up, reassuring his family everything was going to be okay, the briefcase gone from his wrist. He then lit the candle in the middle of the menorah, the shamash, the one raised above the rest.

"I am going to speak our prayer tonight in English, for our guest," he said.

The banging and shouting intensified at the door, but Gershom continued.

"Praised are You, Our God, Ruler of the universe, Who has given us life and sustained us and enabled us to reach this season."

He lifted the shamash from the center of the menorah and lit the first candle all the way on the right, before returning the shamash to the center. Then he got up from the table and answered the door. Gershom's wife served food to the children. His daughter handed out gifts. All while cops swarmed the house, asking questions, looking for evidence, asking about Slavi, and looking for Molly who sat at the table, undetected, and for the first time in her life, prayed.

© JORDAN BRYANT

LISKA JACOBS

Liska Jacobs is the author of the critically acclaimed novels *Catalina*, *The Worst Kind of Want*, and, most recently, *The Pink Hotel*. Her writing has appeared in the *New York Times*, the *Los Angeles Times*, Literary Hub, *Alta*, The Millions, and *Zyzzyva*, among other publications. Born in Los Angeles, she lives in Berlin.

DEAD WEIGHT

Liska Jacobs

It was over. In a couple of weeks, they'd host their annual holiday party together one last time, and then Raquel would have to find somewhere else to live.

She was lying on the Moroccan fainting couch, supine, with the balcony door opened behind her so she could feel the frigid December air. An Alfred Hitchcock movie played on her laptop, Mitzi was curled up beside her. It was one of those cold European days where the sky was like a giant gray light box outside and the cobblestone streets no longer looked quaint, not like they had during summer and fall. Now they were treacherous, icy hazards. Someone could get seriously hurt. Maybe that's what put the idea in her head.

But that came later. Right now, she was rereading Joel's text, his gentle reminder that she needed to get serious about finding another place to live. *I don't want to be a dick,* it read.

Where had things gone wrong? When was the exact moment their relationship shifted and went bad? She'd tried to make herself as small and convenient as any woman living in someone else's beautiful apartment. And it *was* a beautiful apartment. The kind only a trust fund could buy. Did buy. Built in the mid-nineteenth century, when

Germany still had money and artistic flare. There was an ornate marble entryway, like something you'd find in Paris. Double doors and high ceilings and parquet floors. It had ornamental moldings, and two balconies. Sunlight—a rare commodity in Berlin—streamed into every room. The kitchen was large, even for American standards. There was a walk-in pantry; she'd hung herbs from the ceiling, potted a monstera, a saguaro, and great heaving barrel cacti in the winter garden. Raquel's favorite space was what she called her little nook. The Moroccan fainting couch positioned near the bedroom, overlooking Tiergarten park. In the summer it was a sea of green—maple and oaks and trembling cottonwoods. Beneath them cyclists rang their bells at joggers and tourists and the brigades of new moms, pushing cranky babies in strollers; and near the lake a DJ played electronica at the beer garden, couples hand in hand. Raquel much preferred the winter. When the park was silent, and the trees were bare, and the earth frosted over and was hard. On one end of the park there was a famous Christmas market—it was too far for her to hear or really watch any of the goings-on, but she liked seeing the ruins of the church steeple all lit up, and how on the opposite end of the park, almost in direct contrast, was the thirty-three-foot menorah, lighting up Brandenburg Gate.

An icy gust blew in from outside and she shivered. She needed to get up and feed Mitzi, the Somali cat Joel's ex-girlfriend had left behind when she moved back to Ghana. In hindsight, that probably should have been a sign. A girl doesn't just leave her cat. Raquel had written it off as the ex being cruel, something Joel reinforced. *She took all the throw pillows*, he grumbled when Raquel first moved in.

She'd met Joel at a club, the only sensible place for young people in Berlin to hook up. You weren't going to meet anyone staying at home using a VPN to watch the Criterion Channel. Which, incidentally, was what Raquel preferred to do.

She was twenty-six. She was maybe going to be an artist, she was maybe going to be a filmmaker, or an actress. For now, she was a part-time bookseller. Joel was almost thirty. He was British. He was a writer, although that's not what he called himself. On the university website where he taught a course in "Language and Thinking"—after almost three years together, Raquel still had no idea what that meant—his bio read that he was a Nietzsche philosopher. Another red flag. But he was tall and handsome and when he asked her to move in, she was living with three girls in a flat in Wedding, near a crematorium that had been converted into a dance club. In the winter, the gas sometimes shut off in the building; there were rats in the walls. Or, more likely, ghosts.

She couldn't go back to that. The mold in the shower, the smell of hot feet and stewed tomatoes in the stairwell. Apartments with no floors, small windows, no windows. All those house managers who had faces that melted into their necks like fat white thumbs. She spoke lilting, self-conscious German; lacking Joel's blond good looks, she knew the brown undertones of her skin and her overtly Jewish name would have made it near impossible to get a rental contract on her own. And the thought of being a roommate again—the girls in Wedding had all been in a sex collective called Here Kitty, Kitty. An impossible situation. They'd shared a bathroom.

How had it come to this? She traced the rift back to

earlier this year, when Joel had won the Berlin Writing Prize. It meant a ceremony, a little prize money, and a heavy engraved plaque, which he hung above their bed. It also meant he was on his way up, and she was dead weight. Soon he was going to brunch parties with scholars and attending American Academy dinners on the Spree. She tried to acclimate. Elon Musk discourse? Sure, of course she had an opinion. Scandal at the National Book Awards? A quick google search in the bathroom and she understood the basics. Thoughts on coffee? The grow, the roast, the grind, the goddamn way it was served. How did these people care about these things? She skipped one event, then another and another, and soon she was staying home with Mitzi, watching Grace Kelly slink across the room, the phone ringing, ringing, ringing, while the murderer lay in wait.

She opened one of the expensive cans of tuna and plated it for the cat. *Mama only gives you the best*, she whispered into the cat's silken coat.

Mitzi was a kindred spirit. Her shadow. With glossy black eyes, the unbothered way she moved around the room looking for a little warmth, a little sunlight. Somewhere pretty to take a nap. Maybe partake in a little catnip.

Not many Berlin apartments allowed pets. Roommates were never keen on the idea either. And that was *if* Joel allowed her to take Mitzi. She was technically his and he had a childish need to collect things that proved his superiority (the cat, the medal, the apartment). He really wasn't that complicated. Deep down he feared he was a fraud and an idiot and needed constant nurturing.

A fall on an icy sidewalk would do it. Or a slip in the

stairwell, a minor concussion—something that would require another person around to help out. She was good at caring for things—look at the house plants and the herbs; Mitzi adored her. Lately, since the weather turned cold, and Joel had started hinting that things were over, she'd have a pot of glühwein on the stove when Joel returned home from teaching. A few crushed Xanax in it, and suddenly he was content to snuggle up on the couch watching Marlene Dietrich place a gloved hand on a bible and swear to tell the truth, nothing but the truth.

Injuring—*immobilizing* Joel wasn't much of a leap from drugging him. They'd get through the holiday party, and then it would be a cozy winter of Criterion Channel movies, with Joel wrapped in a blanket, Mitzi purring, Raquel's matzo ball soup simmering on the gas range (another reason she couldn't move, the apartment had a gas range!).

JOEL HATED WAITING. HE was edgy, nervous. The guests would be arriving in a couple hours and the cocaine delivery was late.

He was outside shivering. His holiday party was meant to celebrate everything from Christmas to Hanukkah to Kwanzaa, and it was tradition that there be a decent supply of cocaine. But it wasn't here. The sun, somewhere behind the cloud cover, was already level with the trees in Tiergarten park. The guests might have to make do with his stash of acid. He sighed. No one wanted to light a menorah in Berlin while tripping. That seemed like an all-around bad idea.

He struggled with his cigarette, the wrist brace making it difficult to maneuver. The damn thing complicated everything. Writing, typing, carrying bottles of wine or cases of beer. Raquel had to order the alcohol for the party to be delivered. And when the rider arrived, she wouldn't let Joel help unload the bags. Insisting he rest his injury.

It had been a hell of a couple weeks. Ladders slipping from walls, a top-heavy box that sent him spinning off balance, his shirt catching fire when he tried to make tea. All near accidents. One night his Berlin Writing Prize plaque fell while he was sleeping. Pulled the nail right out of the wall. A spate of bad luck, Raquel had told him, laughing it off. But then the fall down the stairwell a few days ago. He must have stepped in something—not uncommon in Berlin, which in some neighborhoods was more slum than cultured European capital, but this something was so slick and slippery that he'd fallen head first down the stairwell. Nothing was broken, but he was pretty banged up. His wrist had taken the brunt of the fall. He could barely put any pressure on it. Thank goodness for Raquel, who had been there to run down after him, bag of ice at the ready. She was almost smiling, telling him that he had looked just like Buster Keaton, twirling about in time with a choreographed fiasco.

That was Raquel for you. Early in their relationship he appreciated her sense of humor. He'd forgotten to laugh at things like Charlie Chaplin slipping on a banana peel, or Margaret Lockwood accidently kicking Michael Redgrave instead of the bad guy in the stock car of a runaway train. But she had no filter, there was no line. She laughed if a baby's ice cream fell on the ground, or when the vice president of the American Academy spilled wine down the front of her blouse. He worried it showed a lack of self-awareness, a determined immaturity.

She was also lazy. Not in her appearance, never in her

appearance. She was alluring in a sleek animal kind of way. But career wise, she had no ambition. Over the course of their relationship, and especially after she moved into his apartment, he suggested meet and greets where she might connect with the Berlin film community, or maybe she wanted to follow him into teaching? He sent her links for online jobs. Compared to him, she'd accomplished nothing. He couldn't rely on a girl like that.

Yet since his injury he'd had to rely on her almost completely. She'd always been a decent housekeeper (not that he thought of her as a housekeeper, she was just home more often, so it made sense that she took care of things like the groceries and cleaning the bathroom grout), but she not only deep-cleaned the apartment, putting fresh flowers in every room, but moved the Moroccan fainting couch so he could elevate his foot while watching the rugby game. She made him breakfast, lunch, and dinner, only ordering out a few times. She took care of the laundry, the cat, and even helped Joel when he couldn't get out of the tub. And through all of it, her light laughing manner had buoyed him. It's easy to get down during a Berlin winter, doubly so if you keep having accidents.

A scooter turned down their street. Was this his dealer? The scooter paused, then turned around, disappearing in the spittle. Joel checked his phone. Messages from writers and artists, people he still couldn't believe knew *his* name. They were all coming to their party. At this point it was more Raquel's party, she'd seen to everything. Even texting all the guests. It hurt his wrist to hold his phone for too long. He was trying to text the dealer now, laboring out w-h-e-r-e when his buddy from rugby called.

"Just seeing if I should bring anything—and since you're an invalid now, I thought I'd call instead of text."

"Ha, ha, very funny. Raquel has everything under control."

"I told you, man. The girl worships you, and that ass . . ."

"Ok, chill."

"You were smart to stick it out."

"Hey, I haven't promised her anything."

"Oh damn that's cold, ha! See you soon, klutz."

He hung up and struggled to light another cigarette. Bouncing up and down a little to try to stay warm.

After the first series of almost accidents, when Raquel was being extra attentive and caring, he'd been a little suspicious. Not that she could be responsible. That would require planning, and a work ethic that Raquel just didn't have. She was a part-time bookseller whose idea of fun was having a movie marathon every night. He knew she didn't want to move, that she didn't want to leave Mitzi— the damn cat followed her everywhere. The pair of them were comfortable in his apartment, and they liked being comfortable.

Then there was the accident with the oven. This was before the fall down the stairs. Raquel was busy feeding Mitzi, and she asked him to take her babka out of the oven, and just as he reached for the handle, the glass exploded. Her exquisite babka, her great-grandmother's recipe, was ruined. Yet all Raquel worried about was his poor face. The glass had just missed his eye.

After that he let himself be cared for, he allowed her to dote on him, to play nurse when he fell and injured his wrist. And then, when he could not sit through another night of film noir, he suggested he might dictate a chapter of his next novel. Now that he was immobilized, maybe this was the perfect time. It was thrilling. She sat in front of him, laptop open, waiting for the words to come pouring out of him.

Then, last night, she announced she'd found an apartment. A studio in Spandau. She could be gone by New Year's Day.

He covertly cancelled on his rugby teammates, telling Raquel the weather had rained out their practice. They watched Veronica Lake bewitch Fredric March, Raquel on one side of the couch, him on the other, until they weren't. Cuddled up together, his injured wrist around her, his bruised ankle elevated on an ottoman.

He tried everything. Offering to massage her feet with his good hand, caressing her arm, nuzzling the soft exposed skin just below her clavicle. *Please baby,* he begged. She pulled away. Reminded him of how upset he was the last time. That he had made her swear it wouldn't happen again. They were broken up.

You can't leave, he said. *Who would take care of me?*

He pointed to his injured wrist, which she kissed. He pointed to his cut-up cheek, his bruised ribs, kisses, kisses. She hadn't wanted to cuddle afterwards. Just slipped from his bed and went to sleep in the guest room.

There was music coming from his apartment. Bubblegum pop. Raquel must be doing another last-minute cleaning. She really had terrible taste in music. He'll have to change it before any of his friends show up.

Just then a VW Golf pulled onto the street and then stopped. Dealers in Berlin were notoriously punctual unless you were blond and tall and looked like a narc, then they sent foot soldiers, or had someone circle the block just to be sure you were alone. The car just sat there idling. He was being checked out.

A kid jumped out and ran toward Joel.

Finally, he had the coke. He'd counted out the cash, thanked the kid, and was just turning away, when he heard— no, first he felt it whish by his ear, and then he heard the crash. It was one of Raquel's giant barrel cacti. After watering the houseplants, she usually put them out on the balcony to dry out. One had fallen, just missing his head. He stared at the mess of soil and cactus spikes and shards of terracotta. He looked up, heart thumping, blinking into that gray lightbox. There was Mitzi. Perched on their top floor balcony. Her head tilted to the side, eyes flashing at him in the growing dark.

IT'S NOT LIKE SHE wanted him dead. Then she'd definitely have to move out. What she wanted was a peaceful winter in her apartment with her boyfriend, and with every failed attempt at achieving this, she'd grown more desperate. The apartment in Spandau didn't exist. She was fairly sure Joel knew this, or at least suspected. He'd had sex with her anyways, without so much as a let's-give-it-another-go afterwards.

A sprained wrist wasn't going to cut it. He didn't *need* her. Not really. Once the party was over and the holidays ended—once January rolled around, what then?

Someone changed the music from R&B to EDM and she snapped to attention. Joel was watching her from across the room. When she smiled at him, he looked away. Not a good sign. Did he suspect her? She'd been careful, she tried to be careful. And she was such an attentive hostess. She'd cleaned the entire apartment. Every surface had a thin, very flammable lacquer of bleach, alcohol, and polish. A little incense to mask the heavy odor. No one could say she wasn't accommodating. All the radiators were cranked. Windows shut out the frigid wind, the sleet and rain. Plates of pigs-in-a-blanket, trays of pull apart garlic bread, of gougères with salmon and caviar, turkey meatballs, something called a sausage wreath—and then there were the dips: French onion, smoked brie, artichoke, eggplant, a fondue. And finally robust crudités. She'd painted her nails and done her hair and makeup with special care. The dress was new and short. There was no reason for the party to not be a total blowout.

Right now, Raquel was nodding and smiling at something one of Joel's buddies from rugby had said. This one's name was Dale. He also did something in publishing. Everyone at their holiday party was in publishing, or what they called, in earnest, "the arts." Out of all of Joel's rugby friends, Raquel liked him the most. He looked like Billy Nolan from *Carrie*—the feathered hair, the soft flannels. Plus, he had an obvious ass fetish, so it was relatively simple to stay in his good graces.

"It smells like a nail salon in here," he was saying.

She placed her gold talons on his arm. "But worth it, right?" Her nails glittered in the dim light. *Mood lighting,* she'd told Joel when he complained about not being able to see his drink.

Before he could respond she gestured to the Christmas tree where a strand of lights had gone out. "They're so finicky," she said. "They were my mother's. A kind of family heirloom."

"I thought you were Jewish," Dale said, running a hand through all that hair.

She forced a dazzling smile. "On my dad's side."

He thrust his chin toward the menorah Joel had bought on the eve of their very first holiday party together. "That's good 'cause who else knows how to light that thing."

"I'm pretty sure you just light it."

She made a show of bending over to adjust the lights. They were really much too large for a Christmas tree. They were meant for a house, something with a two-car garage. Raquel had a six-figure loan from an unfinished bachelor's degree, and her balance had nearly doubled over the last six years; a house probably wasn't in her future. The lights were one of the few things she'd taken with her after her mother's new boyfriend moved in, after there'd been too many hints that they wanted her bedroom as an at-home gym. She'd shown up in Europe with some clothes, a laptop, and those lights. That and Sallie Mae or Navient— she never could keep track of who owned her debt. You can't shake government debt collectors. They called more often than anyone back home.

She twisted each of the bulbs until the strand flickered on. Was Dale watching? Of course he was. The dress was tight in the right places and very shiny.

"My mother converted to marry my dad."

This is what she had once told Joel when he'd asked about her last name. *Cohen is Jewish, isn't it?* They were drinking beers by the river, which in the summer was one of the few places you could cool off. Their skin sticky, hair damp from a recent dip in the water. Raquel was smart enough to intuit that his question had given her some kind of cultural currency that excluded him. She pounced on the leverage. *Yes,* she told him, eyes suddenly wide, *was that a problem?*

No, no, he spoke quickly, holding his beer up. *Of course not.*

The truth was Raquel's mom had gone to Catholic school, her father had gone to yeshiva, and two people who couldn't agree on wallpaper—or on where to get the divorce, on who would get the living room rugs—were never going to agree on which religion to raise their only child. No one converted so much as they just stopped. Raquel had gone to public school; and like all Southern Californian teenagers, she appreciated the end of year vibe shift at Westfield's and Universal Studios. It meant more shopping and peppermint mochas. She watched the movies and read the stories and wished upon a star—was that Christmas? No matter. She got the gist of it. Hanukkah was different. If no one taught you the Ma'oz Tzur, you had to watch it on YouTube the week before your first joint holiday party with your boyfriend, practicing while he was out scouring the city for matzo because ostensibly you had a babka recipe *and* a matzo ball soup recipe passed down from a great-grandmother you never met. (If, like Raquel, your *Bubbe* died long before you were ever born, and your lapsed Jew dad couldn't poach an egg, the *New York Times* recipe is a great substitute).

As it turned out, Raquel needn't have tried so hard. In Berlin, being Jew adjacent, which is what she considered herself, was as good as going to synagogue. As long as she sang pretty, and her hand was steady with the candle when lighting the menorah, Joel's friends were none the wiser. She could have been singing in Greek for all they knew, or, she suspected, cared. But when Raquel sang the Ma'oz Tzur the rugby players, the editors, the novel and short story writers, the memoirists, the academics—they all got very small and very quiet, and she felt she could briefly touch something ancient and mysterious. It was the only time she didn't feel alone—besides when she was with Mitzi.

Where *was* Mitzi? She looked around the room. Too many bodies. Too many voices. Dale was still regaling her with all his "Jew stories," which is what happened whenever the subject of being Jewish came up. *I've been to a bar mitzvah, or was it bat? What's the boy one?*

It was the moment that happens in every party. The pigs-in-a-blanket had that cold soggy look to them, the baked brie had collapsed in on itself. Everywhere were plates of half-eaten small bites and dips and there were rings on the beautiful living room furniture from glasses of glühwein. She'd made the punch especially strong. Shrill laughter cackled and pierced. The noisy pitch of heathens.

Someone was moving to crack a window.

"It's too windy to have them open," Raquel called across to them. She made a face that said, sorry, blame Berlin weather, not me. "If you want to smoke, you'll have to go downstairs."

She turned back to Dale, who was clearly hurt that he didn't have her full attention. Boys in flannel are sensitive creatures.

"Sorry," she dragged her gold nails across his arm again. "You were telling me about the bar mitzvah you DJ'd at?"

He shifted his flannel collar, watching her nails work.

"I was just saying it was a totally different experience than spinning in Berlin. It's much more accepting here."

Raquel tried not to scoff. It was true that before coming to this city, she had a California understanding of its history. Meaning she laughed at Brad Pitt's accent in *Inglourious Basterds* and cried at *Schindler's List*. But it wasn't difficult to draw connections. The S-Bahn that took her to the bookstore or to the movies or to the pet store was the same railways used to deport Jews during World War II. And she did have a great-granny who escaped Berlin as a child . . . she didn't know much else. She didn't want to know. Was it possible that she had relatives buried en mass in the nearby forests? She used to have recurring dreams of a phone ringing. They started soon after she moved to Berlin. It was the rotary kind. Sage green. It just rang and rang.

"Let's get you a refill on that drink," Raquel said, a thin film of sweat beneath her armpits. She'd taken his drink, or maybe he'd handed it to her. He was following her into the kitchen, talking about pastrami at Canter's now.

"Has anyone seen Mitzi?" she asked her guests.

She shouldn't have taken the Xanax to steady her nerves. With the alcohol it was making her spacey and she needed to be alert. The crashing of the cactus—the shattering of all that ceramic and dirt and sharp things. So near to Joel's head. It was exhilarating and terrifying. She could have really hurt him. For a brief moment she felt profound love.

There was Joel, surrounded by his expat writers and editors and a woman Raquel had never seen before. She was leaning all her weight onto one leg, like a flamingo. Hip jutted out, head tilted as if appraising or mesmerized. Another academy head, Raquel figured, and thrust her shoulders back. Kept her head high.

"Joel," she said, Dale trailing behind her. "Have you seen Mitzi?"

The woman crossed and uncrossed her arms. Joel was telling them about his near accidents, waving his bandaged wrist for emphasis.

"I'm in the middle of a story," he told her.

The dreams had stopped after she moved in with him. Part

of the magic of the building. That and Joel had instructed her not to focus on depressing things. *Bad things happen everywhere,* he reasoned. Now she ignored the memorials, the plaques, the cluster of tumbling stones outside their building. To open herself up to them, she reasoned, would be akin to answering the phone. She didn't want to know who, or what, was calling.

"It nearly killed me," he was saying to coked-out laughter. So many tight jaws, black pupils, air forced from somewhere deep inside. Except for the flamingo woman who was looking right at Raquel. Eyes rimmed in thick liner. Hair tumbling in great red waves.

"Maybe someone's got it out for you," she said.

Raquel pretended not to hear her but clocked her outfit: silk pantsuit, statement jewelry. Someone important.

"Maybe it's a dybbuk!"

Joel laughed. "I was thinking of using the dybbuk as a literary device for the symbolism of old and new Berlin—a malicious and possessing spirit believed to be that of a disembodied soul, pretty good, right?"

Whenever he did coke his pupils ate up the blue in his eyes until he looked like a demon. This used to be a turn-on.

"Don't they, like, rape girls?"

"They enter through the vagina," Dale thoughtfully contributed.

"Maybe it's coming for Raquel."

There was that laughter again dislodging those jaws.

"I could use another bump."

"Me too."

Raquel tugged on Joel's shirt sleeve. "Mitzi," she said. "Have you seen her?"

He shrugged her off, not a great sign.

"I put her in the winter garden before the party started—where she can't try to kill me."

"Joel, that's so mean. She could freeze."

"She's a *cat*."

He turned away from her. Back to his rapt audience waiting for more drugs.

Raquel smiled at a nearby group from some literary journal. She couldn't meet the eyes of the woman, who was still watching. She was breathing too fast. Her hand closed around the shamash in her dress pocket. The candle used to light the menorah, also known as the "helper" or "servant." Facts from Wikipedia she recited in her head whenever she thought of the word "shamash."

"Excuse me," she told Dale. But he wasn't listening to her anymore. Deep in game talk with one of the other rugby bros.

The candle pressed against her thigh as she moved down the hall. She just needed to do one final thing. In their bedroom she carefully twisted off the radiator cap, examining where she'd drilled a hole the night before. Outside the wind kicked up. Another storm was approaching. The streets and sidewalks would be treacherous by morning. She turned the gas to high.

In the hall outside of the bedroom the woman was supine on the Moroccan fainting couch—*Raquel's* fainting couch.

"Did you find your cat?"

Raquel shut the bedroom door with a snap. "I'm still looking."

"Joel wanted me to tell you it's time to light the menorah. Did you hear them talking about dybbuks? Fucking *goys*."

Raquel blinked. "Yeah," she said. "I'm used to it."

A faintly raised brow. "You shouldn't let yourself get used to it. Don't confuse apathy for empathy."

"I didn't realize you were Jewish."

She was doing that head tilt thing, sizing Raquel up. The bangles on her wrist clattered against one another as she raised herself from the couch.

"There used to be a hundred and sixty thousand Jews in Berlin and now there's maybe ten thousand. And that's the most in any German city. That's the *high* number."

Raquel never knew what to say when faced with what she considered a real Jew. Someone with a *Bubbe* and a synagogue and an ancestral history that tied her to a cause, to a place.

"It's terribly sad," she managed. Her ears were ringing.

The woman's head tilted the other direction, *clack clack* went her earrings.

"Why don't we sing the Ma'oz Tsur together?"

She was already taking the shamash from Raquel's hand.

"You speak Hebrew?"

"Yes." She was smiling like she was dealing with a child. "I sing in it too, since I was four."

The wind in Berlin was different. It didn't howl so much as it prowled like an animal. You felt its presence just before it pounced. Raquel shivered, a gust battered the windows.

"You do it," Raquel said almost in a whisper. She cleared her throat, "The singing, I mean. Maybe Joel will do it with you, I keep trying to teach him the words. I have to find my cat."

Shabbat shalom, the woman called out as Raquel hurried down the hallway, toward the winter garden. Or maybe Raquel imagined it. There was no one in the hall when she turned to look. No one on the Moroccan fainting couch.

There was only the noise from the party, the wind sighing up and down the streets outside.

In the winter garden Raquel curled up with Mitzi. She'd snuck in just as the first guests showed up, setting up everything she might need. There was a bottle of wine, a thermos of matzo ball soup. Mitzi had her toys, her cat food. A hot water bottle too.

From here Raquel could see into the living room window. Joel had faced the menorah right in its center, facing out toward the city. His way of being transgressive. A menorah in Berlin? So next level. Proof he was worldly and learned and inclusive.

She was an idiot to think he'd let her stay.

There was that wind again. It seeped in from beneath the parquet floors, the frieze-adorned walls, the crown molding. It crawled between the old glass windowpanes, sticking against the curtains and snaking around Raquel's potted plants. It made her lips cold, her nose. The tips of her fingers.

The singing started. There was Joel holding the shamash—tiny helper, little servant. A small flame. Raquel strained to see the strange woman beside him but there were only his friends. His group of expat miracles. All primed for trajectory. Up, up, up, like smoke. Nothing to hold them back. Not history, not someone like Raquel.

All their mouths were open, singing words they couldn't understand or pronounce—and then the pinnacle moment. Candle to wick, flame to gas, to acetone and alcohol and a little turpentine for good measure. And there was the wind, that jealous phantom, right on time, wrapping Raquel in its primeval embrace.

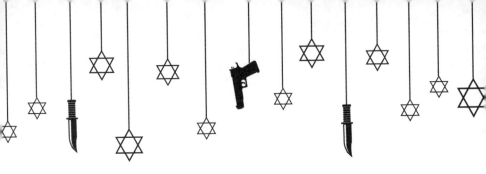

GABINO IGLESIAS

Gabino Iglesias is a writer, journalist, professor, and book critic living in Austin, Texas. He is the author of *Zero Saints*, *Coyote Songs*, *The Devil Takes You Home*, and *House of Bone and Rain*. His work has won the Bram Stoker Award, the Shirley Jackson Award, and the Wonderland Book Award, among others. His reviews appear regularly in places like NPR, *Locus Magazine*, and the *Boston Globe* and he is the horror fiction columnist for the *New York Times*. Iglesias teaches creative writing at the UC Riverside Palm Desert Low-Residency MFA program. You can find him online talking books on X at @gabino_iglesias.

LIGHTING THE REMORA

Gabino Iglesias

"Y'all give each other a bunch of presents, right? It's like twelve days of gifts instead of the jolly fat man with the coked-up reindeer, yeah?"

Antonio took a deep breath. Patience had never been a virtue he possessed, and Mikey had exhausted what little he had within the first twenty minutes of them sitting in his car outside the bowling alley.

"It's eight days of—"

"Right! Eight. That's cool. Never been a fan of the fat man. Not even when I was a kid. Fucker creeped me out a bit, to be honest. I used to try to stay awake. I didn't want some guy walking around my house, touching my toys and shit while I was sleeping, you know? Anyway, I still think Santa has y'all beat in terms of . . . like, quality and stuff. Y'all give each other gifts for eight days, but most of it is socks and shit, right? Like, not really gifts but more like stuff you need. Boring stuff."

"Yup."

Antonio took another deep breath and turned up the radio. The song was crap, some overproduced ditty with a dollar store beat and a young lady belting out something about a club with so much Auto-Tune she barely sounded human. Antonio thought about changing the station, but wanted to wait and see if Mikey had picked up on the message and shut up for a while.

"I mean . . . I guess that's cool," said Mikey, louder now. He had clearly not gotten the message. His talking was like the tides, a continuous, inexorable thing.

"Yeah," Antonio muttered. Maybe "yup" was too small. Maybe Mikey saw it as an acknowledgment, an invitation to continue. Antonio wished it was something else. Maybe a blade he could snatch out of the air and run across Mikey's neck. Maybe that would shut him up, but Antonio wasn't willing to bet on it.

"And then y'all light the remora, right?"

A suckerfish? Why was this motherfucker talking about fish? Then it clicked.

"No, man; it's called a menorah. A remora is a fish. You shouldn't go arou—"

"Cool, cool," interrupted Mikey. His nonchalance was the straw that broke the camel's back.

"Yeah, not cool," said Antonio. "I get it, man. You don't have any Jewish friends. That's fine. You probably don't have any Buddhist friends, either. But I'm not here to explain my faith to you. I've heard all the jokes and all that. We're not here for any of it; we're here to get a job done."

"Damn, man, someone pissed in your cereal this morning?"

Antonio let his chin rest on his chest for a moment and closed his eyes. All he could think about was murder. Bloody, righteous murder.

"I got it!" said Mikey.

Antonio opened his eyes and looked at Mikey. The guy—skinny and somehow resembling a human/rat hybrid despite his round metal eyeglasses and patchy beard—had his phone in his hand.

"Shalom," said Mikey.

"Shalom?"

"Yeah, shalom. Means peace, right? I come in peace."

Murder.

"If you—"

"There they are!" said Mikey.

Antonio had parked strategically: far enough from the door that they didn't seem like a threat and close enough to keep an eye on anyone going in or out of the bowling alley.

The guys Mikey was talking about were climbing out of a dark SUV. Three of them. They'd been expecting two. One little alteration to an already sketchy formula could spell tragedy faster than a bigot dropping a quote from the Bible. The driver was big. North of six feet and heavy in a way that spoke of weights more than beer. The guy riding shotgun was wiry and shorter. He was rocking a goatee and looked mean. He could be bad news. A moment later, the back door opened. A chubby short guy stepped out and pulled a phone out of his jeans. Antonio had never seen any of them and no one had told them who they were. He hated that. He'd have to talk to Raúl about it. Antonio hated having wrong information. Wrong information is what got you killed. Wrong information is what had killed his brother. Thankfully, the three men didn't look like anything he couldn't handle by himself, which was great because he didn't think Mikey could throw a decent punch to save his life.

"Let's wait for them to get inside and then give them a few minutes," said Mikey.

"I thought there were only going to be two of them."

"Same, but no big deal," said the bespectacled weasel. "You're big enough to take all three."

Antonio didn't like the sound of that. He was big, but he was also fairly smart, and three against one was never a good thing.

"You sure we can't bring a piece?" asked Antonio.

"Positive," said Mikey. "See that door? Asshole who owns the place has metal detectors there and at least two gorillas sitting around to make sure no one breaks the rules."

Antonio had heard a few rumors about the asshole Mikey was talking about. Some guy named Frankie. A Puerto Rican who liked to offer everyone in town a safe, neutral place to do business. He got a few bucks for the favor. A win-win.

"What's the story on the asshole? Why does he hate guns so much?"

"Asshole's name is Frankie. Dude had a niece or something that was killed in a school shooting somewhere down in Florida. Girl was apparently the apple of his eye. He figured out where the shooter got his gun and then he tracked down everyone involved and took them out with a Bowie knife or some shit. Fifty dudes, they say. Didn't use a gun on any of them. Then he moved up here and opened this place. My guess? He got some dough from those dudes he killed. Anyway, you know what they call him? The Voice. Hah."

"The Voice? Why?"

"Because no one has ever heard him talk. Get it?"

"Yeah, I get it," said Antonio. "Doesn't make a lot of sense though. If he has all these rules about guns and does business with so many people, he's talking to folks."

"And taking out fifty gangsters with a knife makes sense? Everything is a story out here, man," said Mikey.

"Guess so."

While Mikey talked, the three guys had gotten down and walked into Highland Lanes. One of them, a skinny blond guy who had been riding in the back, had a blue backpack on. That had to be the money. That was why Antonio and Mikey were here. Shitty or not, delivering some Hanukkah gifts to his twin girls and wife was something that'd only happen if Antonio delivered that backpack to Raúl.

"Can I ask you something?"

Mikey's voice put the brakes on Antonio's dark thoughts. He'd quit this life for many reasons—his daughters being the main one—and having to beg Raúl for a few gigs had hurt in ways he couldn't put into words.

"Go for it," said Antonio, angry that Mikey wouldn't shut the fuck up but glad that he'd pulled him from the place his brain was dragging him into.

"You know, since we're talking about tall tales and all that ... is it true that you took on the Colombians a couple years ago? Raúl said you killed so many they sent him a message swearing you were square, that if you stopped coming for them, they'd give you some money and never look your way again."

"Raúl told you all that?"

"Yeah." Mikey's voice was lower now even though Antonio hadn't touched the volume on the radio.

"We were doing a delivery. They fucked up. My little brother died in my arms in the back of someone's car. He was a good guy. I wanted to put enough bodies on their side of the cosmic scale to balance things out. Lots of folks would've done the same."

"Not a lot of folks would even dare take on the Colombians."

"Whatever, man," said Antonio. He was done with that conversation. He hoped Mikey would get the message this time.

"Think we should go in now?"

Miraculously, the man had apparently understood.

"In a minute," said Antonio. "Let's go over this again."

"Okay," said Mikey.

"Guns stay in the car. We walk in like two dudes looking to knock down some pins and guzzle some beers. The three guys who just walked in should be somewhere in there, right? Not in an office or anything else?"

"Nope. Frankie lets everyone do their business out in the open. Those are the rules: everything happens in the open and no one carries any metal."

"Perfect. These three are waiting for someone else, yeah?"

"Yup," said Mikey. "A single guy. No clue who it'll be. Someone's supposed to get in there, pick up the backpack, and walk out."

"Except we're gonna take that backpack and deliver it to Raúl."

"That's the plan."

"Shit sounds too easy," said Antonio.

Mikey reached out and lowered the volume on the radio.

"You're backing down now?"

Antonio didn't like his tone. He thought about popping him in the mouth, but had no clue how much Raúl liked this rat. Maybe the kid was family of some sort.

"I'm not," said Antonio. "I just don't trust easy things. This whole thing smells like shit. How does Raúl know about the money?"

"That's some shit you should've asked him when he offered you the gig after you came back begging for a—"

Antonio pounced. He grabbed Mikey's neck with his left hand and held down his left arm with his right. It was an uncomfortable position, but anger had shot enough adrenaline into his system to make it work.

"I asked for a few gigs; I didn't fucking beg. I stopped doing this shit because my brother died in my arms, but I need some money, so spare me the fucking attitude and pay attention or I'll knock your ass out and leave you here to deal with those dudes after I take their backpack, we clear?"

Mikey made a noise like a cat choking on a hairball. His glasses were shaking on the tip of his nose like a scared animal at the edge of a cliff. Antonio released his throat. Mikey said something Antonio couldn't catch.

"What was that?"

Mikey coughed and said it again, "Shalom!"

That one made Antonio smile.

"You good to go?"

Mikey nodded.

Antonio's parking spot was good for the stakeout portion of the gig, but he didn't want to have to run to his car with the backpack if those dudes got up and decided to come after them, so he moved his car closer to the door. Frankie might have some strict rules about guns inside the bowling alley, but they didn't apply to the outside world. Bullets were dangerous, and Antonio had been having horrible nightmares since his brother's death. He needed the money, but no part of him wanted any part of this, especially the part that could include angry men coming after him with guns.

Leaving the gun in the car seemed like the worst idea

ever, but Antonio didn't want to find out what those gorillas beyond the door would do to anyone trying to sneak in a gun.

Antonio and Mikey left the car and walked to the door of Highland Lanes.

There were two metal detectors right beyond the glass door and one big guy next to each. Mikey walked in first, walking through the machine on the left side. The machine made no sound. The big guy next to it nodded. Antonio walked through the one on the right. There was a beep. A hand the size of a baseball mitt slapped against his chest.

"You wearing a belt?"

Fuck. His belt. Antonio nodded. He lifted his shirt, removed his belt, and, seeing no table or anything else in front of him, handed it to the big man standing next to the metal detector. He walked back out and then walked through again. There was no beep. The big man gave him his belt back and said, "Have a good one, boss."

Past the entrance there was a short dark hallway leading to some stairs. Antonio and Mikey climbed the stairs in silence, listening to the sound of bowling balls rolling and striking pins over their heads.

Highland Lanes, like the few bowling alleys Antonio had been to before, was a sort of time capsule. The air smelled like cigarette smoke, shoe disinfectant, and moldy carpet. At the top of the stairs, the place opened into a long building with a kiosk to rent lanes and shoes in the center, a small opening on the left selling pizza, beer, sodas, and hot dogs, and three arcade games that had clearly been there for way too long—*Street Fighter II*, *NBA Jam*, and *Daytona USA*. To the right, there were ten bowling lanes.

The first three lanes were empty. Two men who looked

like they'd died a week ago and no one had told them were
sitting on the fourth one. A young couple occupied the
sixth one, probably on a date. The guys they'd come looking
for were sitting around in the last lane.

Mikey said something to the lady at the kiosk and she
nodded. "Go ahead then, sugar," she said with a voice that
carried at least four decades of Pall Malls and MD 20/20.

They walked without a word. It gave Antonio, finally,
time to think.

He'd have to take the big man out first. Aim for the nose.
If he didn't go down, open-hand slap to the ear, burst his ear-
drum. That usually kept them down, disoriented, and in pain.
Wiry guy next. Aim for the chin. Most guys had a sleeping switch there. Hit it right, you flip that switch and send
them straight to the land of Morpheus. Lilah Tov. Chubby
guy might be done with the whole thing by then. Or maybe
Mikey would do something. Antonio wasn't counting on it.

"Ready?" asked Mikey. Antonio nodded. The weasel was
annoying, but he had a talent for pulling Antonio out of his
own brain when it counted, and that was something. Antonio nodded and squeezed his fists, the ghosts of every fight
he'd ever been in singing a melody of cracks in his fingers
and knuckles.

The wiry guy saw them coming. He stood up. If he wanted
to be dispatched first, Antonio would be happy to oblige.

Wiry guy said something and the other two turned.

"What's up?" said the chubby guy.

"All good, man," said Mikey. He sounded sure of himself,
confident in a way that surprised Antonio.

"You gentlemen need anything?" The chubby guy again.

Antonio knew it was time to act. Walking over to them

in a relatively empty bowling alley had been their only option, but it was pretty shitty as far as options went. If the backpack was full of money, these guys were going to be on the lookout for trouble.

The chairs and lanes were lower than the floor. Antonio walked around a rack of bowling balls and stepped down. It took just a few seconds, but by the time he was down there, the three men were standing up and looking like someone had called their mothers some awful names.

The big man stepped toward Antonio, whose hands were still down. Change of plans. The uppercut was fast, but it landed well. A loud CLACK came from the big man's skull. He stumbled back. The wiry dude said something Antonio couldn't catch. Antonio moved toward the big man with purpose and threw a straight right and crunched the man's nose. The big guy threw his hands up and covered his face. Antonio reached back and slapped the side of the man's head with everything he had. That finally dropped him.

Antonio turned, ready to deck the wiry guy. He wasn't there.

The punch came out of nowhere. Antonio felt his jaw slide to the left. The light almost went out. He stumbled and turned. The wiry guy was smiling. Antonio threw another right. It hit nothing but air.

The kick to the stomach made Antonio bend over. The wiry guy was there again. The fucker was fast. Out of the corner of his eye, Antonio saw Mikey and the chubby guy with their arms sort of holding each other and grunting. More than a fight, it looked like two drunks dancing a grotesque waltz.

Pain exploded in Antonio's left temple. He didn't even see that hit coming. Another kick? It felt sharper. Maybe an elbow. His knees cracked against the hardwood floor.

He had to get up. He thought about his girls. He had to get that fucking backpack. He stood up.

"You ready, big boy?" asked the wiry guy. He didn't even have his hands up. He was standing a few feet in front of Antonio, bouncing from side to side and waiting for him to get up.

"Yup." Antonio grunted as he got up. His knees threated to give out under him, but they held him up.

The smiling asshole bounced forward. Antonio brought his hands up and tucked his chin into his chest. The guy threw a jab that slapped against Antonio's forearms. It was nothing. It was a kiss from a butterfly. He'd take this guy out with one punch. He ducked to the right and then switched to the left while letting his fist fly. It cut the air like a blind bird and landed nowhere.

The wiry guy was still standing there, the grin still plastered on his face. He threw another jab. Another butterfly—

No. A fist dug deep into Antonio's stomach. Air exploded out of him. He felt his guts move around to accommodate the fist. The ghost of nausea caressed his throat. He kept his hands up and looked forward just in time to see the wiry guy coming down from the sky like some fucking avenging angel, like a mashhit. His elbow slid between Antonio's forearms and landed on top of his right eye. Antonio's brain shook. He went down to his knees again. The pain was unlike anything he'd experienced before. It eclipsed the pain in his knees. He shook his head and the world quivered around him.

He couldn't stay down. He couldn't run away. He couldn't go home empty-handed.

Antonio felt warmth sliding down his face a second before he saw the blood drops hitting the hardwood.

Somewhere to his left, Mikey and the chubby guy were still going at it, grunting like angry pigs with emphysema.

Antonio stood up, but every muscle in his body was screaming for him to stay down.

The wiry guy was still there. He was still smiling, a predator looking at a wounded prey.

Antonio jumped forward. The wiry guy was good, but he was much smaller. Fuck a fair fight. He would smother him with his size.

The guy moved to the side. Fast. He sent out a punch while moving. It landed under Antonio's right eye. Antonio turned in time to catch the next one on the nose. It crunched and the world became blurry. A kick to the stomach bent him over again. An elbow to the side of the head made him see stars. He thought about swinging blindly, a prayer inside a fist, but realized his face was pressed against the floor. He was down.

Antonio tried to sit up. He looked around. The wiry guy was pulling Mikey off the chubby dude. Mikey flailed like a madman. The wiry guy's feet hit the step. He went down with Mikey on top of him. It took the man maybe four seconds to move his hands up, wrap them around Mikey's neck, and squeeze. Mikey's face went red, looked desperate. Then he went to sleep.

"We're done!" The words were out of Antonio's mouth before he knew he'd been thinking about them. They were done. Mikey was out. The world was spinning. His knees were shot. His blood had made a puddle on the floor. His gun was laughing at him from the car. He thought about his brother and didn't want to end up like him.

"Get the fuck outta here and don't let me see you again."

Antonio managed to stand up. He went to Mikey and shook him. Mikey mumbled something. Antonio used the last of his strength to help him get up. They walked out to the car without a word.

The men at the door said nothing. They were used to seeing blood. One of them looked like he was smiling, but Antonio didn't care. Let him have his smile.

Antonio opened the door and dropped Mikey in the passenger's seat. Then he climbed into the car, shut the door, and stuck his key into the ignition. Then he sat there. He thought about grabbing the gun and going back in. He needed that backpack. His girls needed him to get that backpack. Raúl was waiting for that fucking backpack.

No.

He was done. He turned the key and the car purred to life.

"The best-laid plans of mice and men often go awry," said Mikey.

"What?"

"It's a thing my pops used to say when he—"

"Shut the fuck up. Just . . . shut the fuck up, man."

"That cut looks nasty," said Mikey, not shutting up. "I think you need stitches."

"You got a guy?"

"Yeah, we got a guy. He lives near that CrossFit gym on Forty-Fifth. I'll tell you how to get there."

"This is it. You can stay there when we're done. I'm done with all this shit," said Antonio.

"Cool, man. You can get your stitches and clean up. Then you can go home and light your remora."

"Yeah, Mikey. I'm gonna do that. I'm gonna go home, hug my girls, kiss my wife, and light my remora."

© VANESSA RAMIREZT

STEFANIE LEDER

Stefanie Leder is a TV executive producer and writer whose credits include the MTV dramedy *Faking It*, Netflix's *Boo, Bitch*, and ABC Family comedy *Melissa & Joey*. Stefanie has sold multiple pilots to major networks and streamers. Her first novel, *Love, Coffee, and Revolution*, will be published by Blackstone Publishing.

NOT A DINNER PARTY PERSON

Stefanie Leder

"We can't take the drug to Stage Three, Rachel. It increases suicide risk in young adults," says Kai, his voice distorted by my car speaker.

Fuck. I slam on the brakes, just in time to avoid sending a yoga mom flying through the intersection with her oat milk matcha latte. I *need* that drug to be a blockbuster, or Hyena Laugh Lucas will get my promotion. Is it really such a big deal if a drug for depression *slightly* increases suicide risk? If someone's taking the drug, odds are they're already suicidal. I mean, if we save several thousand people, and lose a few, I call that *a win.*

"Did any trial participants actually kill themselves?" I ask.

Kai pauses. I can hear him clicking at his computer. "Two."

"Those poor kids," I say, because that's what a neurotypical person would say. *Those poor kids are fucking up my trial.* "How do we know they killed themselves *because* of the drug?"

"Ostensibly other causes were ruled out."

"*Ostensibly,* Kai. So we really don't know. And that is a very small number of participants who had adverse effects."

"But the adverse effect was death."

I pause. I know I can't say, "They were going to die anyway. We just sped up their timeline," because I said that last year in a meeting about our statin. That got me dragged into my boss Blaine's office. He told me he agreed with me, but during company-wide meetings we needed to use our *inside voices.* Anyhow, I know my reasoning won't fly with Kai. He's sensitive.

"Look," I say. "Maybe those two should never have been in the trial in the first place. Maybe they'd been slicing and dicing their wrists for years."

"Jesus, Rachel." Kai loves me—I make sure of that by bringing him baked goods and sitting on the corner of his desk in a short skirt and sheer nylons—but this is too much for even him.

"Sorry, I get uptight around the holidays." My mind races. Performance reviews are tomorrow, and my drug needs to be in better shape than Lucas's. I need to find a way to exclude those participants from the data. "Go over the case histories of those participants and see what's different about them." I exit the turnpike, passing a painfully slow car on the right. "Carefully. We don't want to make any errors. *For the kids.* I'll call you later."

"Aren't you celebrating Hanukkah with your family tonight?"

"Celebrating is not the right word."

I hang up and turn onto the 870. My intestines twist into a European death knot as I slow down, looking for the entrance. This is the last place I want to be. Thing is, I'm not a dinner party person. Never have been. Sure, I can fake it. I can fake anything—besides an orgasm, that's just self-defeating. But what is *the goal* of a dinner party? To bond? That's way too vague.

It's even worse that it's a family dinner party, because

I'm also not a family person. Sure, I like my sister and my niece, but that is it, and that is only for a limited amount of time. My mother? In an ideal world, the next time I see her would be at her funeral. That's one party I can't wait for.

I turn right, hard, into my mother's over-fifty-five mobile home community. I shiver. I haven't been back here in a year and it's making my fingertips tingle. Like some magic witch sense that something bad will happen tonight, only you don't need magic to know that. Nothing good comes of seeing my mother. I only visit once a year—Hanukkah—and only for my sister.

Someone else is having a party so there aren't many parking spots. There's a handicapped space in front of my mother's mobile home, but that's no problem. Suddenly some basic bitch in a Camry heads toward the spot so I floor my Tesla and veer into it. The other lady hits the brakes. Slams back in her seat. She looks pretty rattled. What, is it her first day driving in Florida? She doesn't even look handicapped. But then again, neither do I. I whip out my black-market handicapped placard and put it on the rearview mirror, then flash her a smile.

I grab my baguette and exit, high heels clicking on the pavement. Ms. Matching Cardigan Set glares at me. Yeah, I know what she is thinking. What you're thinking. See, most people are limited by a misguided sense of "right" and "wrong." I, fortunately, do not suffer from that affliction. I am a sociopath, and everything I do is for my benefit.

You want me to be ashamed? Sorry—I am *proud*. Society needs sociopaths. If someone is slicing into your brain, you don't want their hands shaking because they're worried about hurting you. We sociopaths make life and death decisions without being hampered by emotion. Which is why I'm perfectly suited for my job in pharmaceuticals. All drugs have trade-offs. What makes a hundred people better will make one person very sick. Empaths, or "normals," have trouble doing this math. I do not.

That's another reason I don't care for ethics. What if you have right and wrong confused, like a six-year-old with right and left? What if it's just as arbitrary? Have you ever tried explaining "right" and "left?" How do you explain it without resorting to "*it just is*"?

As I walk toward my mother's mobile home, I decide on my goal for tonight. It's simple: I just have to get through the party without killing anyone. This is metaphorical, obviously. The only things I've ever killed were about five thousand mosquitos and a couple dozen spiders. Violence is for uncreative people, rough people. Me? I'm creative. Elegant. Refined. Plus, beautiful people like me don't do well in jail.

I just need to get in and out of there, with minimal interactions with my mother. And hopefully none with that asshole with Dumbo ears, Jake. Why my sister hooked up with him is almost incomprehensible. Is it because he is a Marine, and that made her feel safe? Until she realized he just had a greater, more official capacity for violence? And a crew of men who will swear on their lives he didn't do it—whatever he did.

I approach the door to my mother's place—it needs a paint job, just like every other unit around here, including my mother herself. Door's unlocked. I take a deep breath and cross the threshold into narcissism, dysfunction, and Burnett's vodka.

The TV is blaring; she keeps it on all day to drown out the noise from the private airport down the road. It's always on Court TV. She likes watching people whose lives are more miserable than hers.

I put my purse down and find her where she always is: in her puke-colored La-Z-Boy drinking a martini, extra dry, no olives. That's right—it's not a martini. It's just vodka. But it makes her feel classy to call it a martini. There is nothing in this world that could make her classy. She eyes me, looking for a fault. She gets her wish instantly.

"That's not challah," she says, looking at the baguette, pissed.

"They were out."

"It's the last night of Hanukkah, Rachel," she says.

"That's why they were out."

She lights a cigarette. "You never do what you're told. Never did."

That's not entirely true. I stole cigarettes for her from Crown Spirits, like she told me. I told the teacher I missed school because I was sick, not because she was too drunk to drive me, like she told me. I hid her credit card bills under my bed so her boyfriends wouldn't find them. Like she told me.

"This is bread," I say. "Challah is bread." I dig into my purse. "Here's a hundo, buy yourself some challah tomorrow."

"You can't buy my affection."

"Wouldn't even occur to me."

She doesn't hear the sarcasm; that takes a level of intelligence she doesn't aspire to. I head to the kitchen where I find my sister, Leah, frying latkes. That's a terrible job. You get covered in grease, you cut your fingers on the grater, but everyone just takes them for granted like you bought them at Publix. Why not just buy them at Publix? Why are people so obsessed with proving they made *an effort*? I care about results.

I approach her and see a blue tinge under her right eye. She's tried to hide it with concealer, but she can't cover it all.

"He hit you again."

She looks up. "Just allergies." She tries to smile but her eyes won't cooperate.

"Allergies affect both eyes, Leah."

She looks toward the hallway, then lowers her voice. "Nina's in the guest room. Can we drop it?"

"If you agree to leave that bastard, I agree to drop it." But she won't agree. She's afraid. Afraid he won't let her. And she's probably right to be afraid. The last time she tried to leave she ended up with a spiral fracture on her humerus. She said she hurt it putting boxes away in the garage, but what thirty-two-year-old gets a spiral fracture putting away boxes? Were the boxes full of angry bobcats?

"Please, Rachel, it's Hanukkah. Let's just get through tonight."

"Funny you say that. It's my goal, actually." I take the spatula from her and start frying latkes. "But my other goals are for you to make it past forty and my niece to make it to eighteen without a maxillofacial injury."

Leah winces. She doesn't like facing the truth. Then again, almost nobody does.

"Why do you want to live this story again?" I ask.

"I'm not."

"Didn't you have enough of it on our first go around?" Because the first go around was bad. Maybe not as bad for

Leah, but that's because I protected her. I had four years and eight inches on her.

"I'm not Mom. Jake isn't one of her boyfriends." She looks down again, because she knows it's bullshit.

"He's hitting you now, he's going to be hitting Nina next. Haven't you heard of generational curses? This is your chance to be a better mother than we had."

Leah tenses. "I would *never* let him hit Nina."

"How would you stop him? You weigh a hundred and twenty pounds."

"That's enough latkes." She takes the spatula from me. Conversation over. "Can you go get Nina?"

I leave the kitchen. There's no reasoning with her. Her self-esteem is so shot she doesn't understand she deserves better. That's the main reason I hate our mother. What she made us think we were worth. Lucky for me, there's something innate in me that won't hate myself. Leah didn't get that gene.

Before finding Nina, I stop in the bathroom and check my cell. Several texts from Kai. That's not good. I'm going to call him. No, FaceTime. He's hot. He doesn't realize it, because he's married.

"Kai." He's wearing a tight white T-shirt, and his hair is falling in front of his eyes. His face is flushed. Maybe he was exercising. Maybe something else. "What's the emergency?"

"Quinn just told me Lucas is ready to go to Phase Three. Thought you'd want to know."

Fuck. I nearly drop my phone in the toilet. Hyena Laugh Lucas lucked into heading the development of our Ozempic rival. Everyone at work wanted to be on that drug. Because it's going to do gonzo numbers. Who wants to diet and work out when you can just get a shot?

"Did he have any problems in Phase Two?" I ask.

"Quinn didn't say."

"I mean, there must've been a few, right? Like at least an intestinal blockage? Those can kill you."

"I would think."

"Do you have access to his data?"

"No."

Shit. Then I need to hack it. Well, someone needs to hack it for me. I pick at my lips. To get that promotion, I either need to slow down Lucas's drug, or speed up mine. I'll try to do both.

"We need to get those two participants out of our data set, tonight," I say. "Before the performance reviews."

Kai looks at me, unconvinced. He wants to beat Lucas to trial, too, but not if it ends up killing teenagers. "I haven't found anything so far."

"Look, Kai, this drug can help a lot of people who are suffering. So maybe we don't market it to teens. Maybe we only market it to adults. But this drug can save lives. We can't let this infinitesimally small subset of people sink a drug that can help so many."

I lean forward a little and tilt my phone down to get more of my cleavage in frame. His pupils darken. It's ridiculous how easy it is to manipulate males. If you're a sexually mature female. If you're a girl, you're helpless. *Vulnerable.*

"We need to find out why the drug affected those kids," I say. "I'm coming over to your house to go through the data with you. Nine o'clock."

I hang up and run my hands under the cold tap. I need to calm down. My blood is pounding in my veins, I can almost see it pulsing. I can't believe I have to deal with this tonight, on top of my fucking mother. My self-regulation is sort of like allergies. Here's how my allergist explains it: you have a bucket. You eat just one peanut, maybe you're okay. You get licked by a disgusting dog, well, that's pushing up the level in your bucket. You're still okay, but you're getting closer to the top. Then you eat another peanut? Now you're in fucking anaphylaxis, because you've overfilled your bucket. That's how I am with stress. Seeing my mother is the first peanut. Finding out Lucas is going to Phase Three is the dog licking me. So now I need to make sure I don't eat any more peanuts. Or I might start saying shit *that I mean.* And that means taking off my mask. This is the number one thing you learn as a successful sociopath: never take off your mask. When the neurotypicals find out what you are, you're in danger.

I straighten my shirt and head to the guest room where Nina's doing whatever preteens do when they're trapped at their grandmother's on the last night of Hanukkah. For Nina, typically, that's hacking. She even hacked NASA once. Girl is twelve and she beat the government! It took *a lot* of favors to keep that kid out of jail. There's a misconception that sociopaths can't love. We do love. Just much, much more shallowly than you. When I see my niece, I feel a surge of pleasure, like when I see my Tesla after it's been waxed. She is mine, and she is beautiful. She even looks like me.

I poke my head into the room. She's on her laptop. A streak of purple hair falls across her face. She does that to signify her nonconformity. I'm the opposite. I keep my hair neat and professional—it's part of my mask.

"Hey AnonGirl347, ready to recount the great miracle of oil?"

"Auntie!" A genuine grin spreads across her face. And for some reason, this makes me smile, too.

"Here." I drop a bag of prescription painkillers on her desk, fresh from our test lab. They're currently in their Phase Three trial. Theoretically, to get approved, a drug needs to be significantly better than what's already on the market. In practice, all these have to do is kill fewer people than Fentanyl. Low bar. "Remember—"

"—don't get high on your own supply."

"Don't get high, period. You aren't meant for this life. You're smart. You can have better." I feel protective of her. The way I am protective of my belongings. Like how I waterproof all my leather bags and never wear suede in the rain.

I look at her screen. She's reading about the ancient Jewish figure Lilith, Adam's first wife. Some say she's a goddess, some say she's a demon. Not sure I see the distinction. "You know why they call her a demon?" I ask.

"She refused to be subservient to Adam."

"Correct."

More specifically? Lilith refused to lie under Adam and wanted to ride him instead. She's a good role model. "So now they say she eats babies. The world couldn't stand a woman who was in her power. It hasn't changed much. Don't be a Mary, Nina. Be a Lilith."

Nina nods.

"Hey," I say. "I need some advice. If you were trying to hack an industrial website, would you use Nessus or Cain and Abel?"

"Neither, they're so basic."

"What would you use?"

She looks at me directly. "What site do you need me to hack?"

I knew I could count on her. I hover over her laptop and type in the department. "Just get me into the R&D database, I can take it from there."

She starts hacking. I text my contact at the FDA, Dax, to see if he's free for a drink in an hour. He's about to get a little tip about how extremely dangerous Lucas's semaglutide is. I peer over Nina's shoulder.

"What are you looking for?" she asks.

"Adverse events."

She's in. She's so good. I take the laptop from her and start scrolling. "*Dammit.*"

"What is it?" asks Nina.

"No adverse events."

"Isn't that good?"

"Good is relative."

"Come on, Rachel!" says my mother from the living room. "It's almost dark." Like I can't look out the window and see.

What am I going to do? I already texted Dax that there was an adverse event. There's *always* an adverse event. Did Lucas find a way to scrub it? *Did he scrub his data before I scrubbed mine?* Fuck. Can I fake an adverse event report in an hour?

Nina and I head to the dining room. The table is set with Target "china," and a box of mismatched candles is out. And the menorah. Meant to look antique but probably from the clearance aisle at HomeGoods. Silver, with Yemenite filigree, eight candle holders plus the shamash. The bottom of each holder narrows to a fine point; they look like little spears. Which is fitting since Hanukkah celebrates a military victory.

"Are you going to do the prayers?" Leah asks me.

"Aren't we waiting for Jake?" asks my mother. But she's not asking, really, she's demanding. She loves Jake. Because he's male. And tall. And not Jewish.

"I don't know if he's coming," says Leah, with a catch in her voice. "He texted and said he was caught up at work." There's no way he got caught up at work. He's a Marine demoted to desk duty.

"Let's do it." I look at my mother. "On account of it being dark. Don't want to anger Yahweh by being late." I grab a lighter. I need to get out of here to fake that adverse event.

"You don't even believe in God," says my mother.

"But I believe in doing things correctly." I turn to Nina. "You want to lead the prayers?" She shakes her head. I stumble through the prayers I learned at the JCC after-school while my mother was drinking "martinis" in a dive bar at the Seminole Bingo Casino with her scumbag boyfriend Cyrus. Why don't we just say the damn prayers in English? What is the point of mumbling syllables in a language you don't even understand? I start out strong, then I really butcher the middle, and then I just give up. "Amen."

"I thought you believed in doing things correctly," says Nina. I crack up. This kid, she's all right. Maybe I will get through this dinner without killing anyone.

Suddenly we hear the heavy thud of boots at the front door. Even his footfall sounds dickish. The door opens and bangs against the thin wall. Jake is a hulking presence, six foot three at least, all muscles, bravado, and frustrated impotence. He enters the room and stares at the lit candles. "You didn't wait for me?"

Leah's face flushes. That's the cortisol. "We weren't sure if you were coming."

"You're not even Jewish," I say.

Leah's back stiffens, on high alert. Jake stares at me, his eyes full of unchecked violence. See, he's not a creative person. He doesn't have vision. He has fists.

"There you go again," he says to me. "Always throwing it in my face. Not good enough for your family, not one of the Chosen People."

"Okay, that's BS," I say. "Chosen People just means Chosen to Suffer." *That's not the reason you're not good enough for my sister.* Did I say that out loud? Sometimes I'm not sure what I say out loud. It takes a lot of energy to constantly filter my thoughts from what I know I'm supposed to say. Neurotypicals have all these rules about what you can say, what you have to imply. That's why I like autistics. They say what they think. My best friend, Reza, he's autistic.

Jake sits at the table next to Leah and looks at her plate. There are three latkes, some brisket, and green beans. "Lay off the latkes, babe. Your thighs are big enough."

I gasp. He's an asshole, but that's such a 1980s way to be an asshole. Leah puts two latkes back on the serving tray.

"Eat the latkes, for Christ's sake," I say.

"No, Jake is right, they're not healthy," says my mother. "So much oil."

"That's the point," says Nina. "This holiday is the miracle of the oil."

"You think that glass of ethanol is good for you?" I ask, pointing at my mother's third, fourth, fifth (?) martini. Why did I bother? The sooner she gets liver cancer, the better for everyone.

My mother smiles. "I'm preserving my organs. Kills the bacteria."

Jake turns to me. "So Rachel, Chosen One, how many people did you kill today with your corrupt pharmaceuticals that you paid the FDA to get approved?"

I have to hand it to him, he's right about that one. We do pay to get drugs approved, both legally and illegally. We pay fees for them to review our drugs. Kind of like paying your professor to grade your paper. Slight conflict of interest. Then of course, there's regulatory capture. FDA worker drones make shit pay. We imply there's a cozy sinecure at the pharmaceutical waiting for them in the future if they just play ball. Finally we straight up bribe them. There's a website where you can look up how much money your doctor has received from each pharmaceutical. Check it out, it's illuminating.

"Ya know, none," I say, serving myself some brisket. "I was having trouble greasing the FDA today." The brisket is falling apart on my fork. Leah must've been cooking all day. Why did she martyr herself for this asshole? What did he bring to the table? Some vague sense of her being "chosen" by him? Being chosen isn't enough. It's who chooses you.

"Must be tough working for the devil," he says.

"Indeed, that's why they pay me so well. How many people did you kill today, Jake? Oh, none, that's right, you're on desk duty. Too bad you crashed that F-35. Do you have to pay them back? How much does it cost? A hundred million? That should take you, what, nine hundred years to work off?"

His fist curls. He wants to hit me so bad. But I can't be the only one mocking him. He wrecked a *hundred-million-dollar plane.* Leah and Nina watch him, nervous.

Jake reaches for the wine and dumps some down his huge gullet. "It was the computer," he says.

"Sure," I say.

"My computer is always malfunctioning," says my mother.

"Does your computer cost over a hundred million?" I ask.

Nina lets a giggle escape. When Jake stares at her, her smile disappears.

He slams his fist on the table and turns to Leah. "You going to let them disrespect me like that?"

Leah looks like a mouse about to be swept up by a hawk. "Rachel's joking, Jake."

"She's not joking."

"Relax, I am joking," I say. "People crash F-35s in perfect weather all the time."

His grip tightens on his dinner knife. He turns to Leah. "If you let her disrespect me, you are disrespecting me."

Leah can't take it anymore. She's soft. There's two choices when you grow up like we did. You hide, or you fight back. Her eyes tear up and she starts to get up from the table. Jake grabs her wrist so hard I see it turn blue right there. Nina tenses. Blood rushes to my head. I want to stab him with my knife.

But I won't. First of all, it won't do much, it's a butter knife, and he's built like a brick house. Second of all, that's how you end up in jail. Thirdly, I'm creative. If I get revenge, it's clever. I'll call my friend Al at Fort Lauderdale PD and ask him to follow Jake home from The Thirsty Merchant tomorrow. A DUI? A DUI will fuck you up way better than a butter knife.

But Nina is angry now, too. She's scared, but she's a fighter. "Get your hand off my mom."

Jake's face turns red. He can't believe he's being challenged by a preteen. A *girl*. "Talk back to me like that again and you'll need braces a second time."

That's it. The third peanut. Adrenaline courses through my body and I have a hard time remembering the calming breaths my ex-therapist taught me. She fired me after she realized I was a sociopath. Because you can't cure a sociopath. Because we don't want to be cured. It's not an illness. It's an advantage.

"Jake." I stand up. "You're done."

"Done with what?"

"Done with this family. You're right. We are the Chosen People, you are not. Get the fuck out of this house."

There's absolute silence. Mother sips her martini, riveted, not sure if she loves this or hates this. Leah is sweating. Nina trembles ever so slightly.

Jake is quiet. That's because he's thinking about killing me. I know he has a gun. It's strapped to the small of his back. I can tell by the way his shirt ripples at the waist. But he's not going to shoot me. Not here. Not over a brisket.

"Please don't do this," Leah whispers to me. "Not in front of Nina."

"Fine." I turn to Leah. "I love you." For some reason it's important to me that she knows. "You know that?"

She nods. She knows it's not the "right" way, but she knows it's the best I can do.

"You want to take this outside?" Jake asks me. Like we're in freaking middle school and going to have a fist fight.

"I do."

This has gone farther than my mother wants. Her eyes are wide open. "Don't be silly. Sit down and have some latkes."

Leah looks at me, silently pleading with me to stay inside. Nina looks terrified. Maybe I should be scared. Maybe I am scared. It's hard to tell with all the adrenaline what is what. Should I back down?

But Jake is already up and heading to the door. I grab the menorah and follow. The candles are about one-third of the way burnt down.

"What are you doing?" He looks at the menorah, confused.

"Bringing light." I point to the dark porch. "The porch bulb is burned out."

He nods, a brief moment of mundanity. Even if you're going to argue, you need light. How will you know if your insult landed if you can't see?

We exit the kitchen and go to the back porch. It is *very* dark out there. No moon. No light from the neighbors either. They aren't home, they always celebrate at their oldest daughter's. The menorah candles cast a faint light on the center of Jake's face, like a Renaissance painting. It makes him look even bigger and spookier than he is. I shut the back door behind us. I hear it click and realize we're locked out. Shit.

"What's your fucking problem with me?" he asks.

I mean, everything. His attitude, his face, his underdeveloped brain. But I really do have a problem now, bigger than my distaste. I've pushed him too far, and now he's going to punish Leah. And maybe Nina. And I can't let that happen.

"My problem is that this menorah isn't heavy enough."

"Heavy enough for what?"

I swing the menorah, smashing him in the forehead,

mostly. The tiny spears slice open one of his eyebrows. A candle sizzles on his scalp. Jake's stunned and a little wobbly. He bends over, feeling his head, seeing if it's on fire. I grab his gun from his belt, toss the menorah.

"Not heavy enough to bash in your brains." I point his gun at him. It's a Glock 19. I don't have my own gun—like I said, I don't like violence—but I practice at the range twice a month. There's just certain things an independent woman should know how to do. Change her own tire. Make a roast chicken. Fire a semiautomatic.

"Whoa. Rachel. What the fuck." He feels his head. There's a little bit of blood, but he's fine. Even a desk Marine is a Marine. "Put the gun down."

I do not put it down.

"What the hell do you want?" he asks, really pissed now. The blood is getting on his white shirt.

"I already told you. I want you to leave my sister."

"That's not your fucking decision. You ask Leah what she wants?"

Leah's too broken and gaslit to know what she wants. I'm her big sister and it's my job to protect her and I always have. Except that time I couldn't. I see Cyrus wrap his thick hands around her neck, her screaming, me trying to stop him, him knocking me to the floor as Dora the Explorer sings in the background. I can't stand it. I can't. I won't. My hand tightens on the gun.

I force myself back to the present. It's not safe to go to the past. Certainly not now.

"Leave." I point the gun more squarely at his chest.

His eyes widen. He wasn't really worried before. He's worried now. "Are you a fucking sociopath?"

"As a matter of fact, yes."

A bead of sweat appears on his forehead. "I'm a Marine, Rachel. Do you have any idea how much trouble you'd get in? There's a security camera here."

I laugh. "Yeah, that hasn't worked since my mother had all her teeth." I see him shaking a little. Good.

"Okay, Rachel, you're freaking me out. Put down the gun, and let's talk about this rationally."

I stare at him, considering my options. It turns out time really does slow down. If I don't shoot him, he'll promise to be better to Leah, then later he'll hit her, and maybe Nina, too. And then he'll get revenge on me. Will he have one of his buddies cut my brake lines? Will I go missing on a nighttime jog? He's not going to do *nothing*. I'm pointing a gun at him.

But shoot him? Do I *really* want to shoot him? There will be blood everywhere, I'll have to clean it up, someone might see something, Leah will be pissed, I won't have time to fake the adverse event and I'll be late to meet Dax, and then even later to meet Kai. And I will have failed my goal: *make it through this dinner without killing anyone.* I'd be letting myself down. I want to kill people all the time, but I never do. I'm a sociopath, but I'm not a common criminal. I'm wearing Chanel. I lower the gun.

"You finally got some fucking sense in you." He takes a tiny step forward. The fibers in his muscles twitch. He's going to make a move. He's going to try to get the gun. He is much bigger than me. *Will he shoot me?* Fuck.

I *hate* inelegance. But sometimes the only solution is inelegant. I raise the gun again and feel for the trigger. I am really not a dinner party person.

JIM RULAND

Jim Ruland is the *Los Angeles Times* bestselling author of *Corporate Rock Sucks: The Rise & Fall of SST Records*, which was named a best book of 2022 by *Pitchfork, Rolling Stone*, and *Vanity Fair*. He is also the co-author of *Do What You Want* with Bad Religion and *My Damage* with Keith Morris, the founding vocalist of Black Flag, Circle Jerks, and OFF! In addition to being a columnist for *Razorcake* fanzine and a frequent contributor to the *Los Angeles Times*, he is the author of the novels *Make It Stop* and *Forest of Fortune* and the short story collection *Big Lonesome*. Jim is the recipient of awards from *Reader's Digest* and the NEA, and a veteran of the US Navy.

THE DEMO

Jim Ruland

Friday, December 18, 1992, 3:07 P.M.

Matt Parvin was the second person to see the body.

The first was Judy Goran, who worked the front desk. Like everyone else at the label, Judy had a million other duties. She answered phones, turned away fans, charmed the label's new artists, and assuaged the old ones who showed up unannounced, demanding to be paid.

Judy had called Matt, the label's get-shit-done guy and unofficial head of security, and told him to meet her at the boss's office. Initially, Matt assumed Judy was calling him about last-minute preparations for the office Hanukkah party. Although Gray Grabowski wasn't a practicing Jew, he liked to do things differently. If all the other record labels were throwing Christmas parties with elaborate Secret Santa exchanges, then Gray wanted a Hanukkah party with food, music, and spin the dreidel—all of which fell on Judy's shoulders to organize.

But Judy wasn't calling about the party.

"It's an emergency," she'd said, but wouldn't go into specifics. When Matt arrived, he found Gray, founder and CEO of Sucks to Be U Records, dead at his desk.

"Are you sure he's . . ." Matt didn't finish, didn't need

to. He knew a stiff when he saw one. Judy did, too. Gray sat hunched over his desk like he was counting to ten in a game of hide-and-go-seek, his long hair covering his face. One hand was tucked under his arm, the other had transformed into a hideous white claw that dug into the desk.

Matt brushed Gray's hair to the side to ensure he wasn't breathing and recoiled at what he found.

"What?" Judy asked from the doorway, a tissue balled up in her fist.

"Come look at this," he said.

Gray's eyes were bugged out and bloodshot. A black ribbon of bile spooled from his mouth. The smell coming off the body was intense, but that wasn't new. Gray had a street punk's ambivalence toward personal hygiene despite being a millionaire many times over.

As if in a trance, Judy walked over and touched the discharge from Gray's mouth, shiny and black under the fluorescent lights. Matt almost stopped her but was transfixed by what she was doing. Judy and Gray had been lovers way back when. Matt had also slept with Judy, but only once and that had been a mistake. They were both married to other people now and their spouses expected them home in a few hours for Hanukkah. Judy and her husband were going to visit her parents in Palm Springs; Matt had shopping to do at Gelson's.

"It's tape," Judy said, peering into Gray's mouth.

Matt leaned in for a closer look and sure enough she was right.

"Why would he . . ." Judy asked.

"He didn't," Matt said. "Someone did this to him."

Four days before Gray Grabowski bit the dust...

Solomon Heinzelmann was in a shitty mood. Even though he'd been up all night and had gone home just to shower and change clothes, he dragged himself into Gray's office to give him the news: he'd found The Intensities.

Gray stared at him with a blank expression on his face. He seemed overmedicated and out of sorts. Solomon wondered if he had gotten an early start on the three o'clock weed break.

"What?" Gray finally asked.

"The band that made the demo?" Solomon said.

"Oh, yeah. Those guys."

Yeah, Solomon thought, those guys. No one knew how long the demo had been sitting in the mail room at the label's North Hollywood headquarters. The cassette didn't come in a box nor did it have a label. Just a black cassette tape without any markings. Most of the time, whoever was working in the mail room tossed unmarked tapes in the trash, but someone listened to this one and liked it enough to pass it up the ladder and somehow the demo made it all the way up to Gray. He didn't play it right away, but once he did he became obsessed with it, and now it was Solomon's problem.

Around the end of the summer, Gray summoned him to his soundproofed office and blasted what sounded to Solomon like a run-of-the-mill thrash band.

"You hear that?" Gray asked with a lopsided grin. "These guys could be bigger than Nirvana!"

Solomon refrained from reminding Gray that he could have signed Nirvana, but that ship had sailed, which was fine. Solomon hadn't liked Nirvana either—not that he had a vote. Gray had final say on all the creative decisions at STBU. Truth be told, Solomon didn't care for the druggy, neo-tribal fuckery that had taken over rock and roll. He hated sounding like his father—now there was a man who hated hippies. Solomon's father had made his mark in the music business turning kids singing doo-wop melodies into teen sensations. Hippies ruined that.

Solomon thought he'd get his big break in the biz with a tight little new wave outfit from Dublin that had a massive synth sound and hooks for days, but it didn't happen. Those Irish pricks blamed Solomon when their album tanked and the label pulled their support. It wasn't Solomon's fault— these things happened. If hits were easy to predict everyone would have one, but Solomon couldn't shake the feeling that despite being a true believer in the transformative power of rock and roll, he lacked some essential quality that great A&R men like his father possessed, some nascent ability to sniff out the hits. When his father fell in love with a band, he pulled out all the stops for them. The bands Solomon loved were too clean-cut, too cold-sounding, too queer—at least for 1992 and probably 1993. Now he was doing time in the independent alternative rock ghetto where you could do whatever you wanted even if it wasn't popular.

Or good.

Or even music.

The last "hit" STBU had was Hondo: The Barbarian from the Future. A maniac pumped full of steroids who played power tools over drum machines and guitar loops. If that was the future of music, Solomon wanted no part of it.

At the end of that fateful meeting last summer, Gray

told Solomon to find the musicians who created the demo. That, Solomon realized as he took in Gray's dead-eyed gaze several months later, was when everything went to shit.

Everyone at the label had a theory about who made the demo. Judy believed it was kids who didn't know any better, teenagers doing what teenagers have done since the first mass-produced electric guitar rolled off the line at the Fender factory down in Orange County. Matt thought the demo was a prank orchestrated by Billy, the label's self-appointed mischief maker; whereas Billy believed it was a plot orchestrated by one of the many former employees that Gray had fired. On his darker days, Solomon wondered if the demo had been made by one of the label's own artists who were operating incognito as a way of luring Gray into the open when he stopped taking their calls. Was that too far-fetched? Too paranoid?

Maybe.

Solomon started calling them The Intensities after Gray rambled about finding the band and harnessing their intensity. It became a running joke at the label.

"Did you find The Intensities, Solomon?"

"Fuck you."

After months of visiting recording studios, rehearsal spaces, and record stores all over LA, Solomon found them. The Intensities were three teenagers from Tarzana. He found them through the shop where they rented massive stacks of Marshall amps for the generator shows they played in the desert. The manager at the shop gave Solomon a flyer for a show that evening with a hand-drawn map on the back and said, "Good luck."

Solomon got in his cream-colored Buick LeSabre, headed north on the 170, and cleared Sylmar around rush hour. He followed the 14 north out past Palmdale, Lancaster, and Mojave to a spot on the other side of the LA County line that wasn't in the Thomas Guide he'd worn out driving all over LA these last few months, but when he got to the end of the map, there they were. He'd found The Intensities.

When Solomon rolled into Gray's office the following morning to tell him that he'd found the band and they were every bit as amazing as they'd hoped, he didn't get the reaction he'd been expecting. Solomon noticed the towering stacks of folders covering Gray's desk. He couldn't recall ever seeing Gray do actual paperwork in his office. Gray did all his deals on the telephone.

"I'll bring them in so you can meet them," Solomon said.

"That won't be necessary," Gray said after a long pause. He seemed genuinely despondent as he stared forlornly at the mountains of papers on his desk.

"No?" Solomon asked.

"We won't be signing any new artists. Not for a while anyway."

"I see," Solomon said, though he didn't. If things had taken a turn for the worse, the least Gray could have done was call off the search. But he hadn't. Instead, Gray had sent Solomon on a wild good chase all over LA. He hadn't told him, Solomon fumed, because he was old and disposable, out of touch with the industry.

I could kill him, Solomon thought as Gray sat behind his desk like a zombie.

He didn't, but he thought about it, and he kept thinking

about it as he drove back to the bungalow he rented in Studio City. The negative thoughts refused to go away as he stared up at the popcorn on the ceiling that night.

Why not? he thought. What have I got to lose?

One day and six hours before Gray gave up the ghost . . .
Billy Gasparro had a problem. He'd been listening to the messages at STBU that Gray didn't bother checking anymore and learned that Hondo was on the rampage again. When Judy arrived in the morning she no longer listened to the messages if she heard Hondo's voice on the answering machine. She simply left a note for Billy to check them, which he did.

There were no new grievances. The complaints were always the same: "Hondo wants what's his." Sometimes it was money, sometimes it was the rights to his records, sometimes it was an apology, but the gist was always the same: you owe me.

There were two messages last week, four more this week, and a bunch last night that all said more or less the same thing: "Hondo is coming. Pay up—or else."

Billy thanked Judy and went back to his office to think about what to do. He didn't take Hondo's threats lightly. Hondo was the lead screamer for an eponymous industrial noise band. On each record he played a new instrument: disc grinder, pneumatic hammer, power saw. These instruments were mostly for show. Hondo possessed the physique of a power lifter and the showmanship of a cage wrestler and when he put his tools to work the fans went nuts. His techno-barbarian shtick played well on MTV—oiled torsos, two-dollar robots, showers of sparks. It was homoerotic as hell, and probably a little fascist, but that's what kept people glued to their TV screens.

Last year, a video for "Hondocore," the single for Hondo's third album, blew up on 120 Minutes, and Capitol Records snatched him away from STBU.

Hondo, however, was mentally unstable. He had a habit of talking about himself in the third person and it wasn't always clear if he knew the persona he'd crafted to go along with his caveman-from-the-future shtick wasn't real. He couldn't get along with anyone longer than it took to record an album or complete a leg of a tour. He was always firing and hiring new players and was sexually aggressive, especially with young men he met on the road. After a string of unsavory incidents during a video shoot in Daytona Beach, Capitol dumped him. Gray reached out to Hondo with a plan to release a solo record under his own name: Henry Isaiah Diamond. Against the advice of the label's lawyers, Gray went along with the plan despite the fact that Henry owed Capitol three more Hondo records. Gray had to know Capitol would come after him if he released a record with Henry Diamond, and they did. Big time.

The old Gray, the one Billy knew, would never put the label in jeopardy like that. It felt like all the money STBU generated went directly to lawyers. Gray seemed to take perverse pleasure in pissing off powerful people and it cost him a fortune in legal fees to fight them off.

Billy wasn't entirely unsympathetic to Hondo. In his shoes, Billy would feel the same way. To some degree, he *was* in Hondo's shoes, had walked a proverbial mile in them. Billy had been in a punk rock band with Gray called Blatant Stereotypes. They'd put out a bunch of records and toured the country a half dozen times. Each time they came back broker, older, and more cynical. The band broke up years ago but were now more popular than ever thanks to the resurgence of guitar rock. Apparently, Kurt Cobain was a big Blatant Stereotypes fan. This should be great news for Billy, Gray, and everyone at STBU, but the label that Billy helped build was on the verge of bankruptcy.

Labels went under all the time, but there was a growing sense at STBU that Gray was responsible for the label's decline. The man who was steadfastly against the notion of "hits" while they were bandmates, was now desperately hanging all his hopes on manufacturing one.

The sad thing was Gray could make all this trouble go away if he wanted to. That's what bothered Billy the most. All Gray had to do was get Blatant Stereotypes back together and start making real music again. They didn't have to put up with lunatics like Hondo, who claimed his songs came from the voices in his head.

Was Hondo actually dangerous?

Billy didn't know. He *looked* dangerous but that wasn't always the same thing. The last thing Billy needed was a homicidal singer stalking the label's hallways looking for retribution—on Hanukkah no less.

Or was it?

Would it really be so terrible if Hondo attacked Gray, an attack that Billy could interrupt just in the nick of time?

Such a scenario would generate a media firestorm: music magazines, newspapers, maybe even TV news. Wasn't that kind of attention just as good as a hit?

The media might celebrate Gray for his stewardship of so many bands that laid the foundation for the guitar rock revival. Or, they might portray him as someone who got rich off the sweat of others and refused to share the wealth with those who made the label an indie powerhouse. It could go either way. But what if the attack scared some sense into Gray? Was Gray Grabowski capable of an Ebeneezer Scrooge-like change of heart? Could Billy engineer such a transformation?

All Billy wanted was his bandmate back. He didn't know what the Ghost of Hanukkah Future foretold, but he feared there wouldn't be a future if he didn't do *something*.

Billy picked up the phone and dialed a number he'd never called but knew by heart.

Thirty-three minutes before Gray kicked the bucket . . .
At three o'clock all work stopped. Hondo knew that. That was nothing new. Gray liked to smoke a little weed at the end of the work day and anyone who wanted to join Gray for a toke or two was welcome at the three o'clock weed break—as long as you were willing to shoot hoops with the G-man in the parking lot.

The G-man called the shots. That's the way it was. Hondo knew that. Everyone knew that. From the bushes next to the loading dock, Hondo had a clear view of the back door from which Gray would emerge with spliffs to share. All Hondo had to do was wait.

The G-man was stingy with his money but generous with his weed. After his second album, on the heels of a brutal summer tour that split up Hondo's band and left him broke as a joke, he pleaded his case with the big boss.

"Hondo broke. Hondo's band quit. Hondo needs cash."

"Come with me." Gray took Hondo to a vault at the back of the warehouse behind the pallets of records that were always coming and going. Hondo thought the G-man was taking Hondo to the bank, the locked door behind which it definitely didn't suck to be Gray. He unlocked the door and took out a bundle of green. Then the smell hit Hondo: a skunky, funky odor he knew all too well. The G-man was paying him in weed.

Hondo should have taken that bundle, sold enough to buy a loaf of bread, a jar of peanut butter, and a bus ticket back to Florida, and sailed on down the freeway. Instead he stayed in LA, smoked all the weed himself, and allowed the voices in his head—what Hondo referred to as The Machine—to talk him into recording another record, which sold surprisingly well, but did Hondo see a nickel of it?

No, Hondo didn't.

Hondo didn't like hiding in the bushes. Hondo didn't like being angry all the time. Hondo liked being on stage with his tools, singing his songs, whipping the crowd into a frenzy. That's when Hondo was happiest: when the noise from the machines on stage drowned out The Machine in his head. Without the noise, Hondo could hear The Machine loud and clear and The Machine told Hondo he was being cheated.

The Machine told Hondo he was being taken advantage of.

The Machine told Hondo to take revenge.

Hondo didn't want to cause problems. Hondo liked most of the people at STBU. Hondo liked Judy. Hondo liked Billy. Hondo used to like Gray, but now he hated his guts and if he didn't give him what he came for, Hondo would make him pay.

Twenty-one minutes before Gray's clock stopped...

No one knows what's in Gray Grabowski's head, Judy thought as she prepared the conference room for the Hanukkah party, but there were a million things on her mind. The warehouse bathroom was broken again and she'd called the plumber to fix it. She'd gone to great lengths to make sure Gray's calendar stayed clear that afternoon. She'd dug the menorah out of the supply closet and had gone to Thrifty to buy new candles. Every year she lost track of the leftover candles and had to go out and buy new ones. For food she'd ordered challah, kugel, and rugelach. The party was scheduled for immediately after the three o'clock weed break and Gray, who didn't eat much, would appreciate the sweets. She'd also bought a case of Manischewitz grape wine, which was more than enough, but the interns loved it and she'd encourage them to take a bottle home with them. Judy hated the stuff. There's no hangover like a Manischewitz Hanukkah hangover.

Judy knew Gray was different the first time they hooked up after a New Year's Eve gig when the calendar flipped to 1980 and it looked like Blatant Stereotypes was destined for stardom. That was the attraction for Judy. Not the fame rushing toward them like a spaceship in a science fiction movie, but Gray's indifference to it. Judy's mistake was thinking there was a plan in place and Gray was its architect. She soon found out that Gray, as driven as he was, wasn't someone who preferred to stay quiet because he kept his thoughts to himself. That's not the way Gray was wired. Gray was quiet because he had nothing to say. Gray lived in a perpetual state of nowness. In his youth, people mistook that for relentless ambition. Someone who was constantly putting one foot in front of the other must have some kind of destination in mind, right?

Not always, Judy discovered, and certainly not Gray. She knew it and Matt knew it. This was their bond. Matt had even less business sense than Gray, but point him in the right direction and he got things done. Judy made sure she was the one who did the pointing. She was the one that made the label grow. After STBU notched its first gold record, Gray offered Matt a stake in the company. The fool turned him down, some nonsense about being happy to be a cog in the machine and not part of the enterprise that made the gears turn. Matt was even more of a punk rock purist than Billy, but Judy never forgave Gray for the slight.

As more people joined the cause, the label acquired its own momentum. Sure, some artists got screwed over along the way, but that was the music business. The feeling was that if everyone kept doing what they were doing, STBU would be unstoppable—and for a while it was.

What happened?

Gray lost his way. He started smoking more weed and became more unpredictable. He broke up Blatant Stereotypes, causing Billy to have a nervous breakdown, and made questionable business decisions, sometimes against the advice of those who'd known him from the beginning. Through all the ups and downs Judy was the one who held things together—like this party, which had become something of an STBU tradition, but it was Judy who planned it and made it a success. When Billy started freaking out, it was Judy who reined him in. Whenever Solomon threatened to knock some sense into Gray, it was Judy who talked him down. And when Matt fretted about making payroll or keeping the lights on, it was Judy who came up with a solution. It was always Judy to the rescue—and she was sick of it.

Judy knew STBU's value resided not in how much money it had in the bank, but in its catalog of incredible music. The location of the label's library of master recordings was a closely guarded secret. Only Gray and his two most trusted lieutenants—Billy and Matt—knew where the stash was hidden.

What no one knew was that Judy knew, too.

Judy was in charge of the three o'clock weed break. In the beginning, Gray would roll the joints himself, but as he got busier and busier those duties fell to Judy. Sometimes Gray would be on the phone all day, talking to producers, distributors, and record labels around the world. His head was in so many different time zones it was easy to lose track. Every day after lunch, Judy went to the back of the warehouse, opened the temperature-controlled vault where Gray kept his enormous and exotic supply of marijuana, and procured enough for a dozen joints.

About a year ago, Judy discovered a door inside the vault that led to a second, secret compartment where STBU's masters were stored. It wasn't even locked. All you needed was the weed key, which Judy had already made copies of since Gray was prone to misplace it. Gray could negotiate a complicated distribution deal involving multiple labels in numerous countries in his sleep, but basic things like keeping track of his keys proved to be a challenge.

Judy could see the writing on the wall. She knew how things were going. When the label was doing well, people saw Judy as an invaluable member of the team, the lynchpin of the operation. When things were going badly, she was little more than an overpaid assistant who asked for too much time off and didn't know the first thing about computers.

Judy wasn't going to sit around and wait for the shit to hit the fan. She cracked open a bottle of Manischewitz, poured a slug into a plastic champagne flute, and tossed it down the hatch.

Eighteen minutes before Gray punched his ticket for the D train . . .
On the first night of Hanukkah, Solomon popped the trunk of his LeSabre. He loved that he could do this from the driver's seat and didn't have to drag his ass out of the car. What would Buick think of next?

Of course, he still had to get up and rummage around his trunk so it wasn't like the button pushing saved him a lot of time and effort. Guys that tooled around in Buick LeSabres—guys like him—needed all the exercise they could get.

There wasn't as much junk in his trunk as Solomon thought. Just a couple of beach chairs, a cooler, and a base-ball bat, which he kept for security purposes and left there in case things got dicey at STBU. The rest of the stuff he chucked into the garage that was too small to park his big boat of a car. There was now plenty of room in the trunk for his surprise visit to Gray Grabowski.

We'll see who sucks and for whom, Solomon thought as he slammed the trunk shut.

Someday they'd invent a button for that, too.

Solomon got in his car and drove down Tujunga toward North Hollywood. He felt better than he had in years. The drive out to the desert to find The Intensities had changed him, like something inside him had awakened after a long slumber. When he went out to the desert there was a point where the map was no longer useful and he had to rely on his God-given instruments. That's what his father used to say whenever someone asked him for his secret.

"This," he'd say, tapping his temple, "is my instrument."

In the desert, Solomon had to use his eyes to follow the curve of the desert hills in the fading light and search for the gap in the mountains that would take him into the canyon where the secret show was being held. Once he found the unmarked road he rolled down his windows and navigated by ear, following the distorted noise echoing off the canyon walls until it sounded something like music.

Solomon pulled his LeSabre onto the shoulder and walked the rest of the way, sand spilling into his loafers. After wandering around in the dark for twenty minutes or so he climbed a hill and stumbled into a clearing where the headlights of a Trans Am—how did they get that fucking thing up there?—illuminated The Intensities: three long-haired teenage boys in dirty jeans wailing away on their instruments to a crowd of fifty people. It looked like a scene that had been beamed out of the 1970s.

Solomon was impressed. This was something. This was music played with passion and, yes, intensity. Someone handed him a beer and when he cracked it open something changed and he understood why Gray was so obsessed with this band. Whatever it was that made musicians special, these kids had it.

After the set, Solomon approached the band as they broke down their gear, not a roadie in sight.

"Boys," he said, "how would you like a record deal?"

They were suspicious at first, but when he told them

he was from STBU they were ecstatic. This was the reaction Solomon had grown accustomed to when he worked in the majors. Ten years at Chrysalis, a dozen more at Polydor, where they kept moving him to smaller and smaller divisions until he was invited to explore opportunities elsewhere. No one had been this excited to hear from STBU before, and he loved these shaggy boys for it, but driving back to Studio City as the sun came up, his brain alert, his hands tingling on the wheel, he realized that STBU was the wrong place for The Intensities. Gray would sweet talk the boys into signing away their rights to both the record and the publishing, and then they'd be fucked.

Solomon couldn't let that happen. It hit him with a strange kind of certainty. Was this what his father felt when he knew he'd stumbled onto something special, something more valuable than money?

When Gray told him that STBU wouldn't be signing any new bands he got angry at him for wasting his time—the disrespect drove him nuts—but he was also relieved. Now he could do right by those boys who'd beguiled him out there in the desert. Could that magic be recreated in the studio?

Solomon intended to find out, but first he had to remove a few road blocks.

One minute before Gray started pushing up daisies . . .
Hondo was confused.

Three o'clock came and went and no weed break. Where was Gray?

Billy said Gray would be there. Why would he lie to Hondo?

It was the first night of Hanukkah. Everyone knew that, but maybe Billy didn't. Maybe they were all gathering inside for a Hanukkah celebration. Maybe Billy forgot to tell him. Maybe it slipped his mind. Billy wasn't Jewish, but Hondo was.

When he was a kid, every year he went to his grandparents' house in Palm Beach to celebrate Hanukkah. He loved sitting in his grandfather's lap while he told him stories about the Maccabees, the warriors who defied the Greeks. Then his parents split up and he was sent to live with his mother in a condo in Westwood. His mother told him it was only temporary, but it wasn't. He never saw his grandparents again.

The Machine said everyone lies to Hondo.

The Machine said the debt must be paid.

The Machine said the time for words has passed and now it is time for blood.

Hondo abandoned his hiding place in the bushes and went inside.

Six minutes after Gray climbed the stairway to heaven . . .
Killing Gray had been easy. He was so zonked on the quaaludes she'd been slipping into the yogurt he ate every morning that he didn't put up much of a fight. She moved behind his desk and garroted him. The rest was easy. She stuffed the tape from the "Hondocore" cassingle into his mouth, got the water works going, and made a frantic call to Matt.

With Gray dead, STBU's assets would be more valuable than ever. Gray never married. He had no children, no heirs. It was possible he had a secret will, but she doubted it. Gray's death meant the beginning of a long legal battle with the label's recording artists. Maybe the terrible contracts Gray forced them to sign would hold up in court, but Judy doubted it. That meant the value of the masters would skyrocket. With the masters in her possession she'd be set for life. She could sell them off to the highest bidder. As the one who pulled the strings behind the scenes at Sucks To Be U Records, it was time to open her golden parachute.

And she would get away with it. Because Matt was simple, Billy was a headcase, and Solomon was a dinosaur. But something was wrong.

As Judy approached the weed locker, she could see the door was wide open.

The door was never open—she made sure of that.

She moved closer, more stealthily now, and could hear someone moving around inside and she felt the first stirrings of panic. Now that Gray was finally out of the picture, she wasn't going to let someone pull the rug out from under her.

The plumber had left a mess and there were tools lying around outside the warehouse bathroom. A new shipment of records arrived yesterday and most of them sat atop wooden pallets, wrapped in plastic like ghost furniture. She picked up a screwdriver and immediately put it down in favor of a claw-end hammer. What if it was Hondo inside the vault?

That psychopath had threatened to take back what was his. What if he was rummaging around, looking for the masters?

She couldn't have that. Judy already thought of the masters as *hers*.

The hammer wasn't going to cut it.

Propped up against a pallet was a pipe wrench. Judy picked it up and tested its weight. It was big and heavy. The key would be to get it up in the air and let gravity do the rest. She rested it on her shoulder like a baseball bat. When she sensed movement inside the vault, she raised the wrench and swung it at the figure emerging from the vault.

Except it wasn't Hondo.

It was Billy.

"What the fu—" was all he got out before the pipe wrench crushed his skull.

Eight minutes after Gray went to the great recording studio in the sky . . .

Matt stood at the free-throw line in the parking lot behind STBU, set up his shot, and let it fly. The ball sailed up into the sky in a prefect parabola and came down through the orange rim.

Nothing but net.

That was eight in a row. A good number.

He spied his ride coming and picked up the duffel bag at his feet and slung it over his shoulder. When the LeSabre pulled up and its trunk popped open, Matt gently deposited the bag inside, like he was disposing of a body.

The bag contained all of STBU's recording contracts. All the proof of a business relationship between the label and its artists was now in the trunk. He and Solomon had cleared out the masters from behind the weed locker the night before. Not just the most important ones—the first recordings from STBU's early days, the game changers and money makers—but all of them. You couldn't tell the whole story of indie rock with these recordings, but you sure as shit couldn't tell it without them.

The plan was to return the tapes to the bands so they could do what they wanted with the music they created. Sell it to another label, put it out themselves, let it sit on a shelf until the end of time. The choice would be theirs to make.

Matt climbed into the passenger seat and nodded at Solomon, who nodded back. There was no need to talk. Ever since he noticed a change come over Judy and guessed at what she was planning, he knew he had to secure STBU's legacy. He knew Hondo would play along and act like he was out for blood, but he didn't expect Billy to be an unwitting participant in Judy's scheme or Solomon to be such an enthusiastic ally. It never occurred to Matt to interfere with Judy's plans and stop her from doing away with Gray. Did that make him a bad person?

No, Gray was the bad guy. He stole a lot of money, ruined a lot of dreams. At the end of the day, what mattered to Matt was the music—both its past and its future.

They drove to Sherman Oaks, where they had a date with a band from Tarzana. A producer was already waiting for them in a tiny little recording studio tucked away in an alley behind a barbecue joint on Ventura Boulevard. He had to pay extra on account of it being Hanukkah but it was money well spent. The plan was to get back to basics, dedicate themselves to the real spirit of rock and roll, and with a little luck, compose a new chapter in the future of music. Matt popped the demo into the tape player and turned up the volume.

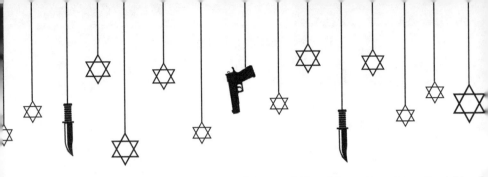

TOD GOLDBERG

Tod Goldberg is the *New York Times* bestselling author of over a dozen books, including the award-winning *Gangsterland* trilogy; *The Low Desert,* which was named Southwest Book of the Year; *The House of Secrets,* which he co-authored with Brad Meltzer; and *Living Dead Girl,* a finalist for the *Los Angeles Times* Book Prize. His short fiction has been published widely, including in *Best American Mystery & Suspense,* and his nonfiction appears regularly in the *Los Angeles Times, USA Today,* and *Alta,* and has been anthologized in *Best American Essays.* He lives near Palm Springs, CA, where he founded and directs the Low-Residency MFA in Creative Writing & Writing for the Performing Arts at UC Riverside.

EIGHT VERY BAD NIGHTS

Tod Goldberg

First Night:

Jack Katz told Doris to run the numbers again. It was just before five. An hour till closing time.

"I could run them five hundred more times," Doris said. "The end result is going to be the same. You'll need a miracle to make payroll."

"How short am I?"

"About fifty grand," she said.

"'About' being more than fifty thousand dollars or less than fifty thousand dollars?"

"More."

Jack got up from his desk. From his perch on the second floor of United Furniture, he could see everything through the floor-to-ceiling window. A young couple looked at dinette sets. A shirtless little boy ran crazy through the sofa section, jumping over ottomans, diving across leather couches, rolling under coffee tables. His sister, maybe eighteen months older, stood in front of a full-sized mirror, licking her reflection.

A man snoozed in a recliner.

Two women examined the wall of hanging area rugs, the same rugs they'd had in stock for twenty years. Maybe more.

His interior decoration consultants—Daphne, whom he dated in high school, and Gil, whom he bullied in high school—literally filed their nails at their desks.

Somewhere, a phone went unanswered.

It was a Sunday, which usually was their big sales day, but nothing was usual anymore. It was also the first night of Hanukkah, which in years past meant a giant company party hosted by Jack's father, Cy, back when most of United's employees were Jews, too. He'd founded United Furniture fifty-five years ago, fall of 1943, right here in Palm Springs. Cy made a point to get as many Jews fleeing the Nazis good paying jobs as possible, which was both a sign of Cy's pure altruism as well as a solid business and protection plan. Didn't matter if it was someone trying to steal a lamp or the Teamsters trying to muscle in: You had to make it through a hundred tough Jews to make it back out alive.

Stayed that way for decades because Cy Katz was a real mensch *and* a real hard case. He set his staff up with generous pensions, which was possible because United Furniture at its height had ten stores, including huge showrooms in Las Vegas and Reno which provided furniture for the new hotels popping up every fifteen seconds. There were even spin-off operations, like the overhead fan store in San Diego Cy put his cousin Arnie in charge of—FanDiego—which did big business for a few years in the 1970s, and then Barstools & More, which sold . . . well, barstools and more. That wasn't as successful, but Cy kept it going for a few years anyway, because its failure was just a rounding error. United Furniture was an empire.

With the empire came the normal problems. Union bosses in Las Vegas and Reno who thought they could shake

Cy Katz down. City planners in Palm Springs who thought they could force him out, turn his prime downtown real estate into shitty condos or an IHOP or another fucking deli. Jack's mom dying suddenly fifteen years ago, followed by Cy getting hitched and divorced three times, once to a mail-order Russian woman who had a sixteen-year-old daughter named Svetlana, who was actually twenty-six and the Russian woman's sister. But they wouldn't figure that out until a significant chunk of Cy's savings was gone.

Each situation chipped at the foundation—financially, physically, and emotionally. Then along came Levitz's western expansion. Then Pottery Barn's. Crate & Barrel's. Then the years when everyone went in on wicker, which Cy refused to stock, opting to double down on recliners, which was a mistake.

Ancient history now.

Cy had been dead for six months and all that remained of United Furniture was the flagship store in Palm Springs, which was now mostly a sinking barge. It was the last days of 1998 and Jack Katz wasn't anywhere near the mood to party like it was 1999. Way things were going, he'd be lucky to enter the year without his head in a noose.

Jack knocked on the window, got Daphne's attention, gave the slit-throat pantomime. She put down her nail file, got Gil to put down his emery board, then flipped Jack a lazy bird.

"I was supposed to be a millionaire," Jack said. He turned to Doris. "How did this happen?"

"Your father should have sold this building to IKEA when he had the chance."

"When was this?"

"Do you really want to know, Jack?"

He didn't. Not really. He already had to drive by the IKEA twice every day, once on his way to work, once on his way home. It was 242,000 square feet. Three stories tall. You could hold the county fair in the parking lot. In fact, when Jack was in his old job as the weatherman on Channel 5, he actually took part in IKEA's grand opening ribbon-cutting ceremony, which was a full-on fair, with a Ferris wheel, people riding fucking elephants and camels, bumper cars, frozen bananas, and a beauty contest, which he got to judge, because he was a bit of a local celebrity.

This was back when everyone knew him as The Weatherman Jackson Storm, which was how he thought of himself, too, always introducing himself to folks who recognized him at Von's as if that was all one word: Weatherman-JacksonStorm. He wasn't a meteorologist, to be clear, he was just good-looking, had a degree in journalism from Cal State Fullerton, and knew how to read a teleprompter, which qualified him to stand up and recite the temperature, banter with the actual news journalists, which he'd done for nearly two decades. He always thought he'd get the call to move into a bigger market—Los Angeles, Seattle, even San Diego would have been nice—but as each year passed, being the weatherman in Palm Springs ended up being a pretty good life. He ate for free everywhere. Desmond's Suits dressed him. He could dependably get an anonymous hand job from any stripper in the region.

Also ancient history. Channel 5 fired him after he showed up drunk for his morning drive-time shift, which was amusing, in a way, since he'd shown up drunk plenty of times over the years, he just hadn't ever been caught. It was the projectile vomiting on air that did him in. Gone were the free meals, suits, and on-call orgasms. He did a two-week stint on KPLM as a morning drive-time shock jock, except he just couldn't think of anything shocking to say at 5 A.M., not without a little help, which got him run from that job, too. With nowhere else to go, he went back to the family business. Jack loved his father. He really did. But working with him was like a bleeding hemorrhoid: eventually, no matter how much you ignored it, you woke up with a persistent pain in the ass.

He sat back down behind the desk—which, like every-thing else at United Furniture, had originally been his father's—and pondered stabbing himself in the fucking eyes with a handful of United Furniture logo pens. Instead Jack met Doris's gaze for a few moments. She'd worked for the company for twenty-five years running their Reno operation, but had only been in Palm Springs for a few months. When Cy died, Jack reached out to Doris and con-vinced her to come out of retirement to help him. She was catching a plane back home tonight.

"If you were me," Jack said, "what would you do?"

"Well," Doris said, "you could start by trying to collect on all these past due credit files." She took a three-inch-thick manila folder from her lap and dropped it on his desk.

"How much is in there?"

Doris shrugged. "Hundreds of thousands."

"What?"

"With interest, it's probably a lot more," she said.

Jack flipped through the folder. He couldn't believe what he was seeing. *$10,412 to Franklin Sommers. Last payment: $25, January 1992. $651 to Lana Shaw. Last payment: $10,*

March 1988. $21,019 to Mandrake Hotel & Suites of Palm Desert. Last payment: $300, May 1989. "Did my father never collect? This is crazy."

"Seems if you needed a dinette set and had a job, he'd give you a dinette set." She cleared her throat. "Flip to the back. That's where it gets interesting."

Jack did as he was told. *Danny Rosen. $59,000. Last payment: N/A*

N/A? Danny Rosen? Jack knew that fucking guy. He owned restaurants and bars in town. Lived in Firebird Country Club, where his neighbors were President Ford and Frank Sinatra, at least up until Frank died. Back when Jack was Jackson Storm, he even had his own signature cocktail at the Sand Trap, Danny's overpriced fake-ass dive bar inside the fucking Marriott in Palm Desert. He also supplied drugs to anyone who lived in a million-dollar home who didn't want to roll up into North Palm Springs to buy coke. A real man of the people. He had to be eighty now.

There were other names. *Dom Zangucci. $25,000. N/A. Charlie Katofsky. $33,000. N/A. Michael Sugarman. $41,000. N/A.*

Rosen, Zangucci, Katofsky, and Sugarman owned some of the most popular night clubs, bars, and restaurants in the city. They were millionaires. They were also the kinds of guys who could get you what you need. Drugs. Girls. Guns. Boys. Whatever.

Well, except for Zangucci, who got arrested the year before on some extortion thing, a trumped-up charge for sure, and now could only get you what you need up in Lompoc.

You're the weatherman, this is your peer group. You can't walk around making God-like pronouncements and then just be friends with accountants. You're the higher power, you surround yourself with muscle.

In retrospect, an accountant or two would have been helpful.

"These guys. These aren't good people."

Doris dug a new pack of cigarettes from her purse, shook one out. "Do you mind if I smoke?"

"You smoke?" Jack said.

"Not in a decade." She lit up, tipped her head back, blew smoke into the air. "I had a feeling today was going to be a bad day."

"These names mean anything to you?" he asked.

"Your father," she began, then stopped. "Jack, how much do you want to know about your father?"

"I don't want to hate him," he said. Fact was, Jack knew enough to know that he could never hate his father. Fear him? Maybe a little. Pity him? Never. But Jack remembered how the station's investigative reporter, Patrick White, dropped a disc on his desk the day he retired.

"What's this?" Jackson Storm asked then.

"Every tip I ever got on your dad," Patrick said. "Thank him for that California King he sold my wife. Saved my marriage."

Now, Doris sighed. "My guess? It's protection money. Everyone shook him down, everyone got a little something."

"He took protection in trade?"

"It's easier to launder a leather davenport than it is cash," Doris said. "Saying from the Old Country."

Jack checked the names again. Danny Rosen seemed

like the least dangerous option. He once saw one of Charlie
Katofsky's guys curb stomp a guy dressed as Santa at a holiday fundraiser for the homeless at the La Quinta Resort,
which sort of made sense now. "This isn't the Old Country.
I'm somebody in this town. And I'm not letting my people
descend into darkness."

Doris smiled sadly at Jack. "You look like your mother,
you know," she said. Doris and Jack's mother, Joyce, had
been the best of friends. They'd grown up together in Walla
Walla, Washington, of all places, two of only a dozen Jewish
families in town at the time. "She'd admire your optimism."
She put a hand to his cheek. "Go home. Light your menorah. Pray. Maybe God will listen." Doris grabbed up her
belongings. "You need me, don't call. I can't be involved in
this shit. I'm too old for prison again."

Jack didn't really believe in all that God stuff—in fact, he
viewed Hanukkah as more of a measuring error than a miracle—but what Jack Katz understood was that some things
exist beyond reason or control and in most cases, it's best
to cover your bases. So he recited the prayer in his head, in
Hebrew, just in case. He felt like he got some of it wrong.
He was dogshit with pronunciation. So he did it again, this
time in English: *Blessed are You, Adonai our God, Sovereign
of all, who has kept us alive, sustained us, and brought us to this
season*—then headed downstairs.

JACK GATHERED ALL THE employees in the center of the
store, by the sofas.

"Everyone," he said, "I wanted to let you know that to
celebrate our great year, the store will be closed until the end of
Hanukkah." The staff looked around cautiously. "Everyone

gets the rest of the week off." More looking around. Doris put a hand to her throat, shook her head slowly, mouthed: "No, Jack, no," but fuck it. Either he was going to get this money or he wasn't. What was seven more days? "Paid!"

Second Night:

Jack hadn't been inside the Sand Trap in at least a year. Fact was, he hadn't been inside *any* bar in the desert in at least a year, not since the end of his Jackson Storm era. He'd gotten sober the old fashioned way—white-knuckling it through a few weeks, followed by some dour Twelve Step meetings in a strip mall in Cathedral City, before he determined that despite the signage, it was in fact a glum lot—but was now California sober: no more drinking, but he smoked a little weed every now and then, swallowed an Ativan or Percocet if he needed it. Took Sudafed for concentration, that ephedrine bump gold for getting shit done. Everything in moderation.

That afternoon, however, he'd found an expired bottle of Ritalin in the back of his medicine cabinet, the label indicating it was for Kristy Lemon, who'd lived with him for a few months about five years ago. It helped him zoom in on what was really important. He'd prayed over his menorah the night before, asked that the oil—metaphorically speaking—get him through the end of the week and that it deliver him some cash along the way. He didn't think that was the purpose of the menorah, or of prayer, but fuck it. The nice thing about Judaism is that it was a religion of questions. His current question was: How can I get some fucking cash? He then spent a few hours online, reading up on what it meant to be a Maccabean warrior back in the day, determined that if he'd grown up in the second century, he'd be fucking dead, did another bump of Ritalin just for the buzz, then topped off with some Actifed so he could get some rest. It was all medicine. Nothing to worry about.

He found a stool at the end of the bar, waived at Posy, the bartender. They'd grown up together, which wasn't unusual. The desert was a boomerang. Everyone came back eventually. He and Posy had gone to the same Chabad Hebrew School together for a few years then found each other again in their teens when both were working retail at the Palm Desert Mall, Posy at Moby Disc, Jack at United Furniture's short-lived chaise longue shop. Now they were both in their forties, Posy serving drinks to golfers, tourists, and defrocked weathermen.

"Well look at you," she said. She set a napkin down, leaned on her elbows. "Thought you might be dead."

"Come on," Jack said. "They would have run a full-page obit of me in the paper, provided I died in the season."

"You think I read the paper?" Posy said. "Personally? If I'd thrown up on live television, I might just kill myself."

"I thought about it," Jack said.

"I bet," she said. "You should get out of here, Jack. I won't serve you if you're sober now."

"I'm not here for a drink," Jack said.

"Just here for the ambiance?"

In a way, he was. When Jack went over Rosen's bill, he saw that thousands of dollars in furniture was earmarked for this very bar. Now, in the dim light of the joint, he recognized a sectional in the corner, several low tables, and, in fact, the very stool he was sitting on.

"I was hoping to catch Mr. Rosen. He around?"

"It's Hanukkah," Posy said. "He's at home lighting candles with his wife. Where we both should be."

"Something tells me he's not observant."

"And we are?"

"Older I get," Jack said, "the more Jewish I feel."

"It's living out here," Posy said. "Growing old in the desert is what we're supposed to be doing." She was probably right. "What is it you want with Mr. Rosen?"

Jack gave Posy the basics, including Rosen's unpaid debts, which made Posy look uncomfortable.

"Let me ask you something, Jack. Do you know who Danny Rosen really *is*?"

"What's he gonna do to me? That bill was to protect my father's business. We're a couple days from Chapter Eleven. Fat lot of fucking good it did."

"Do you know who Danny *still* is in New Jersey? When he goes home in the summer?"

Jack wasn't dumb. Palm Springs had always been an open city for organized crime. You'd run into ancient, retired wiseguys all over the place. But that was the thing: they were ancient and retired. Maybe in New Jersey Danny was a gangster, but in Palm Springs, he was mostly a philanthropist, even if he also ran a high-end drug operation. A couple years back, when the police department was going through budget cuts, he personally paid for five new cruisers. Helped underwrite the local Special Olympics, was a huge supporter of AIDS Project Palm Springs. He surely wasn't out there shot calling.

"He took fifty-nine thousand dollars' worth of merchandise from my father's store. Without interest. That seem right to you?"

"Get a Ouija board and ask your father," Posy said. "Because if I were you? I wouldn't show up at Danny Rosen's house demanding cash."

"And I should just show up at Mike Sugarman's with an open hand?"

"I didn't say that."

"Danny Rosen is almost a hundred years old," Jack said. "I can handle him."

"I'm trying to help you," Posy said.

"I get that. But if I don't get my staff paid," Jack began, but didn't finish his thought. He didn't know what he'd do. He just knew he didn't want to ruin anyone else's life. "Look. I've spent the last year of my life trying to be a better person. Now I'm gonna put families on the street, okay? I can't have that haunting me."

Posy looked at Jack for a long moment. "Are you seeing anyone?"

"Are you asking me on a date?"

"No, I mean, like a therapist."

"Oh," Jack said. "No. I've been reading a lot. I read that book about the talking seagull a few weeks ago. That was interesting. You read that?"

"No," Posy said.

"Read this other book about a woman who lives in Madison County and meets a shitty photographer but she can't get it together to run off with him. That wasn't as good as the seagull book." He paused. "Last night I prayed a bunch. Woke with a newfound clarity."

"I guess I don't associate you with deep wells of empathy," she said. "It's a good look on you." Posy took out a pen, scribbled something on a napkin, slid it across the bar.

There were six numbers scrawled on the napkin: 951238. "What's this?"

"It's the code to get into the staff gates at Firebird, so you don't need to go through the security checkpoint."

"Why do you know this?"

"I've been seeing a guy there for a while," she said, "who doesn't want me showing up on the cameras. I were you, I'd swing by tomorrow night. Danny's usually home after sunset. Show up after dark, he'll have some drinks in him, probably be easier to do whatever you're gonna do."

"What kind of asshole has you come in the back door, like the help?"

Posy stared at Jack with a strange, unblinking intensity, like she was trying to read his mind or bend spoons. "I can't believe I ever depended upon you to predict the weather," she said, eventually, and then disappeared into the back, came back with a bucket of ice, dumped it into a sink, busied herself with the other end of the bar, where actual tipping guests were ordering Sex on the Beach and Lava Flows, like it wasn't even close to Hanukkah.

Third Night:

The staff entrance for Firebird was right up against an outcrop of Mount San Jacinto, a few blocks south of the Frank Sinatra Drive. Half the streets in the desert were named either for dead celebrities or those soon to be. Dinah Shore. Gerald Ford. Bob Hope. Gene Autry. Hope was still hanging on, but Autry had kicked in October, Sinatra at the start of the summer. Gerald Ford was still alive, too, but no one cared about him all that much. Jackson Storm used to play golf with President Ford every year at some charity for one-legged kids or something. Jack couldn't quite remember what it was, only that there was always a one-legged kid on the poster, which Jackson autographed like he was somebody.

In fact, he'd put up a couple of those autographed posters up on eBay that morning, see if there might be someone who wanted some signed mementos. He forged Bob Hope and Dinah Shore's autographs. Who was going to check that?

Jack found Rosen's home, pulled up the long winding driveway in his red Cadillac Seville—well, his father's red Caddie, but it was his now—and parked behind Danny's unmistakable black Jaguar, the one with the personalized plate that said MENSCH. He spent a few minutes sitting there, getting his nerve up, which was a mistake, because another car pulled up beside him.

It was a lowered '87 Honda Prelude, the kind with a purple light underneath it. Rap music thumped out of the open window. Jack looked over, saw Robbie Daulton behind the wheel. Robbie and Jack had gone to high school together, too. In fact, he and Robbie had been in Drama together, had gone up to Sacramento for a monologue competition senior year, after battling it out on the Palm Springs High School stage year after year for lead roles in *Oklahoma!*, *Noises Off*, and *Our Town*. In Sacramento, Jack chose a scene from *A Man for All Seasons*—the one about granting the Devil and law and order—and drank a gallon of coffee beforehand, to be authentically stressed. The judges ate that shit up. Then Robbie came rolling in with Biff's monologue from *Death of a Salesman*—the "Why am I trying to become what I don't want to be?" bit—and owned the fucking house, everyone with a broken dream empathizing with fucking Robbie. Next day, there were photos of them in the *Sacramento Bee* newspaper and everything. First and second prize. Well. Second and first prize.

For a decade after graduation, Robbie managed the Del Taco on Highway 111, and would always give Jack a free quesadilla when Jack hit the drive-thru at 3 A.M., back when Jack was doing overnight shifts at the station, and they'd bullshit for a few minutes, always real cool, but Jack knew Robbie felt like he'd gotten one over on Jack. Then Robbie did a hit-and-run and ended up doing a bid and that was that. He was back, apparently, still driving the same car, a giant dent in the Prelude's hood in the shape of a fourteen-year-old girl.

Robbie turned down the music. "The fuck you doing here, Katz?"

"Practicing my monologue."

"Not gonna win now, either," he said. "You meeting with Rosen?"

"Just here to pick up what's mine."

"*I'm* supposed to be meeting with him," Robbie said and there was that anger he'd channeled as Biff. Uncanny, really. "Unless you're doing the pickup? Are you doing the pickup?"

Jack tried to process all the available evidence. Nope. Nothing processed. So Jack looked up into the night sky, went with an old standby: "Storm clouds are gathering."

Robbie nodded. "Well, fuck." He drummed his fingers on the steering wheel. "I was a little late last week. I guess that matters. You doing middle shit now?"

"Hard to forecast."

"The fuck does that mean?"

"Bring an umbrella, just in case."

Robbie nodded again, thinking. "So you're working with Lil Dom now?"

Lil Dom. Lil Dom. Lil Dom. Who the fuck was Lil Dom? Oh. Maybe Dominic Zangucci's kid. They called him Deuce back in the day. Maybe he was now Lil Dom?

The front door opened and a giant Samoan guy came walking out. Must have been six foot seven, 285, all muscle and tribal tattoos. He had a Priority Mailbox in his giant hand. Looked back and forth to both cars.

"Fuck this," Robbie said when the Samoan started walking toward them, threw up two fingers in Jack's direction. "We ain't done, homie."

"I'm not your homie, Robbie."

"It's a figure of speech, dipshit," Robbie said. "You never were good with subtext. It's why you lost in Sactown. It's why you'll always be a loser." He revved his engine. "Well. Break a leg. Homie."

After Robbie peeled off, the Samoan motioned for Jack to get out of his car. Jack didn't feel like he was in a position where he could deny the man, so he got out, stood by his door.

"What happened to Robbie?"

"He realized he was someone he didn't want to be," Jack said.

The Samoan sized Jack up. Jack tried to roll his shoulders, seem more imposing, but there was no way to make up for thousands of years of genetics. Every man in his family history had been five ten and 175 pounds of pure Jew. The

Samoan had a gun stuffed into his belt, casual, like it was no thing. He also had a teardrop tattoo on his face. A tattoo of claws on his hands. A tattoo of a skull on his throat. "So you're the bag now?" he asked, finally.

"That's right."

"You're gonna take care of Robbie for the fuck up?"

"That's right. Consider it done."

"Good," the Samoan said, then handed Jack the box. "It's all there."

"Oh, I actually wanted . . ." Jack began. The Samoan cocked his head, a real active listening move, which Jack appreciated. But Jack didn't know what it was he wanted anymore. His desire to ask Danny Rosen for . . . anything . . . had dissipated dramatically since this dude walked out. Posy hadn't mentioned this guy.

The Samoan pointed at Jack. "I know you."

"Don't think so."

"You're the weatherman. Johnny Thunders or something."

Shit.

"I was Weatherman Jackson Storm."

"Yeah, yeah," he said. "That's it. I liked your vibe. Lotta these weather people, they're just spank banks for old folks that can't get no porn. That's disrespectful. Weather is science. No need to tart that shit up in red dresses and tight suits and shit."

Jack didn't disagree. Though admittedly he'd made his way through a lot of weatherwomen in red dresses in his time. Almost married Hannah Mountain from Channel 7 a few years back, until it turned out she was sleeping with her own anchorman, Grady Ball, which was gross, in Jack's opinion. Plus, Hannah Mountain was actually named Lucy Morton

and was a Christian Scientist and that was not going to
work.

"What happened to you?" the Samoan asked.

"I was a drunk," Jack said.

"That's bad shit. Gotta keep a pure body." The Samoan
patted the top of Jack's car. "Okay. Well. Boss says it's all
there. Bring back the cash end of the week, no fucking
around, we good?"

Jack said, "We good."

The Samoan looked up into the sky. It really was cloud-
ing over. "It gonna storm tonight?"

Jack said, "You know, I never actually knew."

JACK DIDN'T BOTHER TO wait to get home before he
tore open the box, opting instead for the parking lot of
Sherman's Deli, where he'd called in an order of latkes to
go. He'd already experienced one miracle today—not getting fucking murdered by that Samoan—so he decided to
celebrate a little with some fried potatoes. Inside were prescription bottles, no labels, and a spreadsheet with names
and addresses, dates and times for delivery, and money
owed—which was significant—plus bags of weed—a couple ounces—and a few bags of coke. Not a lot. Not even
a good Saturday night back in the '80s. But still, coke was
coke and Jack was tempted to give it a taste, just for the
hell of it. Instead, Jack opened the bottles. Some blue, some
white, some red, some round, some oval, some octagonal.
Some big, some small, some gel caps.

Jack popped half of a blue pill, just to see what it was,
sort of hoping it was some kind of sedative, shoved the bags
of weed and coke into his glove box, went inside Sherman's

to pick up his latkes. The blue started to hit while he stood in the deli line, surrounded by alta cockers doused in Chanel #5 and looking like they'd robbed a Nordstrom Rack.

It wasn't a sedative.

He got back to his car a few minutes later with a bag of hot latkes and took a look at the paperwork with fresh eyes and a sudden desire to fuck anything that was remotely carbon based. A gentleman named Maury Flanagan had a bottle of reds on order and owed $5,000 for them. No one named Maury could ever be threatening, so Jack decided to start there tomorrow night. And if these red pills were worth $5,000, they must be something good. So, Jack popped one of them, too.

Fourth Night:

Maury Flanagan lived in a house designed to look like an ocean liner over in the Mesa neighborhood, portholes and everything, just down the street from the actress and infomercial impresario Suzanne Somers, which Jack knew because he used to get invited over to her house for charity events and holiday parties, everyone going home with ThighMasters as parting gifts. What a time. No one lived behind gates in the Mesa, opting instead for a private security patrol of trigger-happy ex-cops, stories routinely getting buried about them plugging various stalkers and the like. Palm Springs was like that.

Jack rang the doorbell and the sound of a foghorn blared out, followed by a man shouting, "Come in already, Jesus! It's open! This fucking house!" and a pack of coyotes, somewhere in the canyon, howling in return. Jack stepped inside the foyer. There was a hall tree covered in captain's hats right by the door, a fetish gone wrong, and a series of ornamental walking sticks and canes, a kitchen in front of him, a long hall to the left.

"Hello?" Jack called. "Mr. Flanagan?"

"Back here," Maury yelled. "In the shitter."

Great.

Jack headed down the hall, past two bedrooms, each done up with nautical themes—bent blond hardwood walls, oars hanging from the ceiling, life preservers as art—and found the aforementioned shitter, Maury lying nude in a dry tub, his left leg hoisted up by some kind of rubber tubing that was cuffed to his wrist. At first, Jack thought it was some kind of sex thing, but then realized it was more likely a stretch. Something to relieve back pain? Maybe. There was a martini perched on the soap dish. Despite being named Maury, he wasn't eighty, looked to be in his midfifties, in fact.

"You got my shit?" he asked.

Jack said, "You got my money?" because he figured that's how it was done. Also, he'd taken a full blue and two reds and he was feeling both damn bold and also kind of rummy. Like he could fuck a bull, which he understood was not kosher . . . well, it was not a lot of things.

"You're new?" Maury said.

"Yeah."

"It's in the hall tree. Under the seat. It lifts up. That's how we do it. Now give me my shit so I can get out of this tub."

Jack left Maury in the tub, went back to the hall tree, found an envelope filled with cash, came back to the bathroom, tossed Maury his pills.

"Jesus," Maury said, "I thought you were going to leave

me here." He dry swallowed three reds. "These are the only things that help, other than getting into this tub for an hour or two." Maury pointed at Jack. "You happy to see me, hoss?"

Jack looked down. He had a cement-like erection that he'd somehow not noticed, what with his head feeling like a murder of crows had landed on his hypothalamus and this whole . . . situation . . . and then the thing with the bull was still in his head, too.

Shit was getting weird. This was *not* medicine.

"Adverse reaction," Jack said. He looked around the bathroom. It was covered in floor-to-ceiling wallpaper featuring old sea maps. *Here be dragons.* The room began to tilt. Was he at fucking sea? He suddenly felt like he might throw up. He stared at the wallpaper, trying to figure out where north was, but nothing was helping. The horizon was all fucked up. Dragons fucking everywhere. If he could just find true north, he could get orientation and he'd be fine. "Never been to sea."

"Never been to seed? What?" Maury sat up. His back cracked like lightning, Jack actually seeing the electricity crackling through his skin, rippling into the wallpaper, dragons coming alive, and then Jack was running down the hall, this morning's leftover latkes spattering on the walls as he rushed out.

Fifth Night:

Jack woke up just before noon, his cell phone ringing. His head was pounding, his groin was pounding, his stomach was pounding, and someone was pounding on the door. His back felt pretty good, however, which was probably because he was curled up on a Serta Pillow Top Mattress with Advanced Comfort Quilting and underneath a chenille throw blanket that he'd grabbed from the markdown rack inside United Furniture, where he'd spent the night.

It was Posy. She was also the one at the door. He answered the phone, told her to hold on, he'd let her in.

"Oh thank god," she said when he opened the door. She threw her arms around his neck. "I thought you were dead."

"I'm fine," he said, though he wasn't. But he wasn't fucking dead. Plus, he liked the way Posy's arms felt around his neck.

"The news said it was your menorah," Posy said. "I was so worried when they said they hadn't found any bodies yet."

"My menorah?"

"That caused the fire." She pulled back, stared at Jack. "You don't know?"

All Jack knew was that the previous night, after he finished with Maury and made a few more drop-offs, he headed over to his house and saw that Robbie Daulton was parked down the block, smoking a blunt in the front seat of his car, and decided maybe going home wasn't the move to make. Came back to the office, counted his money. $19,000. Not too shabby. If he made all the deliveries on his sheet he'd walk with a cool $52K. He felt like he could probably extort Danny for the other seven. That's how he was thinking these days.

"Your house, Jack," Posy said. "It burnt down last night. Fire department said you probably left home with your menorah lit and it set your drapes on fire. It was all over the news." She paused. "So you were right that your death would make the news."

Jack fell into a La-Z-Boy. Had he lit his menorah last

night, before leaving? Would he have done that? It didn't sound like something he'd do, not before sundown, anyway, but man, the last twenty-four hours had cooked his brain. "It wasn't me," Jack said. "I wasn't home." Fucking Robbie Daulton. Had he broken into his house and set it on fire? He always was a little pyro.

"You'll have to tell them that," Posy said.

"Who?"

"The police. Your insurance. The news. Everyone. Jack, you took out half the houses on your court!"

That was going to be a problem. How would he explain where he'd been last night? He'd need to get the rest of his money together before he even tried to lie his way through a police investigation. "So, wait," he said to Posy. He got up, reached around her, locked United's door again. Turned off the lights. Did he hear sirens? "Do they think I'm dead?"

"That was the concern, yes."

How much time would that buy him? A day? Two? Four?

"See," he said, "this might help me. I'm sort of in a situation where I don't have an alibi for my whereabouts. If I can be dead for a few days, maybe I can work this out."

"Oh, Jack," she said. "Did you already go see Mr. Rosen?"

"You gave me the code!"

"Did you . . . rob him?"

"No," Jack said. "Some Samoan gave me a bunch of drugs to sell. Shit's been very weird."

"I thought you were going to rob him."

"Why would you think that?"

"Because that makes better sense than selling drugs for him." Now she plopped down in a La-Z-Boy, too, leaned back, kicked the footrest up. "How am I going to unfuck this?"

"Why is this your problem?"

Posy glared up at Jack. "My god. When I said I was see-ing someone who didn't want me showing up on security cameras, did you think I was fucking President Ford?"

"You're fucking Danny Rosen? He's like three times your age!"

"I'm not fucking him," she said. "Not really. He likes to watch me . . . do stuff."

"Watch you?"

"Jesus fuck, Jack, don't make me explain it. You have the internet, for fuck's sake. Anyway. The bar is basically mine now. I have a real life. My debts are paid. My kid is in pri-vate school. This was what I needed. So I took it."

"And then you set me up to rob him?"

"No," she said. "I mean. I knew you'd do something stu-pid. I figured robbery would be on the list. I didn't figure you for violence. So maybe blackmail or something? I guess I didn't take Kitten into consideration." When Jack didn't say anything, Posy said, "The Samoan. He goes by Kitten. Well. I call him that. When he boxed, he went by Tiger, so I call him Kitten."

"Clever," Jack said. "Tell that story at my wake." Jack closed his eyes. The world started to spin. It wasn't unpleas-ant, all things considered. He was dead, plus a couple people probably wanted to kill him. His house had burned down, which meant all he had to his name was on his back and in this furniture store, and he still needed another forty thousand dollars or so. He opened one eye, tried to focus it. Nope.

"He doesn't usually work Mondays."

"Usually is doing a lot of work for you there."

Posy pulled her hair back into a ponytail, tied it with a rubber band she took from her wrist. "Whatever money you're collecting for Danny," Posy said, "if you keep it, you're going to have a real problem."

"I'm not going to keep it. I'm going to pay my employees with it. If Mr. Rosen has a problem with it, I'll just let the police know where I got the product."

"You think cops aren't on his payroll, Jack? He literally bought them cruisers."

"I was the weatherman," Jack said. "What are they going to do? Have me killed? The public would take to the streets. You can't go around murdering weathermen. I'll call the FBI if I have to."

"Did you study at all, like for your bar mitzvah?"

"Of course," Jack said. He hadn't, not really. He mostly memorized passages and made out with Ruth Liebowitz, who had the same birthday as his.

"The Torah says you should have an honest balance. Do you know what that means?"

"Does Danny Rosen?" Jack asked.

Posy sighed so deeply Jack had to check to see if she'd floated off the ground. "I need to take my daughter to the orthodontist," she said eventually. She leaned over and kissed Jack on the cheek, held his face. "Don't do anything stupid without talking to me first."

JACK WAITED UNTIL AFTER the six o'clock news finished before he left the furniture store. He wanted to see how his former colleagues handled his possible demise. It wasn't even in the A block. Fuckers. Wasn't until 6:20 that Brook Sperry did a live remote from his smoldering front yard.

"Tragedy struck Palm Springs early last night," she said, Jack watching her on one of the 35-inch TVs they couldn't fucking move for the holidays, the pricing all wrong. "This house, owned by former Channel Five weather personality Jackson Storm, went up in flames sometime before midnight and ended up taking out three additional houses. Storm hasn't been reached yet but at this hour, authorities are only saying that the lone fatality in this holiday tragedy is a twenty-nine-year-old parrot named Sam . . ."

Jack turned it off before she could continue. Weather personality! What the fuck did that *mean*? Well. Whatever. They weren't saying he was dead. They weren't saying he was alive. And no one had come by the store, other than Posy, which either meant his employees didn't watch the news or they didn't give a shit. Maybe both. And the cops probably didn't know where he worked now. He wasn't even really on the payroll. Which was probably a tax problem.

Now, he needed to drop off the cocaine, which gave him some pause. If he got pulled over with a bunch of coke, that was some shit that was hard to come back from. He'd be looking at real time and that, for sure, would be the end of his time on TV. Not that he thought a return was imminent, but what this week had shown him already was that people kind of . . . missed him? Maybe if everything turned out this week, he'd see about selling out to IKEA, hit the gym, maybe the tanning salon, and really devote himself to getting back on TV. Maybe not as a weatherman. Maybe he could do infomercials? Create some kind of cooking device? Jackson Storm's Miracle Baker? He'd put a pin in that.

But still. He had to be careful. So instead of driving his own car, Jack went over to the airport, parked his

Cadillac, went into AVIS, ordered the least Jewish car ever made, a white Ford Taurus, and made his way to an address in Rancho Mirage he didn't recognize until the very last minute: It was literally City Hall. Before he could turn around, however, a woman stepped out of a Jaguar, waved tentatively. Jack checked his spreadsheet. This was supposed to be someone called "Tammy." No one named Tammy had ever lived in Rancho Mirage, much less worked for the city.

Jack pulled up beside her, took down his window, stared straight ahead. He hadn't shaved all week, so he now had a fair amount of scruff on his face. And since there wasn't a shower at United Furniture, he'd washed up in the bathroom sink, then went foraging in the employee lockers for something more casual to wear, settling on a Lakers hoodie that smelled like all the Lakers had worn it at some point, but which was an improvement over the vomit stench of his own clothes. Finished off the look with sunglasses. A real fucking Maccabean warrior. For fuck's sake.

He put his arm out the window. "Here's your shit," he said. He'd put the coke inside a McDonald's bag.

"Robbie?" Tammy said.

"Out sick," Jack said.

"Wait. Jackson?"

Who the fuck was this lady? He glanced in her direction. Shit. It was Betty Frapman. A city councilwoman. They used to go to pancake breakfasts together. God, she had to be sixty now. He once fucked her in the bathroom of the Penguin's Frozen Yogurt, both drunk out of their minds after a thing at the Lions Club. Shit. That was a night. Or maybe it was a day? All he remembered for sure was that he was supposedly blackballed from all Penguin's after that point.

"Hey, Betty."

"What are you doing, Jackson?"

"Delivering your cocaine, looks like."

"Jesus," she said. "Are we on camera?"

"No."

"Is this what it has come to for you?" she asked. "I thought you'd be in New York. You could have been Willard Scott by now."

"I'm not the one doing coke," Jack said. "You still buying or are we going over my CV some more?"

She stood there, staring at him for a good thirty seconds. "How much?" she finally asked.

The spreadsheet said she'd be paying $4,000, so that would be about twenty grams by Jack's math. But Jack was feeling like there should be a service charge, in light of all this. "Let's call it six Gs," he said.

Betty shook her head, rummaged in her purse, came out with a stack of hundreds. "You work for Danny Rosen now? Is that how it is? I can help you, get you into rehab, whatever you want. You're a local celebrity, Jackson." She handed him the cash. "Will you take a check for the remainder? I'm a little short."

"A check for drugs?"

"We know each other," Betty said. "It's the holidays." She took out her checkbook. "Do you want to see the balance? I'm good for it."

Fuck it. "Make it to cash," Jack said.

She did just that, ripped out the check, stuffed it in his hand. "You look like shit, Jackson."

"I'm having a bad week."

"The holidays can be hard." Betty leaned into the window of his car. "I'm alone tonight. Come over. We'll light some candles. Talk about the old times."

"Aren't you married?"

"Hiram died. It's just me and the cockers now."

He remembered Posy's arms around his neck.

He remembered Posy telling him to contact her before he did anything stupid.

He remembered Posy probably setting this whole thing in motion. That he was like a character in some fucked-up noir movie from the fifties and was now incapable of making the right choices.

He remembered that he probably needed to ensure a little additional income. "Aren't you, like, the mayor or something?"

"It rotates among the council," she said. "So yes, in a few days, I'm the mayor."

He'd never done any blackmail, but it seemed easy enough.

"Lead the way," Jack said.

Sixth Night:

Jack woke up around 4:30 A.M., Betty asleep beside him in her giant California Super King—Jack reached under the mattress, pulled out the tag: Fucking IKEA, he knew it!—a cocker called Burt between them, two more were surrounding the bed. It had been a surprisingly energetic experience with Betty, likely owed to the countless lines of coke she did, and then the barking of the dogs and the way they nipped at his feet added a sense of urgency to the affair, plus they played a slightly sacrilegious game with Betty's menorah, seeing if Jack's oil could last miraculously long, too.

It couldn't.

They'd closed out the night with Betty agreeing to let Jack film their last go, Betty so coked out that he could have asked her if they could fuck on Highway 111 and she would have said yes, and so he found her video camera, caught her doing a few more lines, got some key action shots and then did some arty work involving the cockers howling after Betty fell asleep, slipped the video out of the camera and into his jeans. How much would that video be worth to Betty? Her house was a couple million, easy. Jack saw a whole new future opening up.

Now, Jack wandered into the bathroom, started the shower.

"Care to join me?" he called out. Betty didn't respond, which was great, since Jack really just wanted to wash up and get the fuck out of this place. He spent the next ten minutes scrubbing every part of himself with Betty's collection of soaps and exfoliators. By the time he was done, Jack's skin felt fresh and alive. His hair was clean. He was more than halfway to meeting payroll. Things were looking up!

He got out, dried off, went into the giant walk-in closet, hoping to find some sweatpants or something, only to discover that Betty hadn't thrown away her dead husband's clothes, so half of the closet was filled with golf attire. Hiram had been older, Jack remembered that, maybe seventy by the time he died. Jack didn't feel like he should just swipe something from dead Hiram's collection of garish polo shirts, so he grabbed a white undershirt from a drawer, sniffed it. It smelled dusty, having sat in a drawer since Bush was in office, but that was fine.

"You mind if I borrow one of Hiram's T-shirts?" Jack asked.

No response. Fuck it. He threw it on. It fit nicely. Maybe he'd become one of those guys who in retirement just walked around in undershirts.

He found some socks and underwear, too, decided he didn't need to ask about that, just put them on, fished his own jeans off the floor.

"Well," Jack said into the darkness, "that was a lot of fun, Betty. I better head out." No response. He looked at the clock. It was near five now. Were the cops looking for him? Robbie Daulton? Danny Rosen? Could be no one or everyone in the goddamned city was on his trail. So kindness was the key here. He might need an ally down the line, even with his intent to blackmail her.

Jack curled in behind Betty. Nuzzled up to her neck, buried his face in her hair. "That really was amazing," he said. He stroked her throat with his fingertips and knew, immediately, that something was very wrong.

He'd touched a lot of throats in his life and none of them had ever been cold and sticky.

"Betty?"

Jack tried to tip Betty over, but she wasn't budging.

In his life, Jack Katz had only seen maybe five dead bodies, the advantage of being Jewish being that all funerals were closed casket. The last one he saw was his father, who'd slipped this mortal coil in a bed at Desert Hospital, morphine juicing through his veins, the old man escaping with a pleasant smile on his face, which is sort of what Jack thought he'd find when he flipped on the lamp beside the bed. A pleasantly dead Betty Frapman. *Her heart probably couldn't take the passion.* That was an actual thought Jack had.

Betty Frapman's mouth was stretched open in a silent scream. Strands of bile leaked out of her mouth and pooled in her clavicle notch. Her tongue was ragged and purple. Her eyes bulged wide open, the whites snow white, like a cartoon character being electrocuted. Blood caked her upper lip in a crimson mustache. It was like she'd exploded.

For the second time that week, Jack Katz threw up all over himself. But this time, he also sprayed puke on the corpse of city councilwoman Betty Frapman, one of her cockers, a pricy lamp that Jack had seen at Pottery Barn for $799.99, Betty's garish floor-to-ceiling drapes, and, fortuitously, Betty's menorah, covered in melted wax.

Which gave Jack a miraculously good idea.

IT TOOK MOST OF the day, but by dinnertime Jack finally found out where Robbie Daulton lived. Like everyone else he'd grown up with, Robbie used to live in a gated community in Palm Springs; his parents were lawyers or accountants or maybe they owned an insurance agency, but then they got divorced and Robbie ended up living with his dad in a condo in Cathedral City, which was cool back then, because his dad would let Robbie and his friends smoke weed and have sex in the guest room, all of which seemed to Jack like some pretty irresponsible parenting in the present light, but which he thought was hella cool at the time, back when the drama crew used the joint as their unofficial clubhouse.

Robbie ended up living there until the hit-and-run, and

then he lived in San Quentin, and now the internet said he was living in the Blackhawk Indian Springs Mobile Home Village in Indio, which meant he was living in a trailer park. But like the rest of the desert, Blackhawk Springs was behind a guard gate, since even trailer parks were on golf courses out this way. How else to get someone from Calgary to pay $100K to buy a landlocked mobile home?

Jack told the guard he was there to meet a real estate agent and the guard buzzed him through without even making eye contact. Jack then spent the last few hours weaving in and out of the maze of what they now called manufactured homes, looking for Robbie's lowered Honda, finally spotting him pulling into a two-story number overlooking a pond, Robbie living like the fucking king of the non-mobile mobile homes. From the street, Jack watched him go inside with a bag of McDonald's and then come back out to his enclosed patio to eat, smoke a blunt, make a couple calls, and then leave again.

That's when Jack made his move. He parked his car a few blocks away, let Betty's cockers out of the backseat, casually walked them over to Robbie's house.

The enclosed patio had an unlocked sliding door, which was no surprise. Who was coming to steal the sun-damaged rattan sofa out there or the shitty card table and white plastic chair Robbie called a dining room? The door into the home itself was locked, which made better sense, since surely Robbie had some good shit in there. Drugs, guns, probably a stash of old *Hustler* magazines, that sort of thing. Jack unhooked the cockers from their leashes and they immediately began to run circles around the patio, barking and yipping. They each had a fancy collar with their own name, plus their owner's name, address, and phone number on them. Councilwoman Betty Frapman was such a good dog mom, she even had her office number on the tags.

Jack waited until he was back on the highway before he called the police to complain about what seemed to be some dogs under great distress at Robbie Daulton's address. It would probably take them some time to get over there, what with the conflagration in Rancho Mirage requiring as many local law enforcement officers as humanly possible. That's what happened when someone burns down the future mayor's house with her dead body inside of it.

Jack wasn't sure how he felt pinning a murder on Robbie Daulton. He was sure he didn't feel *bad*, per se. Not bad at all.

Seventh Night:

The Sand Trap was bustling when Jack sat down at the end of the bar, just before 9 P.M. on Saturday. He had on a sky-blue Adidas track suit of Hiram's that he'd grabbed out of the closet. The fit was a little loose, but truth be told Jack sort of liked it, made him feel like the kind of guy who wore track suits and didn't give a fuck, which was never the kind of guy Jack Katz was, certainly not who Jackson Storm would ever become, either. Betty's house had been a gold mine, literally. He'd walked out of there with enough jewelry and watches—plus a stack of sweat suits and golf shirts—that alongside the drug sales had his payroll covered. He'd made a deposit that afternoon. $65,000 in cash after hitting every pawn shop between Palm Springs and the Mexican border. Yeah, there'd be some IRS questions, but fuck it. His employees would be paid.

He'd call Doris in the morning, let her know to process everything. Tonight? He was celebrating. He whistled at Posy when she passed him and she had to do a double take before she realized who he was.

"Where the fuck have you been?" Posy asked. "I've been looking all over for you."

"Lying low," Jack said. Truth was, after the incident with Betty, he'd actually been lying high: He'd slept the previous night at the Strawberry Creek Bed & Breakfast in Idyllwild, up Mount San Jacinto, which loomed 11,000 feet above Palm Springs. It was all hippies and libertarians up there. The mayor of the city was an actual fucking dog. If he didn't suspect his presence in the mountain hamlet tripled the number of Jews, he'd think about moving there full time. People kept to their own. They even cared about the weather. Not that he used his own name when he checked in. He'd found Hiram's old wallet—which still had cash in it, too—and if he put his thumb over the driver's license photo, they sort of looked alike.

"Danny is going to have me fucking killed," she said. "Do you hear me? He is going to have me fucking killed."

"Don't overreact," Jack said. "If he wanted you dead, you'd be dead. This isn't the movies. People that can kill you just kill you and then they're done with it. They don't warn you first. Plus, let's be honest, what eighty-year-old man still calls himself Danny? You have nothing to worry about."

Posy looked at him like he was a space alien. "Who the fuck are you, some kind of gangster? You're the fucking weatherman!"

"It's been a week," Jack said. He reached into his pocket,

pulled out a wad of cash, peeled off a C-note for Posy. "For your troubles."

Posy ripped the bill in half, dumped it on the bar. "I don't need your money. I need you to tell Danny that he's going to get every cent you stole from him and that I had nothing to do with it."

"That would be lying," Jack said. "Wasn't it you who said I should have an honest balance?" Jack reached under his stool, felt around the old pieces of gum, found what he was looking for, yanking a sticker off the bottom of the seat. "Do you see this? It says right here that this is United Furniture inventory. I'm within my rights to repossess every piece of furniture in this bar. But I'm not going to do that. Because I'm a fair person. Danny took something from my business and never paid. I'm taking something from his business and not paying."

"Are you . . . on something?"

In fact, Jack was on a few things. He'd taken a few white pills, a handful of gel caps, a couple blues, two reds every four hours, and drank a Mountain Dew this afternoon. He'd spent the night reading up on the Hanukkah miracle and had come to some determinations, chiefly that it seemed weird that Hanukkah was celebrated for eight nights when the miracle was really that the oil lasted seven additional nights. The one night was the given. Which, to Jack, meant that tonight was the fitting end to his own miracle. He'd made payroll. He was still alive. Yeah, there'd been some hiccups along the way, but that was the point of modern miracles. They didn't come easy these says. No one believed in anything anymore. You really had to put in the time to make shit happen.

"There's cameras in this fucking place," Posy hissed. "He knows you came in here. Everything is recorded."

"Oh yeah?" Jack stood up. "Then listen up, Danny Rosen. I'm a motherfuckering Maccabean warrior! I am the Vengeance of the Jews! I am the oil and I am the light! You owed my father fifty-nine grand and tonight your debts are paid. You got a problem with that? Know this: My menorah never goes out, motherfucker. I'll go eighteen days! I don't give a fuck! Come find me if you got a beef!"

Which is when a big fucking Samoan walked into the bar.

Eighth Night:

For the next eighteen hours, the Samoan periodically tortured Jack and then they'd watch VHS tapes together, Jack zip-tied into a United Furniture papasan chair, which honestly were fucking shitty. Made for college students and burnouts. But Cy loved rattan, so here Jack was. The torture itself wasn't terribly severe in small doses—all of Jack's fingers on his right hand were broken, but the Samoan had done it fast: Grab, snap, *Working Girl.* Grab, snap, *Back to the Future 2.* Grab, snap, *The Fugitive.* There wasn't any kind of information the Samoan wanted, no aim to the torture other than torture, it was just retribution. "When is this going to stop?" Jack asked. His accumulative high was pretty much gone and the pain he was in was significant, though the Samoan had given him a couple Excedrin when he began to weep before the *really* sad part of *Terms of Endearment.* The Samoan was also nice enough to break his fingers and then snap them back into place. So at least they weren't irreparably crooked.

The Samoan said, "When Mr. Rosen gets home from

seeing his wife." He looked at his watch. "So, soon. He likes to be in bed early." The Samoan had an X-Acto knife in his hand. "I need to remove a couple toenails and then we'll call it, okay?"

"A couple?"

"Three."

JACK PASSED OUT DURING the whole toenail situation and woke up an hour into *The Bridges of Madison County*. "I just read this," Jack said, coming alert into darkness, the only light in the room coming from Danny Rosen's big-screen TV. He was woozy and numb, yet also throbbing in pain, though sometime while he was passed out the Samoan had removed the zip ties from his wrists.

Danny Rosen sat on a leather sofa beside the papasan. A menorah burned on the windowsill, Jack able to see the twinkling lights of the Coachella Valley in the distance. Or maybe that was just the glow of the flame? Jack couldn't be sure. His eyes were swollen from the Samoan pulling out all of his eyelashes during *Bill & Ted's Excellent Adventure*.

Danny pointed at the screen. "This reminds me of my wife."

"Oh yeah? She fall in love with someone else, too?"

"Yeah," Danny said. "Me."

"Where is she now?"

"Down the street," he said. "Memory care, they call it. Alzheimer's. Dementia. Whatever. She doesn't know where she is." He shook his head. "But this lady in this? She reminds me of her."

"Meryl Streep."

"She Jewish?"

"I don't think so."

Danny sighed. "Well. Who really cares anymore." He turned and faced Jack. "You owe me an apology."

"You owed my father fifty-nine thousand dollars, plus interest."

Danny said, "Your father was a gangster. Respectfully."

"My father was a furniture salesman."

"You ever wonder why no mom-and-pop furniture stores prospered between Palm Springs and Indio while you were growing up?"

Jack hadn't.

"You ever wonder," Danny said, "why every bar and restaurant in the whole valley had United Furniture? How you'd walk into every coffee shop in town and see a chair you recognized? You never wondered about that?"

Jack sat up. Kind of. He had at least four broken ribs. "I thought my father was a good boss and so his salespeople liked selling for him," Jack said.

"Oh," Danny said, "they loved selling for him." Danny pointed out the window. "You know the history of this place? This country club?"

"No."

"They didn't allow Jews for years. Decades. But that wasn't much of a surprise. Whole area was built by fucking anti-Semites, run by anti-Semites, abetted the fucking Nazis in the 1930s. Look it up. Leni Riefenstahl came out here to play tennis. True story. Your father. He was a good man. Your mother, she was a good woman. You should know that. But they were not the kind of people who would just *forget*. This is back when 'never again' meant something,

Jack. You understand me? My own son worked summers for your father, before you were born. You understand me? United Furniture, it was like . . . spring training. Where you learned to hit. You understand me, Jack?"

He was beginning to.

"You telling me," Jack said, "they *made* these businesses buy their furniture?"

"I'm telling you," Danny Rosen said, "that your father believed in blood redemption. Not killing. Just redeeming. God freed the Jews from bondage in Egypt. A blood redeemer makes sure that the overseers do not go unpunished. That's in the holy books. That's not just me talking shit, you understand." He leaned forward. "You ever been inside the country club here, Jack?"

"A hundred times," Jack said.

"Every piece of furniture purchased between 1965 and about 1990," Danny said, "before all these corporate fucks moved in? Fucking IKEA? Fucking Restoration Hardware? Every lamp. Every fucking candlestick. All from United Furniture. That's redemption. And at a markup. A severe fucking markup." Danny leaned back. "But times change. Business changes. I still need to make my money, you see. I was paying up, too. Your father and me, we had an understanding. It wasn't shared with you. That's his fault. But then you *steal* from me. You understand the situation this puts me in."

Jack said, "I can explain," and then he did, telling him about the payroll problems, about not wanting to put his staff on the streets, about making sure they could all eat, pay their bills, at least for the month. Told him about Robbie burning down his house, about burning down

Betty's house, about pinning it all on Robbie. Danny listened intently, Jack thinking he seemed kind of impressed.

"You did this," Danny said, "for your employees?"

"My people. That's right."

Danny Rosen stood, went over to the menorah on the window sill. "Tiger," he said, "get Jack up." The Samoan stepped out of the shadows—how the fuck someone that big could disappear into anything was a surprise to Jack—and lifted Jack out of the papasan. Gently. Carried him over to Danny. They watched the candles burn for a few moments. "You really burned down Betty's house using her menorah?" Danny asked.

"Had to," Jack said.

"You saved my ass there," Danny said. "That coke was a bad batch. It got traced to me, I'm looking at a murder charge, because you'd flip on me, I'd guess?"

"Probably," Jack said. It seemed like they were being honest with each other.

Danny said, "We're Jews. This mishegoss, it's how wars happen. People misunderstand shit that's been written down for years. You could have called me."

"I wasn't thinking."

"But you were. You took care of your people. That's what we do. That's what we're called to do. It's all your father ever did. I've got a doctor," Danny said, "I'm going to get him to come over. We'll get you fixed up. Lay low for a little bit. Tell everyone you've been in Cabo. Fell off a boat or something. We'll figure it out."

"Thanks, Danny."

"Pray with me," Danny said. He closed his eyes. "I'm

trying to remember the prayer, but it's lost to me now, after all these years."

"I know it," Jack said. And then, to his surprise, it was all right there, his Hebrew school training, his days in the synagogue, these last eight very bad nights collapsing on top of him. He *had* done a good thing, kind of. And so he closed his eyes, too, and said the prayer in Hebrew, a prayer for the living and a prayer for the miracles that are beyond our understanding. אֲשֶׁר עָשִׂיתָ נסים לאבותינו בימיו בעונה זו בָּרוּךְ אַתָּה, אֱלֹהֵינוּ, שְׁלִיט הָעוֹלָם.

ACKNOWLEDGMENTS

EVERY NOW AND THEN, it's important to do something just because you think it will be an incredibly good time. So when I emailed the great and wise Juliet Grames of Soho Press a few years ago, after the success of *The Usual Santas*, which I was thrilled to take part in, and suggested we should do a collection of noir stories centered around Hanukkah, I mostly expected she'd respond with an LOL or an emoji of some kind and that would be that.

A few days later, we had an offer.

Which is when I called my agent, the equally great and wise Jennie Dunham, and told her I'd kinda sorta accidentally sold a book and would she mind, uhm, taking care of that? Fortunately, Jennie thought it all sounded like a cool idea, too, and we were off. So my profound thanks to Juliet for not laughing me off and equal thanks to Jennie for getting in and taking care of business, as she's done for me my entire career. It was a joy to have Rachel Kowal step in to get us over the finish line, and, of course, none of this is possible without the vision of publisher Bronwen Hruska. It's been a wonderful experience working with Soho again.

In order to get to this point, however, I needed to put together a team of writers who shared my vision for what this book could be—which is to say, a book that didn't take itself too seriously, but could, if it wanted to. The first call

I made was to my brother, Lee Goldberg. In all the years the two of us have been publishing, we've never appeared together in a book, so I thought that would be cool, both for readers and our family. But also, I knew if he said no, I was going to have a real problem. Fortunately, he immediately said yes, which was good because I'd already told Juliet he was in. From there, I started compiling the best damn writers on the planet. I only knew James DF Hannah and Nikki Dolson a little bit on a personal level, but knew their work very well and understood that if they were in this book, they'd write short stories that would elevate the form. I wasn't disappointed. David Ulin, Ivy Pochoda, and Gabino Iglesias are my colleagues in the low-residency MFA program at UC Riverside, and all three happen to be some of the finest writers on the planet, each for entirely different reasons. I knew David would bring a religious and intellectual urgency to his work, and I knew he'd surprise me with some sudden violence. I knew Ivy would bring her gritty, street-wise realism that somehow always breaks my heart. I knew Gabino would figure out a way to shift the paradigm. Also, since they all work for me, I knew they'd be on time. Liska Jacobs was my student years ago and though she doesn't write crime fiction normally, all of her books have felt noir adjacent, what the world would be like if the femme fatales were the main characters they've long deserved to be, and so I had to know what she'd come up with, particularly as a Jewish woman currently living in Berlin. Jim Ruland is like a noir character in the flesh. He's over six feet tall, covered in tattoos, has a cold, hard stare, a coy smile, and projects a sense of general menace that runs counter to reality. He's best known as one of the great chroniclers of punk rock, but he's also a terrific crime writer, and I knew he'd find a way into Hanukkah. J.R. Angelella and I went to grad school together—along with Ivy!—and we've been good friends ever since, our text messages probably enough to get us both incarcerated or institutionalized. It's been a few years since he's been out there, life taking precedence, but he's coming big now, as I knew he would. Give me something hardcore and bad ass, I told him. Oh. He delivered. And then, finally, I wanted you to meet the next big thing, a writer on the come up, and that's Stefanie Leder. She's been making TV shows for over a decade, but now she's jumping across the aisle into the book world, her debut coming out next year, and I knew she'd bring the weird, the dark, and the disturbing and do it with a cinematic flair. I cannot thank these wonderful writers enough. They all showed up when I called. I'd have them over for kugel anytime.

Finally, I am nothing without my wife, Wendy. She hears every idea and only ever picks the good ones. I am a better man because of her love.